George Farenden followed in his father's foot   and joined the fire brigade in Birmingham at the age of twenty, rising to the rank of station officer at Birmingham's Central Fire Station. After serving his thirty years, he retired but was never far from fire brigades, or firefighting, as his life took another path. He started a new career working for DuPont de Nemours, Inc. as an emergency response consultant. After fourteen years with DuPont he finally retired to Somerset, where he now lives with his wife, Jane, and their dog, Coco.

To the men and women of the world who turnout and fight fires, so risking their lives for us. Service beyond the call.

George Farenden

JACK WOLF

The Recruit

AUSTIN MACAULEY PUBLISHERS™

LONDON • CAMBRIDGE • NEW YORK • SHARJAH

A CIP catalogue record for this title is available from the British Library.

ISBN 9781398408654 (Paperback)
ISBN 9781398408661 (Hardback)
ISBN 9781398408678 (ePub e-book)

www.austinmacauley.com

First Published 2022
Austin Macauley Publishers Ltd®
1 Canada Square
Canary Wharf
London
E14 5AA

The Recruit

John Wolf stepped off the bus in Birmingham city centre on 10 July 1972; it was a thirty-minute ride on the cream and royal blue number fifty double decker bus that brought him into town on the fine summers day, having said that there had just been a brief shower which washed the air clean and lightly wetted the city streets.

He walked up Bull Street then right onto Corporation Street, the smell of damp tarmac and city was familiar to him. After all, he was Birmingham born and bred this town was his playground, he knew most of it. He had been born in its heart, just off Broad Street. He had never been far away from its centre; even when he left school at fifteen years old, his work as an apprentice electrician often brought him back to the city centre he knew so well. On reaching eighteen, the introduction to the pubs, clubs and nightlife deepened his knowledge of the 'City of a thousand trades'.

As the wide street opened up, the sun burst from behind a leaden grey cloud that was hastily making its way northward, the heat of the bright sunlight made the glistening black tarmac of the roadway steam in appreciation of the sun's warmth. To John, this just increased the familiar smell of the city. He was wearing his favourite summer clothes, pale blue washed and worn Levi jeans with matching Levi jacket, a plain white tight fitting Tee shirt, his light tan suede desert boots completed the outfit. When the sunlight hit him from a gap in between two tall buildings, he felt its warmth, briefly he was comforted and self-assured. This was the look he was going for; this would impress his new employers even the weather had obliged in showing him off at his best.

Walking now, briskly, for no other reason than he thought he was a little late, he would see the white clock tower of Central fire station any minute; it was an impressive building for its age, dominating the end of the street and a landmark from the day it was built. The station also doubled as the brigade headquarters. This was a big investment for a city which like everywhere else at the time was emerging from the great depression, a pile of red bricks on a triangular site with Portland stone detailing gave work to many a skilled tradesmen in an era when work was scarce, with eleven bays it was said to be the biggest station in Europe in 1935 when it was completed.

Little did the city fathers or anyone know that within five years of the station being built, it would prove a great investment for the city as war spread across Europe. Passing the great terracotta façade of the Victoria Law Courts on his left, the tall white fire station clock tower was now in plain view. He passed a trendy boutique, instantly recognising the music that came from the open glass doorway, Hawkwind's, Silver machine; his brother liked this music but it was not for him. As the music faded, a wave of doubt swept over him. His arms straightened, his fists became clenched, the brisk walk almost turned into a march; he pushed his doubt aside, make a decision and stick to it, he almost said it aloud. The short walk took him closer to his new life.

John had been a contract electrician in a factory which, to him, seemed a sentence not a job, deep down he knew what had triggered his decision to change career. A few weeks earlier, he had been part of a 12-strong gang of electricians on Loan Labour to the giant Austin motor works at Longbridge. At eight o'clock one Monday morning, the portly, balding Foreman dressed in a siren suit which was years old and soaked in smelly suds oil, was detailing the week's work as he had done for the past three months. John was an electrician in name but due to his only being twenty-one he had no apprentice to fetch and carry for him. He would have to wait until the company could afford to employ another apprentice. Everyone else was man and 'mate', he was nothing more than an 'Improver', his 'mate' may be months away. The week's tasks were called off.

"And lastly, John, you're this week's Lamp Tramp."

In his five years as an apprentice, he had worked mostly on new build sites and commercial buildings in the city. Maintenance in huge factories was still new but mundane, another new was 'Lamp Tramp'. He waited until the gang had dispersed, drifting away to their allotted tasks.

"Boss."

"Yes, John."

"What the hell is a Lamp Tramp?"

"Great job, son, get yourself a pencil and a piece of paper. Here, you can borrow my notebook. You walk the factory, even the offices."

8

He said 'even the offices' with great glee because to him that meant female contact.

"Anyway, note any lamps that are out. When you have a dozen or so, get yourself off to the stores, sign out the lamps, then go and fit them, then walk the factory again, find more lamps that are out and so on. That's your job for the week, the cushiest job on the site, you owe me a drink."

"Boss, this place is big, maybe hundreds of acres, thousands of people work here and I alone change the blown light bulbs?"

"I know, great, isn't it? What a cushy number, and John, you know better, bulbs grow in the ground lamps, light things up."

John turned away, then hesitated and turned back to the foreman, trying hard not to show emotion but not really succeeding.

"Boss, five years an apprentice and college, all to be a Lamp Tramp, is that it?"

"John, you're not moaning, at being given the plum job in the Gang, are you?"

"I'm not moaning, boss, but I'm not jumping for joy either."

"John, I've been watching you, you have potential, give it another few years, keep your nose clean and you may make Foreman by, say when you are fortyish."

John stared at him, should he apologise to this well-meaning guy, or should he point out that a smelly siren suit and a paunch was not the sum total of his ambition. No, he couldn't upset him, the Foreman had only ever been kind to him.

"Okay, boss, I'll be your Lamp Tramp."

John smiled and turned away, knowing this was the end, another forty-five years of this was not going to be his future.

John had an older brother and sister, both of whom had achieved grammar school and then went onto university. John had failed the eleven-plus examination and left school with just two very minor O levels from his secondary school. He was more interested in Soul and Blues music than examinations. Otis Reading was a special favourite. Perhaps, if only to please his parents, he should have tried harder at his studies. Although nothing was ever said of his lack of achievement, he knew they were disappointed in not sending all three children to university. He thought back to the day he left school, his father never mentioned his schooling but his mother, in an attempt to praise him for his two O levels had a very short chat with him.

9

"They maybe the clever ones, but you're more practical, not educated to degree level as your brother and sister but at least you're good with your hands. You are a good lad."

She meant well but this was not what he wanted to hear. His mother was not helping, it did nothing to quell his feeling of being mediocre; the pat on the head seemed to make it worse.

Through the huge wrought iron gates of the station and onto the wetted granite cobbled drill yard that shone now in the strong sunlight. The station was huge, the drill yard was flanked by the double layered balconies of the flats that were married men's quarters, the inner face of the station was proudly 1930s in design, something the more formal exterior only hinted at. With a lump in his throat and a feeling of trepidation in his chest, he made his way into the centre of the drill yard which formed the working heart of the fire station; he was now lost, emotionally and actually. Walking as if he knew where he was going, he realised he was on a converging course with a fireman in overalls; he pressed on. The fireman stared at the blond-haired youth walking across his path.

"You look lost," he chirped.

"Yes, Sir."

Start with a 'sir', he thought, *this chap could be the cleaner or an officer, best to aim high.*

"I'm looking for the training school. Could you direct me?"

"Oh, another lamb to the slaughter."

Raising his arm, he pointed. "North-west corner, you'll see the sign on the door."

He looked John up and down, but the fireman didn't break step, then he was gone through the back of the station and into the engine house. Walking toward the training school doorway, John looked back over his shoulder at the clock tower; good, not late; in fact, five minutes early.

Sitting in the training school's number one lecture room behind an old oak school desk which was a little small for a grown man, John looked down at the polished brass inkwell engraved 'Birmingham Corporation' that gave away its age. He felt he had slipped back in time, his apprenticeship meant nothing, one of thirty young men in the room, now he starts all over again. His mind drifted for a moment, should he have stuck to his electrician's job?

It was a trade after all and his mother had told him, "You will never go hungry if you have a trade." He thought of the five years of college studying electrical engineering. Had he wasted five years learning something which in his new career, to him at least, had no obvious use? He was starting again back at square one, everyone in the room probably knew more than him, about his new life.

He had disappointed his parents at school, then he quit his chosen trade to be a fireman, once more his parents had looked disappointed when he told them what he had done. What happened if he failed this recruit's course? What if he was scared of heights? What if he was just plain scared of fire? *Oh shit, I've messed this up*, he thought to himself. He considered walking out. He looked around the lecture room; he might be able get out without being noticed. But he knew what had to be done. Make a decision and stick to it, once more he almost said it aloud.

As the entrance door at the rear of the lecture room burst open, someone shouted, "STAND!" Everyone in the room unconsciously jumped to their feet. Training Officer Bianchi walked, well, almost marched to the front of the classroom flanked by two officers, one each side of him. They seemed to mirror his every step. John watched the training officer closely. He had no idea of his rank but he had pips on his shoulders rather than the bars worn by the other two, which surely meant something. He walked with a swagger or was he strutting? This guy was full of his own self-importance.

He mounted the small dais which was placed in front of the two wall-mounted black boards, standing behind the centrally placed plain wooden lectern. He deliberately took a long breath; his chest swelled, pulling his shoulders back. He grasped each side of the sloping lectern top, as his chin came up his mouth seemed to droop downwards at the edges. He curled his lips, slowly he looked down his nose with heavy lidded eyes at the assembled recruits. The gaze held nothing but disdain for the men in front of him. It was pure theatre.

"SIT!" It was one of the officers with bars on his shoulders shouting the orders.

The arrogance of Benito, '*Il Duce*' came to John's mind. The room of recruits sat as the training officer's chest and ego swelled even more in preparation of his speech.

"You are joining the fire brigade, my fire brigade. That is, if I decide you are good enough. We have a long tradition of service, we are a family."

This wasn't a pep talk or a lecture; it was a well-rehearsed piece that he had delivered many times and he was getting into his stride.

"You will be brothers, you will see death and destruction, you will be expected to run into fire when every other living thing runs away, you will work shifts, days, nights, Saturdays, Sundays, high days and holidays, Christmas days and your birthdays. You will be injured and burned, and don't kid yourself it won't happen to you; it will, and consider this, on average two firemen are killed each year due to service. You are expected to do this job for thirty years. Nobody wants to pay you decent wages. They will tell you that you sit around all day, play snooker and squirt water for a living. You will be as Cinderella…you will live, eat and sleep behind the red engine house doors and when called to stand too, when the fire-bell rings, you will answer their call, their fear, their alarm. You will risk your life for a stranger, someone you never knew or will ever know and when the alarm has passed, when you are exhausted and done, you will return to the fire station, close those engine house doors behind you and lick your wounds. We are their insurance policy; they never want us, until they want us, then briefly, we are heroes. At fifty years old, you will not be able to keep up with operational firefighting, you will be old and slow. So you will retire on a pension, which, they will begrudge you. Yet, on average, firemen die within ten years of receiving it, so statistically you should be dead before you reach sixty five, any more will be a bonus." He paused and scanned the room once more.

"Now, remember this all of you. I don't know you, I don't want to know you, and I don't like you. I am not your friend, I am not your mother or your nursemaid, and you are shit to me, the lowest of the low, mere sprogs, so remember that. You will stand whenever I come into the room, you will not talk to me unless I talk to you first, then you will call me 'Sir', nothing else. Do we understand each other?"

The thirty young men mumbled a begrudging "Sir."

He paused and looked around the room at thirty sullen-faced youths all of which looked as if they had been hit with something rather heavy.

"Now is the time for a decision; if you have doubts this is your chance, you should leave, I will not think any less of you as that is not possible."

He paused, again deliberately scanning the room, his head moved slowly from left to right, still with his chin high in the air, he looked into their eyes searching for the fear, the insecurity in every individual and, maybe, he was feeding on it. He paused a long pause. Then, as if he'd had a change of heart, he spoke again.

"There is tea at the back of the room. I shall be back in fifteen minutes to sign in those that remain."

He left the room with the swagger and pomp of his arrival. John had been watching him closely; it was as if he had two personalities. Was he separating the wheat from the chaff? Or was he enjoying too much the small amount of power he held over this, his latest batch of unsuspecting new recruits? Whatever it was, this man wasn't going to intimidate him. John had taken an instant dislike to the horrid man. If the training officer's speech was supposed to rattle him, it didn't; it did the opposite. Twenty-eight sat down after tea; Training Officer Bianchi had got to two of them already. The remainder would be split into three squads. Little did they know that four of them would not make the grade; the winnowing had begun.

By 1000 hours of day one, Training Officer Bianchi was detailing the squad's two tens and an eight.

"And Squad three will be: Brown, Edison, Ford, Harvey, Marchant, Nelson, Wolf, and Wright. You eight sit in this row of desks. You are all Birmingham so get to know each other. As for the rest of you, from brigades all over the bloody place, Staffordshire, Warwickshire, Holland Counties and not forgetting some of our local friends and neighbours. Make two rows of ten, here and here. Okay, move."

The scrapping of chairs and the shuffling of joining papers took a few minutes to die down; the three neat rows filled the classroom, now, everybody was in place.

"Squad instructors will be; Squad One, Sub-Officer Martin, Squad Two, Sub-Officer Hughes and Squad Three, Sub-Officer White."

Sub-Officer White picked up eight bundles of papers from the floor, approached his recruits and started walking the Birmingham row of desks.

"Course notes, one for each lecture, just one hundred and twenty. Read them, write on them, colour in the pretty pictures, if you want."

He dropped a pack with a hefty thump on each desk.

"They're all yours, gentlemen, study them, keep them, never be caught without them." He continued down the row.

Bianchi was at the front of the room again.

"Right, you bunch of bastards, you look like some hippy drop-outs from Woodstock or somewhere, so all of you get yourselves short haircuts, a crew-cut would be best, by next Monday at the latest. If you can't get it done by next

Monday, don't bother coming back. Now, today before anything else I want everyone out of civvies and into uniform, each of you will find your issue in the basement, the leading firemen there will sign you out with your undress uniform, your fire-kit and your working rig. You have thirty minutes to be back up here in working rig, okay? Move."

Thirty minutes later, they were back in the lecture room in blue overalls. Bianchi was still there, looking agitated. He had probably been waiting for them on the dais and that hadn't come easy to this impatient man. There were no preliminaries; he just barked his next orders.

"Squad One, stay where you are. Squad Two, go to lecture room Two. Squad Three, drill ground, full fire kit. Go."

The wooden chairs scrapped the floor once more, and a queue of excited chatting recruits quickly formed at the rear exit door. They jostled each other to get to their posts, nobody wanted to be last to arrive.

Squad three was on the drill ground feeling very uncomfortable, dressed in full fire kit for the first time, the smell of their new woollen tunics and freshly waxed leather fire boots filled the air. The eight Brummies' had raced down to the basement locker room to change once again within minutes, they had little time to talk to each other but a series of nods and smiles was a good start. Sub-Officer White stood in front of them looking at each man in turn as they took up their places in the squad line, then he walked the line in front of them, then behind them, returning to the front and centre, he shrugged his shoulders as if in resignation of his lot.

"You will call me Sir, when we get to know each other I may let you call me Sub-O which is short for Sub-Officer; note the two bars on my epaulettes. I'm going to teach you how to be a recruit firemen, how to use the pumps and ladders and the basics of firefighting. True firefighting will come during your four years qualifying on station. We don't have time to do all that here and now. I'm going to turn you from ignorant little shits into something that resembles a fireman, a fireman that can be let loose on a station without killing himself or more importantly somebody else. This is initial training, nothing more nothing less. The next twelve weeks you're mine, you answer to me. Do you understand?"

"Yes, Sir."

"Let's start with running hose."

Death of a Salamander

A crisp morning in late October at Aston Fire Station, Fireman Wolf was the complete fresh out of the box recruit, in his undress uniform, a woollen double breasted reefer jacket and trousers complete with his peaked cap tucked safely under his left arm, he looked every bit the fireman on parade. He was excited at this being the real start of his life as a fireman.

Fire school had been good but this was the pay-off for three months of running around a drill ground, of completing the initial course successfully; he had made it. Some had fallen by the wayside, but he was here, his first shift on a station. No more being shouted at by impatient training officers, no more Sub-Officer White making him run ladders or running out endless lengths of hose. He was going to ride fire engines around his town and maybe pose a little. He was confident of his newfound abilities; this was going to be so much fun; how could anything possibly go wrong? Directly off the engine house was the station office, knocking purposely on the half-glazed door he felt self-assured, he had been posted to a busy inner city fire station. He was envied by the other recruits who had been posted to less busy fire stations on the edge of the brigade. *How good is this, to be on his three-engine fire station? I'm going to be right in the middle of the action.* There was a short pause.

"Come in."

A high-pitched voice commanded. Jack's confidence instantly evaporated, he was nervous once again. The station office was small, no more than twenty feet square. Behind a large mahogany desk in the centre of the room sat Station Officer Sidney Jackson, standing on his left was Sub-Officer Dwyer and sitting at a very small desk in the corner of the room tapping away at an ancient imperial typewriter was Leading Fireman Miller. John took it all in quickly and bringing himself to attention, he gave his salutation.

"Fireman Wolf, reporting for duty, Sir."

The station officer's stare seemed never ending and unnerving but, the tap, tap, tap, of somebody who had never been trained to type but was doing okay with just his two index fingers was somehow comforting. The station officer broke his stare.

"Very well Miller enough typing get yourself a tea."

Leading fireman Miller looked John in the eyes as he passed him by; he smiled and went out through the entrance door.

"So, Jack Wolf, brigade number 1834. Well, aren't the brigade numbers getting high."

The station officer started thumbing through Wolf's thin file.

"John, Sir, its John Wolf."

It was at this moment, John realised, he wasn't supposed to speak. Slowly and with great purpose, Station Officer Jackson's head rose from reading the very thin file.

"What?" in a loud voice the station officer replied.

John noticed the officers' voice had raised by at least an octave, maybe two, and was he growing in size? John was transfixed as the station officer rose from his desk. Station Officer Jackson stood up, reaching his full height, paused and lent forward putting his clenched fists' knuckles down on the large desk. He must surely be at least six feet four inches tall, with snow white cropped hair, yet weighing no more than twelve stones. The tall thin giant stood before him in a uniform that had obviously been tailored to fit, complete with two rows of medal ribbons on his chest. It was a sight to behold, unfortunately the giant had a thirteen-year-old girl's voice.

John considered a smile but thought that would it be taken as an insult and be a certain disaster. Things were bad enough as it was, humility was the only answer.

"You little shit, how old are you?"

"Twenty one, Sir…Twenty one."

His nerves made him repeat himself.

"Twenty bloody one! Do you know what I was doing when I was twenty bloody one?"

John went to speak; thankfully it wasn't necessary.

"I'll tell you what I was doing. I was with the Guards halfway up Monte bloody Casino, that's in Italy in case you don't know. I was trying to stay alive, that's what, and you have arrived on my station and the first words out of your mouth are to correct me?"

He paused. Was his voice even higher? John considered a reply but decided his silence was working well for him. He glanced at the sub-officer who was smiling and enjoying the dressing down of the recruit. The sub-officer had been at the end of Sid's tongue-lashings several times and knew it would quickly pass as in fact it did. The station officer seemed to have a switch that he could turn on or off from mad to normal, normal to mad. The station officer sat down as fast as he got to his feet.

"Right, let's have a look at your file. Practical ability – excellent, Technical ability – excellent, Hydraulics – average. And, of course, position 12th out of a cadre of 24 students. Hmm, so you really are average. Summary comments, Wolf has potential and could do better if he tried, blah de blah de blah... The rest is the usual training school standard waffle, which amounts to, we did our best to train the little shit and it's not the school's fault if you're no good."

Wolf had the feeling history was repeating itself. Was it possible his mother was involved in his training school marks?

"Well, Wolf, you start today. I'm paying no attention to that training school bullshit. You have been posted to the best watch on the best fire station in Birmingham, the UK's second biggest city, and we are going to make a fireman of you, but most of all you are now part of a watch, my watch. Welcome Jack."

He held out his hand, John reciprocated; it was the firmest handshake he had ever felt and brought pain with it, but it was also somehow reassuring. Perhaps the switch had a third setting, mild and fatherly.

"Well, Jack, here at Aston we attend on average two thousand calls per year. We also do a fair number of assists to other stations, however, on the station ground we have a mixed race community, mostly Indian, Pakistani, Chinese, and Irish in terraced or back to back housing."

Now, his chest was swelling.

"But, we also have our share of big Victorian houses."

John stared intently at him yet frowning, awaiting the secret of big Victorian houses but nothing more came. *Why was the station officer proud of big Victorian housing?* His thoughts were cut short by a short ring of the fire bell which made him physically jump.

"Ah ha, Jack, your first shout."

John stood to one side as the two officers made their way quickly out of the office. John followed. Leading fireman Miller was waiting for him just outside the office door.

"Your fire kit is on the back of the pump. Jump in."

Someone shouted, "Full house, Aces and Queens, everybody goes."

One six-litre Rolls Royce engine fired up, then a second, then a third, filling the engine house with noise and part burnt petrol fumes. The fire engines had come alive and were straining at their leashes as the drivers revved the engines in a bid to warm them up in the short time available. The officer of each engine was in the watch room, closely watching the attendant copy down the telephone message from fire control; the short ring had been a warning that a fire call was coming through. Now the message was complete the fire-bell sounded in earnest a full forty-five seconds long. John knew where to sit, centre seat in the back, the pattern was always the same. Driver/Pump operator and officer-in-charge in the front, two breathing apparatus wearers on either side in the back with the fifth man in the centre. John was dressed in full fire kit by the time the sub-officer jumped into the front seat; the two breathing apparatus men smiled at the lad's keenness.

"Salamander on fire, Jacques Garage 274 Aston Lane, no BA."

The sub-officer seemed calm considering a Salamander was on fire and he did not even want breathing apparatus. *Salamander, what exactly is a Salamander?* John was sure it was an animal or was it a mythical dragon? But that didn't make sense. The station officer's words were still in his ears, mixed race community Chinese, Indian, Pakistani, Irish, where do salamanders come from? The roar of the engines grew louder and one two three automatic doors rolled up and across the ceiling, in sequence, adding to the noise and excitement. A small green light came on in sequence by the side of each door indicating the door was fully up and the engines could go. The pump escape led the charge, followed closely by the pump, and bringing up the rear was the turntable ladder.

Then the real noise came; John had never heard three sets of two-tone horns used in anger before, but he was on a ride he had never dreamed of, being thrown around in the back of a fire engine. Powering down the Witton Road, three great fire engines weaving through the parting traffic was a spectacle. Traffic, left and right, parted like some biblical scene, the driver was throwing the twenty-ton truck around like a toy. Why had he not realised how thrilling this could be? As they turned left into Aston Lane the tyres let out a great roar as rubber was scrapped off the tread and onto the road surface, a pall of dense black smoke was rising high into the air, no more than five hundred yards to their right. He wondered if the Salamanders had managed to escape. Would he be seeing his first burned or dead body? The sub-officer turned in his seat looking back at Jack.

"Stay close to me. Do nothing until I say."

The pump escape with its huge escape wheels spinning freely turned into the wide driveway that led down to Jacques' Garage, down the drive it stopped some 30 feet short of the burning building the driver of Johns' pump knew his job and stopped at the top of the drive, knowing the turntable ladder may need to get in closer. Amongst the mess of buildings was a large brick and wood structure with a Belfast roof which had thick black smoke rolling out of it. This wasn't the smoke of a bonfire, this was evil looking stuff. It was heavy, it rolled as it came through the open vehicle entrance doors, it was melting a Goodyear tyre banner that hung across the façade, as he watched the melting banner broke in two, each side sweeping to the ground as if it was the grand opening of some hellish theme park. But there were no flames; this smoke was strange it looked alive, it had a centre core that moved up faster than the outside, it kept rolling as if deliberately mixing itself with fresh air so it could breathe. The sub-officer looked back at his crew. "We're going to lose the roof. Jack, get a hydrant in. Go."

Oh, this staying close didn't last long, Jack thought. He ran to the pumps water locker, grabbed a standpipe and hydrant key then looked up and down the road for the nearest hydrant. He glanced back to the fire scene. The pump escape crew had a main jet working and with heads down, they were trying to get in through the vehicle doors. He did a quick calculation, one main jet, a thousand gallons of water in the on board tank, he had less than four minutes before they ran out of water. Then he saw the plate, the bright yellow hydrant plate. Running up to hydrant, he flicked off the lid in one smooth move, following up with the standpipe three turns and it was tight on the street main. He cracked the hydrant open, brown, rusty, muddy water at first erupted from the standpipe, then fresh clean, town's mains water. It was then he realised a fireman was standing next to him holding out the male end of a seventy-five foot length of coiled delivery hose, easily enough to reach the pump. "Good day to you, 'Conkers' the name, pray tell, who may you be, my good fellow?" knowing full well it was the new recruit.

"Jack Wolf."

Came the automatic reply. "Jack, I'm calling myself Jack now. How did that happen?"

"Hi Jack. Welcome to Blue Watch. Ready for some fun and jeopardy?"

Conker must be 50 years old but he ran back to the pump like a twenty-year-old, laying the hose as he went. Jack was just about to run after him when he remembered that he was expected to turn on the water, when it was called for. Conker connected the supply hose to the pump and gave him the hand signal to turn the hydrant on; he had learnt them at fire school. Fireman used them to communicate to each other if they had no hand held radios. When the hydrant was fully open, Jack caught up with Conker at the back of the Pump which was now feeding the pump escape so the guys on the first jet never lost water.

Jack followed Conker as they ran down the drive towards the garage together. They could see another two firemen wearing breathing apparatus, ready to go inside the building and the original two now working just inside the doorway. Then it came, it had been waiting for the untrained, for those that think they know fire, it was waiting for someone to make a mistake, the foolhardy, the irresponsible, the reckless. It was ready, it was to take the building for its own. It wasn't an explosion, it was more a deep primeval thunder that rolled to a roar, the superheated rolling smoke changed instantly to flame, then the heatwave came. Jack watched the guys in the doorway cower, they seemed to shrink in size in an effort to shield their faces and bodies from the incredible radiated heat, he could feel it and he was a good fifty feet away but they never moved. *Surely they will pull back,* Jack thought, but no, it was a battle of wills, them versus the beast.

Sub-Officer Dwyer was now in front of them. "You two get another line of hose in and cover those guys."

As they laid out their jet outside the garage entrance, Jack noticed two things, both new to him, the ground he was walking on was steaming like the surface of a volcanic island but even stranger was the sight of the station officer, who stood legs wide apart, fists clenched on his hips in the centre of the scene, white helmet tilted back on his head, his woollen double breasted tunic buttoned to the neck, but no wet legs just his office trousers. The fire was on the offensive, it was trying to take charge, the station officer was defiant, he accepted and relished the challenge, they were squaring up to each other like boxers in a ring, this was Sid's fire ground and he was not giving an inch, Conker looked at his new friend.

"So, I hear you have met 'Screaming'."

It dawned on him instantly, one octave, maybe two 'Screaming Sid'. The second jet was quickly followed by a third, then a fourth. Handsworth, the next closest station to Aston, had sent their pump to assist and the weight of attack was growing. With tons of water a minute being pumped into it, the beast was hesitating. Two of the Handsworth guys were running out of the building, pulling a wheeled oxyacetylene welding set behind them. Conker, backed up by Jack, pushed into the building with the other jets, they were now breathing smoke. He knew the other guys were only feet away but he could see nothing, his eyes stung, he was crying buckets of tears, his nose was now running so badly he could taste the snot in his mouth. The heat was burning the back of his gloveless hands, the back of his neck and ears must surely be burnt.

"Down," Conker shouted, "get down."

At a 100 psi the jet reaction of the branch was so great, it took at least two men to control it, one on his own would be thrown around like a rag doll. Conker had to go first, he dropped to his knees, Jack hesitated for only a moment, then a wave of heat passed over him forcing him to follow. Instantly, Conker shouted again, "Down, down."

There was no panic in his voice but this was not a discussion. Jack and Conker were now on their bellies lying over the rock solid canvas hose, they were lying in an inch of hot water that flowed past them. Jack's ears and hands tingled with pain.

"Feel the water," Conker shouted.

Jack pushed his hand forward into the ink black water; it was hot and bought more pain to the back of his hand.

"You know what that means? That means we're on it, got to be careful, we don't hit the BA crew with the jet though, that does piss them off."

Jack closed his eyes, he gave up trying to see through the smoke, his eyes felt like they were being burnt out of their sockets by acid. He lay on the hose with his mouth open, as close to the water as possible without drinking the foul stuff. Conker was directing the jet, an eternity seemed to pass, he considered getting Conker's attention and telling him he had to get out, but he couldn't do that on his first day and definitely not in his first fire. His face was now on its side, touching the water. It was almost comforting, perhaps he could rest or even sleep, he wondered if he was losing his senses. Is this how death comes? His eyes no longer burned, he thought he could breathe easier, maybe he should sleep, and it was getting quieter and even comfortable lying on the workshop floor, this wasn't so bad after all. Conker pushed Jack's head into the deepening water.

"Hey, Jack, Jack, come on. Where are you going?"

The shock of inhaling shitty black water brought him coughing and spluttering back to his senses. Conker was staring him full in the face.

"Are you okay, son?"

Jack dug deep. "Yep, yep, yep."

"It's venting through the roof. Stay with me Jack, it will get better."

Suddenly, a wave of cold fresh air passed over them. It was wonderful, it tasted sweet. Jack's senses came rushing back to him. Conker knew the building was failing, he pulled them tight up against the sidewall.

"Head down, son. It's on the move."

Jack could now hear a rumble, the sound of a few bricks hitting sheet metal then a few more and then an almighty deafening crash that seemed to shake the very ground they lay on. Then a rush of superheated smoke passed over them, complete with burning embers that felt like red-hot needles being stuck into his face and hands.

"Bet you, that's the end wall," Conker shouted through the din, in a matter-of-fact way.

Why wasn't Conker on the edge of consciousness like me, Jack thought. But with the end wall now gone, the smoke layer was lifting fast, the draught had changed direction completely. Fresh air now washed over them, things were better, deep inside the building, he could hear the BA men working their jet. They could only last twenty minutes with the air cylinders they had, but twenty minutes deep inside a burning building felt like a lifetime. It went quiet, the sound of the heavy jet of water hitting metal had stopped. The two BA men came towards them through the now steamy smoke, pulling off their masks and shaking them empty of sweat. They walked up to the two kneeling drowned rats.

"It's all yours guys, we got it, despite you two trying to drown us."

"You got it. You cheeky bastards. Who do you think was covering your backs?" Conker replied.

"Well, thanks to you two our backs are soaked." The two BA men walked out laughing.

Not too soon for Jack, things were returning to what could be called some kind of normal. The hot water he had been lying in had worked its way through his woollen tunic to his skin. He was sodden, he had a dull headache and the

22

back of his hands were brilliant red. They looked as if he had too much sun. As he raised his hands to touch his ears, he realised each ear had a blister the size of a cigarette end across the top. Conker noticed him wince as he touched the burns.

"Lucky we got down when we did, we may have burnt our ears otherwise."

A wry smile flashed across Conker's face. The large hole in the roof and the missing gable end was easily venting the garage now. As the smoke thinned, they could see a good half of the roof had in fact burnt away and fourteen cars were burnt out wrecks. Yet, around the edge of the workshop, equipment and other pieces of stock were remarkably untouched by the fire but everything was dripping wet and smoke stained. The small dancing, brightly coloured flames that remained amongst the debris indicated the cocktail of paints, metals, solvents and definitely smoky oil still burning.

"Now, that's what you call a good stop," Conker said, shutting down the jet. They both lurched forward as the one-inch stream of water was shut down.

Jack stared at the ruin; he was not sure what a good stop was, but evidently Conker was pleased with the outcome. Jack looked him in the face. Was this the same man he met outside thirty minutes ago, a face as black as the ace of spades, white streaks from his eyes where the tears had washed the soot away and, like Jack, two snotty candlesticks ran from his huge bulbous nose.

"How come you can take that shit, Conker? I was struggling back then."

"Smoke eater, Jack. Lungs are shot, don't feel it, forty Capstan full strength a day makes this a walk in the park."

The two drowned rats stood together in silence, looking around the burnt-out workshop. Jack thought he should ask.

"What about the Salamander?"

"Yeah, it could be what started it. It's over there."

Conker nodded towards the heart of the fire. Now, the heart of the rubble, climbing over the debris. Jack found his Salamander; a giant paraffin heater lying on its side, stood upright, it would be six feet tall with a tank at the base that must have held at least five gallons of paraffin. *Reversing into it when it was lit with a customer's car was sure to get a grease monkey the sack*, thought Jack, making his first fire scene investigation summary.

Screaming Sid came walking through the smoke.

"Okay, let's get a line on these cars so we can get them out from under this rubble; it's still going underneath there."

23

The Handsworth crew was already there, with 50-foot line, rope to everyone else but lines to firemen, it was tied to the back of their truck and they pulled the first car out of the garage. Jack walked forward and looked at something floating in the water that was revealed by moving the burnt out wreck, but was unable to work out just what it was.

Conker and Screaming were now at his side. Screaming didn't speak to either of them. Lifting his walkie-talkie radio up to his mouth, he spoke casually to his sub-officer.

"Tumble, you there?"

"Yes, boss, go ahead."

"Send a message from me in brigade, speak to fire control. We've got a stiff, we'll need the circus."

"Okay, boss."

Jack's brain was racing, trying to decipher what was happening. Were these people speaking English? Conker, Screaming, Tumble, Stiff, one by one it fell into place.

Conker, the big nose, Screaming, the high voice, Tumble – Dwyer, Stiff, a dead person, preferably with rigor mortis, the thing floating in front of him was a dead mechanic. But what was the circus?

"Conker, Jack, get him over here. Let's have a look at him."

Screaming moved away, seemingly unmoved by finding a dead man. Jack had been mulling over the possibility of dead Salamanders and what they were. Dead mechanics hadn't entered his thinking. He went to walk forward but was stopped in his tracks as Conker's arm was flung backwards across his chest. "Be not so hasty, my little friend."

Jack looked at him. Why was Conker looking so intently at the dead mechanic?

Conker pulled out a packet of plain Capstan cigarettes from inside of his fire tunic and slowly put one in his mouth, with a flick of his wrist he flipped the top off of a zippo lighter and lit the strangely white cigarette. He drew on it thoughtfully. Then he exhaled a deep lungful of blue tobacco smoke.

"Look, what do you see?"

"I see a dead man floating face down in shitty black steaming water."

"Yes, so do I, but that's not right, is it?"

"Why not, he's dead and floating, so?"

"That's my point, how deep is the water we are standing in?"

Jack looked down to the black water.

"Half an inch, maybe an inch."

"Exactly, then pray tell, dear fellow, why is he bobbing up and down like a cork in a bathtub?"

"You're right. How strange? The floor must slope away really quickly over there."

"No, that's not it. I reckon we cannot see what lies before us, the obvious."

Jack was wet to the bone, yet burnt, physically exhausted and just about to give up mentally. He had been on the station no more than a few hours and had managed to piss off the station officer, almost pass out from smoke inhalation, deciphered a language known only to firemen, now through the haze of a smoke induced headache, he was expected to solve puzzles.

"What's obvious? I don't understand."

Conker stared intently at the corpse and again he pulled deeply on his Capstan. He took the cigarette from his mouth and holding it between his index and middle finger, he pointed toward the place where it lay.

"There be a pit, there be an inspection pit under him, there maybe half an inch of water here but I reckon we've just dragged a car away that was over a pit and Sonny Jim was in it; that pit is six foot deep and full of water."

Jack looked at the scene afresh.

"Conker, you're right there is something, there is a pit."

"Not only is there 'A' pit, it's just one pit. How many pits are there around us?"

Jack froze to the spot and looked around. He didn't want to go swimming with Sonny Jim.

"Get a ceiling hook off the truck, Jack, and we'll drag him out. Be sure to go back the way we came in, no short cuts or you may find another pit."

When Jack got back with the hook, he noticed the water level had dropped a little. There it was, the definite rectangular outline of the inspection pit. He handed Conker the ceiling hook, Conker snagged it through what was left of the mechanic's clothes and together they pulled him across the garage floor to a spot that was clear of debris. Conker laid the hook down and knelt on one knee beside the body. He paused as if paying his respects, the cigarette hanging from one side of his mouth.

"Give me a hand. Let's turn him over, give him some dignity."

They rolled him onto his back.

"Oh dear, he's burnt," Screaming said, peering over their shoulders.

To Jack, it was a burnt tailor's dummy, no hair, no features, just a burnt semblance of a person. Screaming walked off again to survey the entire scene.

So this was the circus, it had arrived. Three police cars, two marked, with uniforms in them, and one unmarked, with two guys in plain clothes, a black Mariah, a police doctor and a police photographer, not to mention a divisional fire officer and an assistant divisional fire officer.

Jack was outside with the pumps' crew and the crew from Handsworth, most of which were puffing on cigarettes. They seemed good guys and worked well with Aston's crews without any shouting or fuss. Jack listened in wonder at the banter that passed between the two fire stations' crews. There was rivalry, yet a great respect that came with sharing the danger and adversity they all went through. They could insult each other in a way that made them closer, it acknowledged their bravery and suffering but somehow belittled it at the same time. Jack found it strange to listen to, but enjoyed the camaraderie it brought; he felt part of it. If he wanted to be called a fireman, by firemen, he had to pay a price. He had started paying his dues.

The assistant divisional officer appeared at the garage doorway and called across to the resting crews. "The two men who found the stiff over here and inside."

The inside of the garage was lit with floodlights, although it was the middle of the day. The circus was standing in an open circle in the centre of the workshop. The occasional flash of a camera lit the corpse. One of the policemen in plain clothes spoke up.

"Tell us what you saw, from when you came in to the point when you recovered the victim here."

He made it sound like they had strolled in wearing shorts and tee shirts on a fine summer's day and had struck up a casual conversation regarding the unseasonably pleasant weather with the now deceased. Yet, it was the use of word victim that pricked Jack's ears; why victim and not casualty? Perhaps firemen had casualties and policemen had victims. Conker went through their actions as if writing a report. He started giving his account of the fire from the moment they entered the building with their jet, in his quaint version of old English and in the third person. Jack thought he could make it sound more dramatic, more heroic, or even just as plain shitty as it was and he hadn't yet mentioned Jack's burnt ears.

26

"Hold it there, bud."

One of the uniformed police officers held the palm of his hand up, a little too close to Conker's face, whose narrative came to an abrupt stop.

"I have worked it out, this is what went down."

Everyone looked in amazement at the cop who had broken Conker's flow.

"I reckon this guy is working alone and he needs to get under the car for whatever reason. He gets in the pit and pulls the car over the pit so he can work on the underneath. He was probably welding something when he set fire to the car, maybe he cut through a fuel pipe.

"In his panic he attempted to, but couldn't move the car, he's alone and trapped, the fire spreads easily, loads of petrol around and he burned to death under the car, then the whole building goes up, the rest is what you see. Oh, and another thing, if he isn't dead from the fire, these two firemen finish him off by pumping so much water in here, they drown him in the pit. Then, to top it all, they manage to move or wash away any evidence of the accident in the process of playing firemen. Brilliant, thanks lads."

Jack raised his open hands and was about to speak but Conker, looking directly at him, shook his head just once. It was a 'say nothing' shake of the head.

The doctor who was to officially pronounce death and record the time, looked at the cop long and hard.

"Good stuff, officer, an interesting summation, but should you not wait for my report before insulting the intelligence of just about everybody here?"

"Hey, doc, I'm sorry for stealing your thunder, but what do you think killed this man who was burnt to a crisp under the car? Old age? Come on, you don't have to be a rocket scientist to work this one out."

Jack had decided. This cop is a fool. He had also created a weird atmosphere, a silence that was almost embarrassing. Were the doctor and the copper about to argue about the cause of death with each other? The doctor held himself together; he was to ignore the fool. Surprisingly, Conker broke back into the conversation.

"Well, in my humble opinion, and I would hate to jump to conclusions like my erstwhile friend here" – gesturing toward the fool – "but it may have something to do with the bullet hole in the back of his head, and a clever little bullet hole it is too, small calibre, probably a .22 or a .32 with maybe, a homemade low energy bullet, the assassin's choice, it goes in, races around inside the skull turns the brain to mush, instant death, no exit, no mess, he was dead before he hit the ground."

The doctor smiled, the two officers in plain clothes glanced at each other but said nothing. The fool, mouth open, stared at Conker.

THE HOME DELIVERY LIBRARY SERVICE WILL VISIT YOU NEXT ON

Tues 11th JUNE

PLEASE LEAVE YOUR RETURNED ITEMS OUTSIDE IN THE HOME LIBRARY SERVICE BAG PROVIDED.

WHERE POSSIBLE, PLEASE AVOID LEAVING THE BAG ON WET SURFACES IN SEVERE WEATHER.

FOR ANY QUERIES, PLEASE CONTACT 01926 851031.

The Birmingham Boys

Back on station, the roll was called which they had missed at the beginning of the shift. Sub-Officer Dwyer called the parade to attention and detailed the runners and riders as Station Officer Jackson looked on. Jack, by roll call, was introduced to the Blue Watch.

Leading Fireman Miller (Dusty)
Fireman Shakeshaft (Will)
Fireman Johnson (Johnny)
Fireman Fowles (Conker)
Fireman Taylor (Toot)
Fireman Clark (Nobby)
Fireman Jones (600)
Fireman Harrison (George)
Fireman Hall (Bert)
Fireman Wilson (Harry)
Fireman Smith (Smudger)
Fireman Woods (Fatal)
Fireman Batchelor (Horace)
Fireman Wolf (Jack)

Will, Fatal, Jack and Conker were cleaning the breathing apparatus sets in the backwash, the section of the engine house directly behind the garaged fire engines, where engines and equipment are cleaned, breathing apparatus recharged and everything prepared for the next shout, Jack could wait no longer.

"So who do you think shot the mechanic?"

Jack asked the open question to everyone within earshot. Will and Fatal looked at Conker.

"Sometimes, my little friend, no knowledge is an asset, ignorance is bliss. You know nothing of gangs, bookies and the workings of the Birmingham underworld do you?"

29

Jack shook his head. "No, is there an underworld?"

"There were, and maybe still are, gangs in Birmingham. The big gangs have all gone now but down Summer Lane there are a few who won't let it go, the Sabini or what's left of them. My money says that stiff was the owner of the garage. Mr Jacques, he's probably double-crossed someone, someone he shouldn't have and that someone is sending a message."

As he spoke, a car pulled into the station yard and up to the backwash. Jack had seen the car before and the two plain clothes' police officers who climbed out, they strode directly to the station office. How did they know their way around the station. Jack was still unsure of his way around it. Minutes later, the Tanoy came to life.

"Fireman Fowles, Fireman Wolf, to the station office."

Screaming looked annoyed at something or someone but was holding himself under control, he spoke through gritted teeth.

"These two police officers are going to ask you some questions; tell them all you know."

Neither officer showed any emotion, the younger, taller one, spoke first with a slight London accent.

"So you are the two who found the body?"

"Yes, you know that," Conker replied.

"Went straight to it, we understand and fished it out of the pit?"

Again, Conker replied, "Yes, we've been through this once."

"Seventeen firemen at the scene and you and the first day recruit find the body; strange, don't you think, Fowles?"

"T'was that somebody would happen upon the poor fellow. Why should that not befall we two?"

Jack smiled at Conker's turn of phrase, was he winding these guys up? He was not sure but Jack was getting used to Conker turning it on and off. The police officer turned to Screaming.

"Sir, how much does a fireman earn a week?"

"£20.50p for a standard 56 hour week," came Sid's exact reply.

"£20, you earn £20 a week, Fowles."

Conker stared at the police officer.

"Then can you tell me why you have £200 in used bank notes in your locker?"

Conker said nothing.

"Okay, moving on, how did you acquire knowledge of guns, bullets and assassins' tools of choice?"

A long silence, as Conker looked around the room looking at everyone in turn. Jack could stay silent no longer.

"What the hell is going on here? Are you forgetting we are the good guys? We took a gut full of shit, fought the fire and put it out. First, we have to listen to the half-baked ramblings and insults of your boy, the fool. Now you two clowns arrive and accuse us of being hit men, for the, the underworld Are you stark raving mad?"

He pulled himself up and looked around the room. He remembered that it was his first day, there were very experienced firemen and fire officers at the fire and it was probably not his place to attack these plain clothed C.I.D blokes or whatever they were, but this was not going to stop him. He started to open his mouth to continue, then.

"Fireman Wolf," a thirteen-year-old girl's voice shouted.

"You will stay quiet until you are spoken to. Do you understand?"

"Yes, Sir."

Jack stiffened and looked at Conker pleading him to say something, now the second cop spoke, Jack was boiling with rage, good cop, bad cop here it comes, *this is ridiculous,* he thought.

"Fowles, Fowles…where do I know that name from? Do you have relatives in the town?"

Conker looked him up and down and was considering questioning his parentage, his quaint way of phrasing had gone.

"Really? Is this all you've got? You've an obvious execution under your nose and you're fishing with a name linked with gangs fifty years ago. Wow, you are lost aren't you? Boys you really must try harder."

Conker was on the offensive; he was now questioning them.

"I bet you found the gun in the bottom of the pit, didn't you?"

"We cannot say."

"Of course, you did, no one that does this stuff stays close to the weapon or uses it twice, that would be stupid. Someone is pissed off, he has used a fresh gun, and he likes fires. He thinks they tidy up after him, and you" – turning his attention back to the taller cop – "you Sir, are up from London, on loan to the locals, are you? Could it be, you've got a turf war? Congratulations boys you've thought of that, haven't you?"

31

"Okay, that's it, this interview is at an end." Screaming had had enough.

On his way out, the tall cop turned to Conker and offered him his Police calling card. "If you remember anything, call me." Conker smiled and slid the cheap white card into his top pocket.

On the fire station's first floor, the kitchen and mess room were either side of the passageway that led to the top floor staircase; the kitchen overlooking the drill yard and tower, the mess room overlooking the front of the station and Ettington Road. In the bay window, Jack sat with Fatal, listening to an old brown Bakelite radio fixed oddly high on a plywood self between the chimneybreast and the front wall the smoke stained dial was set on the light program.

Fatal was fortyish with a beer belly that hung over his black leather belt which was twisted and straining with the weight it was under. He saw humour in just about every situation, constantly joking, he even spoke with a smile. He must have had an infection as a child as his face was pockmarked with odd patches of colour making him look more like a fifty-something-year-old. They each had a huge mug in front of them with two rounds of soggy toast that had been kept in the kitchen plate warmer. Jack was not keen on tea and the blue watch mess only had coffee syrup, which would do until he brought his own coffee into the mess.

"What did you do before you joined, Jack?" Fatal asked.

"I was an electrician."

"Sparks, eh, very useful, you may come in handy."

"How about you, Fatal, what did you do?"

"Bit like you, Jack, I have a trade, I was a carpenter."

Jack shot back, "Chippy, eh, very useful you may come in handy."

Fatal laughed aloud.

"What about the others. What did they do?"

"Well, Jack, me and you, oh and Harry are the only ones from civvy street. I was too young and missed it, the war that is, all the others went through the war in one service or another, not many fly boys, mostly Navy, like Tumble, Nobby, 600 and the others, some Army, like Screaming and Horace. Horace got his dicky leg in North Africa shot in both legs and a piece of his arse is missing, he does whine about it when it rains, he reckons it's the damp it gets in his wounds, fancy becoming a firemen and you don't like water or damp! Anyway, it gets him out of drill often enough when he don't fancy it, but to be fair to old Horace, he can work a turntable ladder and he's a good cook."

"You're not calling this toast cooking, are you?"

"Well, perhaps not this toast, but old Horace is a good mess man and a good bloke."

"As for me, after the war there wasn't much work around, reparation had only just begun when I started as an apprentice, I got pissed off fixing bombed out terraced houses so I joined the job along with Smudger."

"What's with all these nicknames? I don't know half the blokes' real names. I'm only getting nicknames."

"Well, it's kind of a tradition, it makes us the watch we are, nobody but your friends know your nickname and if someone isn't your friend and they use it that tells something about them. It's a bit of fun that's all, it gives us a bond."

"So where does Fatal come from?"

"Well, when I joined and came on the watch the first ten jobs I went to all had a stiff, fires, road traffic accidents, industrial accidents like, people trapped in machinery, everyone, all ten had a fatality involved, so they called me Fatal."

Jack looked Fatal in the face, unconsciously checking the amazing story, ten jobs and ten dead. Wow. Yet something was not right, the perma-smile was there as always but there was also a glint in his eyes, as Jack frowned, the perma-smile grew wider.

"Bullshit, first ten jobs and everyone a stiff. I don't believe it."

"Ha, good for you Jack, do you want the real reason?"

"Yes."

"Well, you see…My first name's Alan."

Jack looked at Fatal and burst out laughing. Fatal slapped him on the back.

"Good man, Jack, don't take no shit from nobody."

Fatal took a big draw on his mug of tea and looked out of the window watching the traffic on the road outside.

"What's with Conker, the Sabini, the underworld, and guns, Fatal?"

"Good old Jack, you don't miss much do you? Well, no one's quite sure what Conker did during the war. Some reckon he was lent to the Secret Intelligence Service and went to Taranto, Italy, in operation 'Slapstick', but he reckons he was just an ordinary parachutist."

"How come he knows so much about the Sabini family and gangs?"

"Ahh, the Sabini connection. That's his wife's side of the family. Don't know much about them other than they was more into horse racing and illegal gambling, but he did take me to a family do of theirs once, some years ago, and wow, what a family, like stepping into a bar in Naples, kids everywhere, the women dressed in black, men strutting around like peacocks drinking that red wine shit. I had to ask for a pint of mild, special like, and did they give me dirty looks and to cap it all, pasta as the food, I mean, who eats pasta?"

"That would be mainly the Italians, I guess."

"Well, yes, I know that, but what the hell is wrong with a proper buffet? We was in Highgate for Christ's sake! Not dear old Napoli. It was a party, weren't it so, sausage rolls, cheese on sticks, you know those hedgehog things and some pickled onions, pork pie and maybe pickled beetroot. Now who doesn't like a bit of pickled beetroot on a sandwich? Proper party food."

"I can see you're a gastronome and a lover of the finer things in life, Fatal."

Fatal laughed out loud, he seemed to laugh loudest at himself.

"So when did the Sabini start their family enterprise? Is it still going?" Jack's interest had awoken.

"Well, going way back, probably well before the first war or maybe as late as the early 1920s there were several rival gangs in Brum, the two biggest being the 'Sabini' and the 'Birmingham boys', not only the general gang stuff, but they really didn't like each other, they spent more time beating each other up or stabbing each other to death than anything else. Apparently, the cops were quite pleased with that state of affairs as it was naturally thinning them out and they left them pretty much alone. Conker reckons there are one or two dregs left but who knows."

Dusty approached the table and sat down.

"Hi, lads can I join you? Whoa, good ears Jack, How did you get them? Can I burst them for you? I'm good at burstin' blisters."

"No, no I'm fine thanks."

"That'll teach you not to stand up in fires, won't it, Fatal?"

Fatal decided to change the subject and save Jack any quizzing about his burns.

"Where you bin' with the TL Dusty?"

"Just a run into Central for stand-by cover, seems Ladywood have got a job on, made pumps five following an explosion while they were fighting a building fire, they requested two ambulances, that's the last I heard. Horace is sitting on the TL's radio in the engine house listening to the messages."

"I'm going down to listen."

The two old hands understood the lad's keenness and watched him go without speaking. Jack made his way down to the engine house as he approached

34

the turntable ladder he looked up and saw Horace sitting hunched over the steering wheel listening intently to a message. He climbed into the front officer's seat; beside him, Horace held a finger up and pointed at the brigade wide radio, a man's voice was hard to hear through the static but the tone was constant and controlled, he was calling control and identifying himself by the call sign of Ladywood's pump escape. The message started.

"Informative message from Station Officer Kent at Frederick Street. This incident involves a single storey building of timber and brick construction measuring approximately a hundred feet by fifty feet with a pitched corrugated asbestos roof, the building being used as a workshop. The building is fully involved and on fire severely, four main jets in use and one turntable monitor, we have experienced the explosion of an acetylene cylinder, which resulted in injuries to two firemen both of which have been conveyed to the Birmingham Accident Hospital by service ambulance, details of personnel injured will be sent by landline shortly."

The message was short, it had no emotion and ended as abruptly as it started.

"Why didn't they tell fire control who the men were and what injuries they had?"

"It's an open radio, Jack we're listening in, who else is listening in? Newspapers, radio stations, even relatives and wives sometimes listen in especially if it's a big job, not the best way to find out your husband's been blown up, is it? So, it's done on a landline. HQ can control who gets what news and when."

Horace lent forward and turned the little blue knob to the off position on radio. "Anyway, it's half five; only half an hour left of the shift, time to mop the engine house before we finish. Fancy a pint on the way home?"

Horace had mentally switched off as he switched off the brigade wide radio. He knew not to get emotionally involved.

"Yes, why not."

Jack fancied a pint.

Dancing with the Devil

"Parade, Parade, attention."

At 1800 hours, the men of Blue Watch Aston came to attention in the backwash of the engine house, runners and riders were called off for the fifteen-hour night shift. Jack was the fifth man on the back of the pump escape, after checking all the equipment on each engine was present, clean and working, the watch met up in the mess room for tea and the reading of the latest orders from HQ. The orders were read by Sid who ended with, and today is 30 November; does that mean anything to anyone? Jack knew what was coming.

"Happy birthday, Jack."

Screaming was in fatherly mode.

"Arrange a drink after work with the boys one evening and I'll buy you a pint."

"Thank you, S. O.," replied Jack in amazement.

"In the meantime, you have to put a birthday pint in for everyone behind the bar upstairs. Its tradition."

Up another two flights of stairs from the first floor mess room and kitchen was the top floor domestic area where firemen relaxed during stand-down periods. It had two brass poles that dropped some forty feet to the engine house floor below, one from the dormitory at one end of the building and the other from the games' room and bar, the bar was open to on duty firemen just the same as any pub, all were allowed to drink during stand-down except the drivers.

Sid had not said more than half a dozen words to Jack since he came from training school and now he was offering to buy him a drink. He would take him up on this kindly offer. The drawback was he would have to buy everyone a drink first.

"One last thing men, just thought you would like to know, the two guys from Ladywood caught in the explosion are doing okay. Both have blast injuries but unfortunately the Leading fireman broke his Back, they say they have to wait for

36

the swelling to go down before they know if he'll walk again and the fireman that was with him, Crompton, Firemen Crompton or Compton. I'm not too sure of his name, was hit by flying shrapnel from the cylinder that severed the femoral artery in his thigh."

Dusty broke into Sid's briefing.

"They reckon the pump operator realised what was happening and saved him from bleeding to death by standing on him, well on his leg anyway, he wouldn't keep still, writhing about he was."

Screaming knew Dusty well and it was time to stop him talking.

"Yes, thank you, Dusty, enough about the writhing. Everybody on the drill ground full fire kit, 1900 hours."

The three officers stood up and left the room.

Across the mess table from Jack sat a new face, a young face, he looked Jack straight in the eye, the stare was solid but kindly, yet unflinching and confident.

"Hi, I'm Harry, been on leave and missed your baptism."

Jack offered him his hand. "Nice to meet you. How long have you been on Blue Watch, Harry?"

"God, you're a bit formal, aren't you? Handshaking and all, not long just coming up to a year now. I came top, got the silver axe, best student, where did you come?"

"Pretty much middle, pretty much average, pretty much expected."

"I hear you hit the ground running though, a stiff on your first shift, good stuff, it took me six weeks before I had one, a floater in Handsworth Park, Lake."

"A floater, I have to tell you Harry I'm struggling with the new language, what the hell's a floater?"

"Oh, sorry mate, I struggled too at first, a floater is a drowning on the surface; drownings apparently, have two types, those that take on water as they drown, they're sinkers, and those whose throats naturally close up as they drown, they basically suffocate and float."

Harry paused mid-sentence, considering what he had just said. Jack instinctively leant forward waiting for the next nugget of information. Harry was back from his deep thoughts.

"However, sinkers decompose depending on the time of year and water temperature, then they gas up and come to the surface and become floaters, mine was a sinker that became a floater."

"Are you sure about this? You sound like an expert in drownings. How come you know this stuff?"

"It's the old guys, they are amazing, they have seen it all. Wars, fires, accidents, the lot, they are as hard as nails, honestly, don't bother telling these guys you've got a minor injury, cut your finger or the like. You don't get no sympathy, if your finger is missing in action, you may want to mention it, they would help you look for it, maybe. Anyway, enough about that stuff; when we going for this drink?"

"Yes, I've been thinking about that, what about after Friday's day shift?"

"Great, we could have a few in the Barton Arms, then on to the Longboat in town and maybe a Ruby."

"Sounds good to me. Friday it is."

The short ring of the fire bell sent the engines' crews to racing downstairs to the engine house like Pavlov's dogs, they would respond to their allotted tasks.

"Pump escape only, police request assistance, person locked out," the attendant shouted from the watch-room doorway.

The pump escape pulled up to a halt quietly, no lights, no two tones, outside the three story Victorian house on Albert Road, it was easy to find with the Police Panda car and two bored coppers standing outside in the early evening darkness. Screaming approached the two young constables, one-stepped forward.

"Evening, Sir."

Good start, Jack thought. In Jack's mind there was some confusion over the equivalent ranks between the services. Jack had decided from the beginning; if in doubt throw in a 'sir' that keeps everyone happy, massaging Sid's ego should work well for these cops too.

"Evening officers, what have we got?"

"Apparently an old man lives alone here and he hasn't been seen for a few weeks, we've had a look around and the place is closed up tighter than a drum we can't get in, thought you could help us."

"Certainly, happy to help the boys in blue."

"Harry, Jack, around the back check for entry points up and down."

They made their way down an entry, then through a side gate and after checking the rear doors and windows returned to the front of the house where they found Sid standing in the small overgrown front garden. Harry spoke to Sid through the very overgrown tall privet hedge.

"Nothing around the back, SO unless you want to break a window."

"No, I don't think that'll be necessary. Who's the smallest Harry, you or Jack?"

"How heavy are you Jack?"

"Just 12 Stones," Jack replied, instantly.

"Ha, 12 Stones 4lbs."

"Jack SO he's a good half a stone lighter."

Jack wondered if Harry was inflating the numbers to avoid the task at hand.

"Okay, Jack, get yourself around here."

Jack stood by the side of the station officer who was staring down at an ornate cast iron grating that was directly under the stone bay window, the two friendly cops were also staring at the grating and Jack realised they had the same look on their faces as he must have, that puzzled but interested look of something new.

"Do you know what that is, Jack?"

"No, SO Is it an air vent?"

"No. It's a coalhole, well the chute down to the coalhole this house has a cellar and in the cellar is where the coal for the house was stored. When the coal was delivered in hundredweight sacks you didn't want them traipsing through the house making a mess with all that coal dust, so the house was built with a chute from the outside directly into the cellar. The coal wagon turns up, you tell the coalman how many hundredweight sacks you want and he tips them down the chute as he does, so he leaves the empty sack by the side of the grating. When he's done you count the empty sacks and pay him accordingly. Hey, presto cellar full of coal and no black dust in the house, and that is how we get in, smallest man down the chute. That's you, Jack, down the chute though the coalhole up the cellar steps and let us in through the front door, then we'll search the house for the missing resident."

The two young cops looked at each other and nodding thoughtfully as if this was a well-considered plan, even better it was a plan that didn't involve them in going down the coal chute.

Jack stared at the two foot by one foot grating that hadn't been used for well over fifty years and was much less enthusiastic.

"Okay, lads let's have this grating off. Jack get yourself a torch off the truck and take your axe and belt off, it will help you slide down the chute easier."

On the back of the pump escape. Jack rolled his axe and belt up and stowed it away. He started going through the torches looking for the brightest, they were at best pathetic torches, little green right angled things with two U2 batteries powering them, in fresh air they were nothing more than a pale yellow/orange glow, in smoke you couldn't even read your breathing apparatus pressure gauge with it. Jack took the brightest yellow glow available and made his way back to the now open grating.

"Okay, Jack, in you go, but first take your helmet off; you won't fit in there with that on."

Jack was so concerned with sliding down this dirty, damp, hundred-year-old chute that he could barely fit into, that he had forgotten it was on his head.

Taking off his black fire helmet, he said, "Here, Harry, hold this for me."

Harry smiled and taking the helmet shook his head. "Yes," his eyes said, "I'm glad it's not me."

Jack raised his arms above his head and was helped into the chute feet first. He wriggled and slid to the point where his head was at ground level, he could smell earth and the stronger smell of decaying wood and the dampness of the cellar, he tilted his head slightly sideways to stop his nose hitting the lintel supporting the bay window, bits of debris fell onto his face. He clenched his mouth shut; as he started his slide, his tunic started to rise up his back. He was now in near and total darkness with dirty cobwebs sticking to his face, he lowered himself to the point where his arms were at full length outstretched above his head but his feet were in free air, nothing solid no floor yet, he waived his legs in an attempt to find something solid but nothing, he thought of bringing his arms down to his side to control his descent but couldn't, there wasn't room, they would have to stay raised above his head until he was out of the chute. He waited for the situation to miraculously change but nothing, he was half way down, he couldn't go back but, how far would the fall be? A large black spider whose web had been destroyed by this invader made his way across Jack's face. He didn't even have enough room to shake his head, he tried blowing jets of air from his mouth to blow it away but the spider slowly made its way undisturbed across his face.

"You okay in there, Jack, not stuck, are you?"

"No SO It's just a little awkward."

Jack knew he had no choice, time to let go, it could be a ten-foot drop or a ten-inch drop but he had to let go, he had stalled long enough. Holding his breath he released his grip on the lintel and shot down the cute. The ride into the unknown was probably only four feet, then a drop of maybe two or three feet but just as the chute ended and the drop came, Jack hit something big in the pitch-blackness. He had no idea what it was, instinctively he flung his arms around the cloth covered thing, his feet hit the floor, he stumbled but held on tightly to the punch-bag like thing, they pivoted in the cellar in a weird dance which came to a slow graceful half circle end. He was upright and pleased he had made a good landing, not dropping tens of feet and breaking legs or ankles, he had made it safely, the hard bit was over.

It was probably due to this punch-bag or whatever it was suspended from the ceiling that broke his fall, fancy that, an old house in working class Aston having a gym in the cellar he thought. He held onto the punch-bag with his left hand and flicked the torch switch on with his right, bringing the pale yellow torchlight upward to shine on the punch-bag.

Jack didn't remember getting from the coalhole to the front door; an ashen faced Jack opened the door. The station officer looked at Jack.

"You okay, Jack?"

"He's in the cellar; he's hanging in the cellar."

Jack stepped aside and lent on the hallway wall. He thought he may well faint, the pump escapes crew and two young cops filed past him. Jack paused and took several deep breaths hoping it would clear his feeling of nausea, a minute later, he made himself follow the crew and go back to the coalhole.

The escapes crew had run the searchlight cable down the chute and lit the Victorian cellar and the hanging man, underneath him was a moving pool of creamy white, then he noticed the creamy white drops that fell from the clothing adding to the dinner plate sized pool of maggots.

Jack was trying his hardest to keep himself together; to him the only way was to rationalise what had happened. He must take pity on the hanging man, not fear him, he should look his dancing partner in the face, he pulled his gaze up from the maggots on the floor and with purpose looked the corpse once more in the face. The eyes were gone, they had been eaten by the maggots, there were no eyes, Jack couldn't take much more, he felt himself swaying, he was cold and sweating.

Sid, who had been watching his newest recruit, shouted, "Conker."

"Sir."

"Take Jack out, get him some fresh air."

Conker led Jack up and out, back to the roadside, the pumps escapes engine was ticking over, supplying power for the cellar searchlight. They sat on the blue brick front garden wall lit by a nearby street light. Jack watched the traffic passing to and fro, going about their business the headlights lighting up his face as they passed, they had no idea of the hellish thing in the blackness so close by.

"How you feeling, Jack?"

"I thought I was going to throw up, I don't feel too good."

"You've had a rough few weeks, thrown in at the deep-end a bit, Jack, hold it together, take some deep breaths, get some air, it will help."

Conker put his arm around him and they both sat silently watching the traffic. They must have looked a very odd couple to the passing motorists; for minutes nothing was said. Jack was the first to speak in a voice that was trembling as much as his body.

"I touched him, Conker, I held him, we danced around together in the cellar, bits came off of him in my hands, I think I dismembered him."

"Easy, Jack, easy. He's a stiff, he isn't a person anymore."

Jack suddenly stood up. "I need to wash my hands, I must wash my hands, I've got bits of him on my hands. Please, let me wash my hands, please, Conker."

"Okay, son, it's okay. Come to the back of the pump and you can have a wash."

Jack sobbed as he scrubbed rotten flesh off his hands under an outlet of the pump escape. As he shook the freezing cold water from his hands, he looked at Conker and coughed a short snotty laugh. Conker was watching him closely, he was worried for his young charge.

"It's my birthday, Conker. It's my birthday."

"I know, son, I know."

The Train to Nowhere

Off-going watch dismissed, Blue Watch half turned neatly and made their way to the locker room, all the watch were changing into civvies when Harry burst through the locker room swing doors, wearing the brightest red and white striped boating blazer anyone had ever seen.

"Everyone to the Barton Arms, Jack's buying," he announced loudly.

A small cheer went up, probably for the entrance of the blazer more than anything else. Jack had one foot on his locker shelf tying his shoelaces when Toot, Nobby, and 600 approached him.

"Belated happy birthday, Jack."

Toot Taylor was holding out his hand, Jack shook each man's hand in turn.

"Have a good time tonight, but we won't be joining you, long drive home and we know what these sessions can turn into. We'll have a pint for you when we get closer to home."

"Are you sure, this is not going to be a session, just a few beers?"

"If you believe that, you'll believe anything."

When they walked into the Barton's Arms, Jack was stunned by what he saw. This unassuming pub in the heart of run down Aston was a time warp, the outside hinted at the style of the nearby Tudor Aston Hall but the interior was pure High Victorian, everything from the wrought iron staircase, to the fabulous mahogany bar and Minton tiles everywhere, Jack looked around him, to his eyes it was beautiful, he was spellbound.

The group of fireman walked towards the bar where Screaming, Tumble and Dusty were already standing, each with a pint of mild, they had not got changed but just thrown a jacket over their uniforms. Sid seemed genuinely pleased to see the men, these were his boys, his surrogate family and he was proud of them. Sid sought out Jack from the crowd.

"What can I get you, Jack, what'll you have?"

"Pint of bitter please, SO."

Jack was expecting, 'Call me, Sid, we don't have to be formal off duty,' but it never came.

"Bitter? Are you sure, Jack? M&B do a nice pint of mild and they keep a good cellar here."

"No, thanks. I'll stay with the bitter if it's all the same to you."

"How you getting on with us old farts on Blue Watch, Jack, think you'll stick it?"

Dusty was asking the question but Sid bought his gaze from the pretty barmaid to Jack for the answer.

"I love it, thanks L.F."

Jack paused, waiting for, 'Call me Dusty', but, as before, nothing.

"Having said that, the bloke that hung himself, scared the living daylights out of me."

"So I hear, not a pretty sight even if you expecting it, that's the trouble with people that commit suicide, they never consider those that find them, or the state they may be in when they are found, they're very selfish when you think of it. But then again, they probably have more on their minds than worrying about the tidy up afterwards, or perhaps to them there is no afterwards, perhaps there is no afterwards for any of us, only a now, and if there's a now, when exactly was the beginning?" Dusty seemed to be having a very deep conversation with himself.

Sid shook his head slowly from side to side.

"Very well, Dusty, thank you, before we end up discussing the meaning of life, let's join the others at the tables."

The guys had pulled two small round cast iron tables together so they, all eight, could sit together. Jack walked over to the assembled group, sat down with his back to the bar placing his pint on the table.

"Where's ours?" Harry shouted out loud, pointing at Jack's pint.

"Just got yourself one, did you, you tight git."

"No, not at all, the station officer bought me this."

"Oh, did he? Teacher's pet, are you? You and the SO big mates, eh."

"No, of course, I'll buy a round."

Jack swivelled in his seat to face the bar. As he did so, he saw Dusty flanked by Sid and Tumble, carrying a tray of beers. The group laughed as one and grabbing a glass each they tapped them together over the centre of the table.

"Cheers gaffer and happy birthday, Jack," was the chorus.

Sid took one look at Harry's blazer and was transfixed.

"What do you think, SO? Great, isn't it? I bought it from the rag market only yesterday."

"It's a very interesting choice for a night out in Birmingham."

"Do you think so?"

"Yes, especially as we have no river to speak of, in Birmingham, but I'm sure it's fashionable or dare I say trendy, however a trifle sudden for my taste."

Still staring at the blazer, Sid sat next to Jack. "Do you smoke, son?"

"Well, yes, sometimes. I do like the odd Benson with a pint."

"How about a pipe or cigars?"

"Never tried a pipe but cigars I have. My father smokes Tom Thumb cigars, only at Christmas though, my mother buys them for him. When I became sixteen, he gave me one to try, now we always have a cigar together at Christmas, it's almost tradition."

Harry shouted out, "Oh, listen to her, Mommy! Daddy! He'll be telling us he was a choirboy next, mister goody two shoes."

Sid ignored Harry, opened his coat and reached into an inside pocket. He pulled out two cigars, not big maybe four or five inches long, from another inside pocket, he pulled a silver cigar cutter, clipping the end of the first cigar, he handed it to Jack. Jack took it and rolled it between his thumb and forefinger, testing the tobacco for moisture content then ran it under his nose inhaling the aroma he looked across at the guys sitting around the table, all were deep in conversations of one sort or another although Jack was sure the barmaid was high on the list of topics.

"It's a Cohiba, Jack, fine cigars, Cohiba, and what you're holding is a Panetelas, not too big, not too small in my opinion, that is."

A Dunhill lighter followed from Sid's pockets, Sid flicked the lighter into life and lit Jack's cigar first, Jack took a small drag on the fine cigar, and the ritual much cherished by Sid was complete.

"Happy birthday, Jack."

Another pint of bitter was plonked on the table in front of Jack, he finished the half an inch of beer left of his first pint and tasted the fresh one, a sour taste came to his lips, he held the straight pint glass up so the light from the stained glass window would show the clarity, it looked clear enough but tasted foul.

Jack looked across to the bar to see if the barmaid was free, rising he pushed his chair back and started the walk to the bar to complain. He realised the barmaid was watching him. She had no real interest in him, she was waiting for a reaction;

45

the group of firemen had gone strangely quiet. The barmaid fixed her gaze on him and continued polishing the same glass. Jack stopped, looked down at the pint and turned to the table. "Who's put what in my drink?" Everyone looked at Harry.

"Harry, what have you done?"

"Me, nothing, I've done nothing."

Jack walked to the bar. The barmaid was smiling. She expected him.

"Would you throw this away and give me a fresh pint, please."

"You ain't getting one for free, you'll have to pay for it."

"I'm happy to do that, but I'm not drinking one that's spiked with I don't know what."

She tipped the beer down the bar sink and picked up a clean glass. "Bitter, is it?"

"Yes, please. What was in it anyway?"

"A half gill of our finest malt and that's not cheap."

"And they thought I wouldn't taste it?"

"I did try to tell him, but he reckoned you wouldn't notice."

"Him, which one?"

"Who do you think? Harry, of course."

"You know Harry?"

"Oh, yes, I know Harry."

At that moment, Jack was slapped on the back by Harry as he bumped into his side.

"What you up to Jack, chatting the barmaid up, are you? I've tried it, you don't stand a chance mate. She's immune to that stuff?"

"Harry, what the hell were you thinking putting malt whisky in bitter?"

"Ah, it's nothing just a stiffener to get the evening going. Where is it, anyway?"

"Down the drain, where it belongs. If you want to buy me drinks, I'll drink one for one with you but let's not ruin both the whisky and the beer."

"Aha, great, two large whiskies, please, darling."

Jack downed his in one, and as he slammed the glass down on the bar top, he shook his head; the change of taste assailed his senses. He looked at the glass, *why did I do that? I don't like whisky.*

"What are you talking about, Jack? You're mumbling."

"Oh, nothing."

He took a drag on his cigar and his head spun, instantly, he realised he and all the pumps' crew had missed lunch, two slices of soggy toast at eleven o'clock; that was the sum total of his food for the day. Now, he was drinking beer and downing large whiskies, not the cleverest thing to do.

After three fast pints of beer, Harry stood up and pointed at his empty glass. "Who's for another?"

"No, I'm done."

"And me."

"And me." One by one, they all refused more drink.

Finishing their drinks, Blue Watch made their respective ways homeward, wishing Jack a happy birthday for the final time. The three officers were first to leave and Conker was last. Jack stood to say goodbye to his new friend, Conker shook his hand and drawing him in with the shanking hand whispered in Jack's ear, "Watch yourself, Jack. He likes practical jokes and you're heading the right way to be his next victim, let him get ahead of you in the drinking stakes."

Harry approached the table with two pints of beer in one hand and two glasses of whisky in the other.

"Good night, you two, look after each other."

Conker pulled on his coat, placed a grey cloth cap on his head and left.

"Right, just me and you, off to town, a couple in the Longboat and a Ruby, what do you say, Jack?"

Jack went to speak but noticed Harry was looking straight past him over his shoulder towards the entrance door.

"Bloody hell, Tony Bianchi, just the man, wait here, Jack."

Jack stared at the large whisky and the table full of empty glasses with dregs of beer inside. He looked over to the bar, Harry was in deep conversation with Bianchi. He swiftly grabbed the large whisky and began sharing it out between the empty glasses, with half gone, he stopped, looked at the half-empty glass, the rest went into Harry's glass. Jack looked at the bar once more, no change, Harry was in full flow, Jack took up his pint of bitter and managed to pour a little into the spirit glass but spilt more on the table than went into the glass. The table was a mess, he re-arranged the glasses and beer mats, so it didn't look so obvious and looked back to the bar. The two were in a very deep discussion about who knows what.

Then he noticed he was being watched, she was polishing glasses again. Jack realised, he'd been caught. She smiled, lifted the flap in the counter top and made her way over to the table, smiling.

"Shall I clear the table for you?"

"Thanks that would be great."

Her first tray of empties were the ones Harry was most happy to see go. When she returned for the rest, she was accompanied by Harry, and Bianchi. The barmaid wiped the table dry.

"Thank you, gorgeous, what time do you finish? Fancy a drink, maybe a Ruby later?"

"Piss off Harry."

"I'll take that as a maybe, shall I?"

"What are you two sprogs doing in here, in my local?" Bianchi asked.

'Sprogs' was not a word Jack liked, it seemed sharp and mean and when aimed at him it came as an insult. Jack had decided pretty much from the beginning that there was something about Bianchi that made him uneasy, the swagger, the air of superiority, Bianchi was to be watched closely.

"Me and my new mate, Jack, are off to the Longboat in town to have a drink for his birthday; do you want to join us?"

"No thanks, I don't want to be seen out and about in town with two sprogs. Anyway, as I told you, I'm meeting my brother here for a pint, bit of business to do, maybe some other time or maybe never." Jack was sure now he didn't like Bianchi and he didn't want to drink with him. As Bianchi spoke, his doppelganger walked in through the entrance door. He was the same in every respect, he made a spectacle of his entrance, he wanted to be seen and admired. The clothes and shoes were surely Italian, the look was finished off with a 'Borsalino' broad brim fedora, it was a sight to behold. *Did he doff his hat to the room as he removed it?*

"Franc's in the chair, who's drinking?" he announced loudly.

Tony bid the two sprogs farewell and joined his brother at the bar.

"Well, that's a surprise, I wasn't expecting that at all."

"You mean the identical twin thing, yes, amazing, isn't it, nine minutes apart so they say. Franc was first then Tony."

"Franc's got the Bianchi swagger all right. Are they both arse-holes or has Tony got the monopoly on being a shit?"

48

"Come off it, Jack, don't be like that, they are all right when you get to know them."

Jack was unconvinced; he grasped his spirit glass in his fist obscuring its contents and downed the glass in one.

"Come on, Harry, keep up."

Harry didn't flinch, he did the same with his glass, the barmaid was in plain view again and smiling.

Just up the canal from gas street basin, along a wharf the Longboat pub boasted its 1960s' architecture, inside blue brick arches acknowledged the canal-side heritage and that of nearby canal tunnels, the lack of light increased the effect, Jack wasn't keen on this pub he preferred the old pubs in town but Harry seemed at home here.

Harry, sitting with his back to a full wall mirror, which was supposed to increase the tunnel effect, he sipped his pint of Davenports Lager, the trompe l'oeil effect was totally lost on Jack as it appeared that there were two Harrys drinking with him and as the Bitter and Whisky from earlier, were beginning to take hold, this double Harry effect was not helping.

"Jack, you into cars?"

"Yes, well engines, and the like anyway. I re-built my BSA bike in my dad's garage, it was in bits when I bought it."

"No, not that old shit, not bikes. What do you want with that old crap? I mean proper cars."

"Like what?"

"Well, I've asked Tony's brother to help me find a Jaguar, he's in the trade, he buys and sells motors and I might get one cheap."

"One what? A Mark ten or something?"

"Oh god, you are boring Jack; a proper car, a sports car hopefully an E-type, even better an E-type convertible."

"Good grief, Harry, you aren't messing around, won the pools or something, have you? An exhaust for that would cost more than my bike's worth."

Jack sipped his pint and looked at Harry who seemed to be getting a little drunk.

"You really are serious, aren't you? Wow, an E-Type, it drinks petrol faster than I drink beer. How the hell can you afford it?"

"Well, Franc reckons if I do a little driving for him, as a part-time job when not on duty, ferrying cars between auction houses and picking them up from spray shops, that sort of stuff, he will take money I earn off any money I will owe him. It would be beneficial for the two of us. He gets more time doing his business sourcing cars and I get a new car; well, new to me. I'm not talking about a brand new one, I mean a second-hand one, that's maybe been in a bump and been fixed or repossessed, you can get a real bargain, he reckons. Franc reckons if I give him a little time something will turn up in the trade and he'll jump on it for me."

"Franc seems to be doing a lot of reckoning for you."

"He's a good bloke, Jack, don't be so negative. The only problem is, he wants a wedge up front and I don't have it."

"The only problem, that's the only problem, how big a wedge, how much?"

"A ton."

"A ton, £100.00 for something you haven't seen, well nobody's seen, it might not even have had its crash yet, you must be mad."

"I know, I know, but think about it, Jack, we're talking an E-Type, that will pull the birds, bound too, look at it my way, I'm thinking of it more as an investment in my future marital happiness."

"An investment in your imminent poverty, I reckon, Harry. How come Tony's twin can get motors like Jags? What exactly does he do anyway, this all sounds a bit vague to me?"

"Gor-blimey, keep up Jack, he's in the trade, do you want me to paint you a bloody picture? It's what he does, he buys and sells cars, sometimes write offs and sometimes repo's does 'em up, you know, repairs them or whatever, then moves them on. Being ex-fire he has contacts in the job and with the cops, so he gets first pick of the car wrecks in town. He's in with the car insurance guys too, so it's a win for everybody."

"Franc was a fireman?"

"Yes, I thought everyone knew that Francesco and Antonio Bianchi joined together, had their picture in the Birmingham Evening Mail, and everything. Didn't you see it in the paper? They were famous for a day; well, just the evening edition actually."

"'The Birmingham boys at the double.' That's what the line read, was in the local interest section, 'Twins join City Fire Brigade' blah, blah, blah. Franc sailed a bit too close to the wind though, he got into a bit of trouble with missing petrol."

"What do you mean missing petrol?"

"Yes, well, when he was newly promoted to sub-officer, he was left in charge of a station and he decided to fill his private car up with petrol from the station fuel pump, while the gaffer was out on a shout one morning, got caught red-handed when a divisional officer came for an early morning visit; apparently he also had a few cans in the boot as well for good measure. When they went back through the petrol tally books, they had him down for hundreds of gallons."

"What, are you serious?"

"The brigade was good to him though, gave him a choice, gave him a way out. Resign and walk away, no pension, no nothing or, they call in the cops and have him charged with theft. He walked. But for God's sake, never mention a word of this to him, he's really bitter about the whole thing, reckons he should have been given a second chance, he offered to pay for the 'missing' petrol but the chief wasn't having it, he got the order of the boot and he didn't like it."

"I can't believe what I'm hearing; and this is the guy you are going to work for part time? Have you thought this through, you're seriously going to give him £100.00 in addition to working for him, that's the equivalent of two months' wages as a deposit in order to maybe, get a second hand E-type that may have been in a crash and written off at best, all this from someone who you have just described as a petty thief! No wonder he was smiling when we left, he's taking you for a fool. Harry, you must be pissed you haven't heard yourself. Don't be so gullible, it all sounds ridiculous."

"Oh thanks mate, thanks for your enthusiastic support, no imagination, that's your trouble. The way I look at it is, I'm getting a bargain, an E-Type, hopefully a convertible, a bird pulling machine for £100.00 down, I'm an optimist I'm a glass half full sort of guy."

"That maybe metaphorically correct, Harry, but your glass is actually empty."

"If you're going to take the piss, Jack, you can drink alone."

Harry got up and walked to the bar, empty glass in hand, and called for another drink.

Jack thought it was time for peace-making and even more important, time for something to eat. Walking up to the bar he placed his empty glass next to Harry's.

"Come on, aitch, I'm sorry, I didn't mean to be so blunt, cheer up, it's my birthday drink. I'm going to let you buy me a curry, where you taking me?"

Harry looked at Jack, not sure if he should forgive him for his scepticism; perhaps he could show Jack who the gullible one was.

"Erdington, that's where we're going, great curry house, my favourite the chef's from Sylhet, great Bengali food."

Jack turned towards the door. "I'll get a Taxi."

"No, we don't need no taxi, we'll take the train from New Street, dead cheap the way I travel. Stay with me and just buy a platform ticket."

Down on platform two of New Street Station, the old train was waiting, a carriage was directly in front of them as they came down the staircase. Harry reached forward and opened the well-worn handle to the slam door carriage and gestured for Jack to climb in first. Jack obliged and made his way to the nearest pair of available seats, which wasn't really difficult as they were the only two people in the carriage. They sat down on the dusty, maroon coloured heavy wool seats which smelled of old age and stale tobacco, after a couple of minutes' conversation about the types of curry available, Harry Jumped up.

"Just off to the loo mate, must have a piss, won't be a tick."

Harry was gone from the carriage. Looking around, Jack thought, how lucky they had been at finding a train so easily, but he did not feel comfortable with just a platform ticket in his pocket, what did Harry have in mind when they got to Erdington? How would they get out of the station? Anyway they had made it just in time as Jack could hear the last few doors slamming shut and whistles blowing as cries of farewell filled the air.

In that instant, it dawned on Jack, he was being set up. He was out of his seat as the train started to move, running in the opposite direction to Harry, he leapt from the carriage door as the train gathered pace, given extra speed by the moving train, he ran headlong into a white ceramic tiled supporting column. Grasping it, he swung himself around, pressing his back against the tiles, hiding himself from where Harry must surely be, he waited a good thirty seconds before looking around the column. There he was, Harry, with his back to Jack, watching the train to Erdington pull out of the station, Harry gave the train a mock wave as he walked forward towards the exit stairs.

Jack followed at a distance.

Jack was finding following someone without being seen extremely difficult, staying close enough to watch which way the person is going, but out of sight, was harder than he ever imagined, but Harry was unknowingly being helpful, wearing his red and white boating blazer he stood out like a sore thumb, he had no idea he was being tailed. He was convinced his gullible friend was on his way to Erdington and maybe even further afield if he fell asleep, Harry was pleased he had pulled off his practical joke, he allowed himself a wry smile. It was thankfully a short walk from the train station out onto Stephenson Street. Harry crossed the road and joined the end of a small queue of people outside the rear entrance of the Midland Hotel. The queue was being controlled by a rather large bouncer dressed in an ill-fitting black three piece suit, who held a clicker in his left hand, numbers in the bar were restricted so when the bar was full, no one goes in until someone comes out. As Jack watched, Harry turned around and looked in his direction. Jack froze, luckily, he hadn't been seen. Leaning back against the wall Harry took out a cigarette and lit it waiting patiently for his turn to enter. It was at that moment the plan crystallised in Jack's mind, he knew the front way into the hotel and he knew some of the door and bar staff, it might just work.

Turning his back on the growing queue, Jack, almost breaking into a run, crossed Stephenson Street and made his way up Stephenson Place then left into New Street, just a few more yards and left again was Burlington Arcade, through the arcade and down the stairs to the Midland Hotel front reception, standing close by was a large friendly face dressed in the same ill-fitting suit as the guy on the back door. Donald was an old classmate from Queensbridge School, he instantly recognised Jack as he approached.

"Hey John, how's it hanging buddy. I haven't seen you in a while."

"Hi, I'm good, thanks Don. Any chance I can come in and have a pint at the back bar?"

"What you doing here around the front, Jack? You know, it's 'residents' only' this way in, walk-ins have to go around the back."

"I know, I know, but I'm running late and I'm meeting someone special, if you know what I mean. I can't be late, I'll put a pint behind the bar for you. What do you say?"

Don smiled a huge smile. "Okay, pint of larger and lime, make sure you tell and pay Rona, no one else, she's working the downstairs bar tonight."

"Is she now? That's even better. Thanks, Don."

Just inside the doorway from the hotel to the rear bar stood yet another ill-fitting suit, as Jack opened the door and stepped into the bar, he was surprised by a "Good evening, Sir." This suit naturally assumed Jack was a resident.

"Good evening indeed." Jack heard what he just said out loud and thought it may have sounded a bit pompous; anyway he was in, so far so good.

The rear bar was packed. Jack made his way to the end of the bar where Rona was standing punching numbers into a till, Rona was in her mid-forties and not unattractive, she had worked a few bars in the town as manageress, that's how Jack had come to know her. She ran a tight ship, a plain no nonsense woman. Jack knew her enough to pass the time of day with her, but she lingered with no one, she was pleasant to all, but business came first.

Rona looked up and saw the familiar face standing next to her. "Well, Well, John Wolf. Well, last time I saw you was when I was running 'The Hole in the Wall'. Where have you been? Come into some money now, have you, drinking in hotels?"

"I've been working shifts, working nights means not so many free evenings. You don't want to hear my sob story so first things first, would you put Don on the front door, his usual behind the bar for me. I'll have a pint of Ruddles and have one yourself, and one last thing, I've a favour to ask you."

"Ask the favour before you buy me the drink and I'll decide if I'm drinking with you."

"My mate is about to come through the back door. I want him to think I work here. I just need to stand your side of the bar for two minutes when he comes in. I'll touch nothing, no drinks, no till. I just want him to see me behind the bar."

"It'll cost you a large vodka and tonic, touch anything and I'll cut your hands off."

"Thanks, Rona."

Jack pushed open the low bar end door and took up his position, with his back to a rack of spirit optics, he kept out of the way of the busy bar staff, sipping his Ruddles, he waited for Harry. It didn't take long, Jack heard him before he saw him.

"Excuse me, excuse me, coming through, man with a thirst, let me get to the bar, excuse me."

Holding a ten pound note aloft, Harry got to the bar and squeezed himself unceremoniously between two large groups of office workers, waiving the note in the air, he scanned the long bar for available serving staff. Then his gaze froze, his head stopped dead, then slowly returned to the far end of the bar. There he was sipping a pint of beer and nonchalantly waving with his free hand. Harry's jaw visibly dropped; what he was seeing could not be possible. As Jack watched, Rona snatched the ten-pound note from Harry's grasp.

"I take it you're John's friend and you're buying the drinks. Cheers."

Harry was stunned. This was all happening too fast, he was still staring at Jack.

"Yes, that's fine, that's fine." He could say nothing else.

"Good, that's a lager and lime, a Ruddles, a very large Vodka and tonic and yours is?"

"Mild. Mild, a pint of Mild, please."

"We don't sell Mild here, we're a hotel not a working men's club."

"Bitter then, Bitter is fine."

Harry watched as she walked over to Jack, who had not moved an inch. Standing close, she turned and waving the ten-pound note in the air she pointed to Harry. Jack raised his glass in mock salute. Rona was quick witted but Jack didn't realise how quick she caught on to developing situations. She turned back, drew herself up to Jack and kissed him on the right cheek. She turned away, moving slowly and somehow alluringly, off to pour the drinks. Jack was surprised by the kiss yet stayed cool and played his part. Harry could only watch in disbelief.

Things couldn't be going better but Jack wanted to get away without speaking to Harry. He had to leave him wondering how the hell he managed to get not only here before him but behind the bar. Harry was now again shouting, "Excuse me, excuse me, coming through," making his way towards Jack. Jack had to be quick. He slipped out from behind the bar.

"Thanks Rona, I owe you one."

Rona smiled and carried on serving drinks. Jack made his way not towards the back door but toward the hotel door from where he had come in. The same suit was still working the door. Jack looked at the big guy barring the way, his sole job was to stop revellers from entering the hotel proper. As he approached him, the suit walked across his path and took hold of the large ornate brass door handle. Jack slowed and considered his options; it was a dead end, and Harry was undoubtedly coming up behind him, the suit all of a sudden smiled.

"Good evening, Sir, I do hope you enjoyed your drink." He swung open the heavy door for Jack to pass through.

"Thank you, yes the Ruddles is very good tonight."

Making his way out, Jack was now in the hotel foyer once more and passing Donald.

"Thanks Don, your drink's behind the bar."

At that same moment, back in the bar, Harry approached the Hotel doorway in an attempt to follow Jack. The suit stepped in front of him.

"Sorry Sir, residents only passed this point."

"But I'm with my friend, the guy you just let through."

"Yes, of course you are, Sir, he's a resident here. You show me your room key and I'll be happy to let you through."

"I haven't got a room key, anyway. It's a fire escape route, it has to be available for everyone to use when the premises are open and in use and I want to use it."

"And it will be Sir, just as soon as fire breaks out. I'll be the one to make sure you're first through this door. Until that time, I would be obliged if you would use the rear door."

To the drunken Harry, being patronised by a mere Neanderthal was extremely annoying, and a Neanderthal, even one in a suit, was not telling him what to do.

"I demand to use this doorway. Get out of my way."

"Sir is demanding, is he?"

Harry sized up the suit, surely this guy would not risk his job by fighting over one person using the door, although the suit was a good six inches taller and heavy set, to Harry he looked muscle-bound, no quick reactions so maybe a bit thick in the head, slow and docile like all Neanderthals. Harry leant forward and took hold of the brass door handle.

"I'm coming through and you're not stopping me."

The suit lent forward to whisper in Harry's ear.

"Let me explain it in plain English for you Sir, as you seem to be having trouble understanding me, me being so polite and all. You see, it's like this. Pull that handle and you'll wake up in hospital."

The suit pulled away but kept eye contact with Harry. He left Harry with the decision.

Harry looked the Neanderthal in the eyes and quickly thought his options through, an easy decision, he decided. Bluff, he could read this guy like a book, this bouncer was full of crap, and idle threats. He tugged at the handle.

The fist that hit Harry full in the face was larger than normal considering the size of man swinging it, this guy must have practiced, maybe it was his time as an amateur boxer that helped, he was fast, he never telegraphed its imminent arrival, Harry never saw it coming.

The Family Man

At Aston, the tour of duty was about to start, it was fifteen minutes before parade when Harry walked into the locker room sporting the biggest black eye anyone had seen for a good while. Everybody looked but Dusty was the first to ask the question.

"Whoa, how the hell did you get that? What a shiner! You need to get a beef steak on that."

"Yes, I know, I know, I've had lots of advice and old maids' remedies and shit from everyone. The constant comments are beginning to piss me off, okay. So you all know I got hit by a bouncer in a bar. That's it, story over."

"Okay, Harry, don't get your knickers in a twist. I only asked, perhaps we should rename you, maybe we'll call you Shiner."

Conker looked across the crowded locker room towards Jack, he frowned and moved his head down and slightly to one side. Jack didn't know why but he could read Conker's expressions easily and it was reciprocal when Jack pursed his lips, raised his hands and showed his palms with fingers spread to Conker. Conker knew the answer. Clean hands, not me.

As Blue Watch made their way out of the locker room for morning parade, Harry waited for Jack by the doorway. As Jack walked towards him Harry put out his hand offering a handshake. Jack smiled and grasped his friend's hand.

"I have no clue as to how you did it Jack but good on you, no hard feelings."

"No hard feelings from me, Harry, it looks like you came out of this the worst, anyway."

"Yes, and I've been barred from the Midland Hotel, me barred, the bastards, I've never been barred from anywhere."

Sid was standing in front of the paraded Blue Watch. The station officer had not failed to notice Harry's black eye which he seemed to be staring at with interest. The parade was standing at ease. After the sub-officer had taken roll call and the runners and riders had been called off, Sid bringing himself back from wondering how Harry had acquired his black eye, pulled himself upright.

"Just one thing from me, men, it's an update on the spate of workshop fires we've been having. It would seem that there is a possibility that they are all connected. Handsworth had another last night which contained several cars which were shut and cuts and that was definitely arson. Well, a fire of doubtful origin anyway so, with our Aston lane job, Ladywood's job where the two guys were injured and now Handsworth, it would seem someone is targeting workshops."

"Was Ladywood's job arson then, SO?" asked Conker.

"Yes, apparently they made a very good job of torching the place. The investigating officer says it was a professional job. When they eventually found the pieces of the oxyacetylene set, the torch and the cylinder head were turned on, probably playing on the wall of the cylinders virtually guaranteeing an explosion. Nasty evil thing to do, no thought of us, when we have to get into the building to fight the fire."

"How's about the chaps who were injured, SO?" Smudger asked.

"Good news there, the leading fireman that broke his back is not as bad as first thought. He is walking a bit, it's doubtful that he will get back to full duty but at least he's walking, the fireman is on the mend as well."

"Thank you, sub-officer, dismiss the men."

The rest of the shift was pretty much uneventful. The usual false alarms from kids calling from phone boxes. The operators in fire control tried to keep them talking until an engine could get to the box but the serial offenders knew only too well this ruse, and could time their escape to perfection after abusing the control staff, they were rarely caught.

Just as lunch was being served, the fire bell rattled into life.

"Rubbish chute on fire. Sapphire Tower, everybody goes."

Jack looked down at his lunch, boiled codfish mashed potato with a few peas smothered in parsley sauce served on a snow-white plate. It was probably the most unappetising meal he had ever seen. Surely this couldn't be the work of Horace. Jack pushed it away leaving it on the table, the call was a great excuse for throwing away the congealed blob, when he returned, which hopefully would be long enough to declare the meal cold, stale and inedible, so not upsetting the person who had created it. As he left the mess room, he noticed some of the plates had names hastily scribbled on their rims in black china graph pencil.

When the owners returned, they actually wanted to resume eating the white thing and the names made sure they returned to the right plate. Jack would be happy to throw his away anonymously.

The short ride to Sapphire Tower was almost a weekly run so there was no frantic drive to get there in record time. It seemed to the crews that someone enjoyed lighting rubbish and dropping it down the rubbish chute, sending it tumbling into the huge, galvanised bins housed at the base of the tower deliberately setting them alight, the chute would then act as a chimney funnelling acrid smoke to the upper floors where the tenants would berate the firemen as if it was their fault for letting the smoke enter their lobby. Was it to watch the fire engines and crews arriving or was it just to see firemen? Perhaps even meet one and maybe talk to him, was it to relieve the boredom of living in a council tower block full of unemployed and unruly youths that made someone repeat their stupidity?

No one really knew, but if someone was getting enjoyment or satisfaction from it, the fire crews would do everything possible to disappoint them. So as not to make it a spectacle, the ride and approach was low key, no two tone horns, the blue lights turned off as they approached the tower and the whole event would be treated as mundane, each time the bins would be wheeled out and filled with water and each time the station officer picked out four firemen to walk the floors checking for other fires. The order duly came.

"You two, walk the floors top down to ten and you two ten down."

As the crews turned to their tasks, there were three loud pops as apples exploded amongst them. The crews all moved instinctively close to the wall of the tower.

"Okay, the bastards are throwing stuff, move the engines out into the street and stay close, and no wandering about." Sid was as cool as ever.

Jack watched as the fire engines were moved, no one seemed at all concerned that someone was throwing fruit at them, he looked up the tower but he could see no one on a balcony or at a window. He was scanning the face of the tower when 'pop-pop', another two apples exploded on the pavement in front of him. 'Johnny' Johnson was standing next to him his back pressed against the tower wall.

"It's best not to look up this close to the tower, Jack. Do you know an apple thrown from the twentieth floor is doing about a hundred miles an hour when it reaches the ground and, believe me, that hurts if it hits you, even with your helmet on. Having said that, we've had worse thrown down onto us."

"Like what?"

"Oh, general stuff, rubbish usually. The pump roof got hit by a tin of baked beans last year. No, tell a lie it was alphabetti spaghetti, not beans. Oh and dog shit, Smudger got hit with that a while ago, we've had dog shit a few times."

"But I didn't think you could keep dogs in a council tower block."

"You're right, they can't. I'll let you go up and explain that to the drug dealer living up on the top floor who has a very short-tempered 120lb Rottweiler called Diablo, which he keeps for protection. I'll let you tell him he really shouldn't have a pet dog in a tower block, shall I? Best of luck with that."

"Yes, good point, but why throw dog shit?"

"Who knows, perhaps it's because we represent the establishment, we're in uniform, all the things they don't like, who knows."

Conker walked from the entrance door, keeping close to the wall and stood by Jonny and Jack, all three now standing with their backs pressed against the tower wall. He looked across to the station officer who was standing on the other side of the road, well out of the drop zone.

"All clear ten down, SO."

"Thank you." Sid gave a wave of his hand.

"Are you on your motorbike today, Jack?" Conker asked.

"Yes, I certainly am, a bit chilly this time of year but at least it's dry."

"Any chance of a lift home this evening? I want to get home smartish. I'm taking the misses out for a meal tonight. It's our anniversary and don't want to be late."

"Of course, if you're happy riding pillion. Where will you be taking Mrs Fowles tonight?"

"Up town. It's all booked, The Berni Inn, Stephenson Place. Prawn cocktail to start, then a nice juicy Sirloin steak, followed by a big wedge of Black Forrest gateau, all washed down with some Mateus Rose, it's her favourite."

"Very nice, I know it well, and the Midland Hotel is just around the corner for pre-dinner drinks if you have time."

Conker laughed. "Oh yes but you have to watch the bouncers there though, they're handy with their fists, I hear."

"Apparently so."

The sound of Smudger's voice came from the entrance doorway.

"All clear, from the top down to ten SO."

"Okay men, let's go home."

Everyone moved quickly, heads down, mounting their respective fire engines. Jack decided to take Jonny's advice and not to look up again. He didn't like the thought of being hit in the face by a fifteen-ounce tin of alphabetti spaghetti or, for that matter, by one hundred mile an hour flying Diablo shit. The three trucks left as unceremoniously as they arrived.

At five past six, Jack and Conker were weaving through the city traffic on Jack's 650cc BSA Golden Flash motorbike. They looked quite a sight; Jack in blue jeans and a world war two flying jacket and flying helmet and Conker in a rather large gabardine mackintosh, fire boots and his grey cloth cap on backwards, which stopped the wind getting under the peak and blowing it off his head.

Making their way through a huge, post-war council housing estate in Kings Heath, their journey ended in a small quiet pudding bag cul-de-sac. They were just six miles south of the city they worked in. Jack kicked the bike stand down and turned off the ignition. Reaching under the petrol tank he pushed the petrol tap to the off position. The tank did leak a little and this prevented a pool of petrol gathering underneath the bike. He pulled off the leather helmet and stuffing it into his jacket pocket, he looked around the cul-de-sac, it had no more than a dozen semi-detached houses arranged in an open ended circle, all of which were owned by the fire brigade.

"Thanks Jack, that was great fun, it's a long time since I've ridden a motorbike. I'd forgotten how much fun it is. Come in and meet the misses and the family."

"Are you sure it's all right? You need to get yourself changed and off to town. Maybe another time."

"Of course, I insist you have a coffee. I've a real Italian percolator. You can chat to the misses while I have a quick bath."

"All right, thank you, if you're sure you have time."

"Don't worry about that, come on in."

The front door of the small semi-detached house led into an equally small hallway. Conker pointed out the coat hooks and Jack hung his jacket on the only free hook. Straight ahead, beside the staircase, was the kitchen door. Pushing it open Conker announced loudly, "I'm home you lot and we have company, I hope you are all decent."

You lot, all decent, Jack had not asked and Conker had never mentioned the family he was about to meet. In the kitchen, totally un-impressed with their father, were the fifteen-year-old twins, Sara and Alice. They were introduced to Jack, looking at each other they giggled and laughed as Jack held his hand out as a greeting. Was it shyness that made them giggle and reluctant to shake hands with Jack or, was it their father standing in the kitchen in a gabardine mackintosh with his hat on backwards that was making them laugh? Whatever it was, it made Jack look and feel a little awkward standing as he was in the middle of Conker's kitchen with his arm outstretched and no hand to shake. Luckily, at that moment, a tall, attractive woman with short, dark hair came through the back door of the house and firmly grasped the outstretched hand. "Ciao, welcome."

"Ah, here she is, the love of my life, my darling Giulia. Happy anniversary darling, this is my new friend, Jack."

"Welcome Jack. Joseph has told me all about you and your exploits together. I see you have met the terrors. Have you met Sophia?"

"Thank you, Mrs Fowles. No, no I haven't."

"Ah, there you are, Sophia." Giulia then looked down to see a black smudge mark on the back of her hand left by Jack's thumb.

Sophia, hearing her father's arrival, had come down the stairs from her room and entered the kitchen and was now standing behind Jack. Jack turned and froze to the spot. Jack had never seen a more beautiful girl. The biggest, darkest eyes he had ever seen. Sophia was just twenty years old, she stood five feet six inches tall, long dark hair reaching down to her waist, and the longest legs. To him, she was perfect; then she smiled, an enticing, tantalising smile that lit the room. It captivated him, Jack was in a trance, he was dumbstruck.

"Sophia, this is Jack."

Jack's hand naturally shot out again to shake hands. Why? He did not know, it was a habit, men were okay with shaking hands but girls found it rather old-fashioned and awkward. Yet, here he was again, standing in the kitchen, with his hand outstretched. Thankfully, Sophia smiled and offered her hand. Jack grasped it eagerly and a little too tightly. She winced as one of her finger rings dug into an adjacent finger.

Quickly returning from his trance, he said, "Oh, I'm sorry, I didn't mean to hurt you." He looked with alarm at Sophia's hand.

Sophia also looked at her hand, the back of her hand had a black oily smudge mark, maybe lighter but nevertheless similar to her mother's. Lifting it upwards towards her face, she looked at Jack.

"Petrol?"

"Two star petrol, my bike's an 'A10' so, a four stroke engine."

What the hell am I doing, he thought. Jack hoped the ground would open up and swallow him. He couldn't believe what he was saying. He had just met the most beautiful girl he had ever seen and within thirty seconds had made her wince with pain, marked her hand with engine oil and struck up a conversation regarding the different grades of petrol and types of combustion engine most suited to them. Just when he thought it could get no worse, he blurted out another gem.

"Swarfega, have you got any? That will get rid of that, works every time."

"Does it, Jack? You are a mine of information, unfortunately, mostly useless, I'll check my make-up bag for Swarf... Whatever, I'm bound to have some; it's probably in my purse with my set of socket spanners."

Jack had to admit defeat. He was lost for words. He just looked again at the oily smudge mark on her hand and slowly shook his head. His moment to impress Sophia had quickly passed.

Conker saw Jack was floundering and decided to come to his rescue, but before he did he glanced at Giulia. She smiled knowingly and raised her eyebrows; women know these things, they can feel the chemistry way before men know what's happening.

"Is it best if I leave before I say anything else stupid or hurt anyone else?"

Sara and Alice giggled some more.

"You don't escape that easily, Jack, you're not leaving yet. Sophia when your hand is clean would you be as good as to make Jack a cup of coffee."

"Yes, papa."

Giulia started giving orders. "Joseph, go and have a bath, you two, homework and I'm off to get myself dolled-up. Back in a few minutes; you two, enjoy the coffee."

Jack sat at the small bright yellow Formica-topped kitchen table across from Sophia. They looked at each other and smiled. Nothing was said; they both looked down at their coffee cups, then they both looked up at the same moment, almost mirroring each other, Jack managed to speak first.

64

"Could I start again? But could I first apologise for hurting your hand and for being so oafish. You caught me off guard, you being so, so..." His voice tailed off to nothing.

"Of course, apology accepted, but you were saying? Me being so, so...so what?"

In for a penny in for a pound, Jack thought. It was now or never, this was his chance.

"For you being so pretty."

Sophia was full of confidence for her age, she looked at Jack and smiled. She felt the chemistry, her look was full of compassion. He looked so vulnerable, his blond hair short on the sides but a long mop top and a face much younger than his years which added to his appeal and charm. She liked the look of him and she had heard of his first few exploits in the fire brigade from her father. Even before she met him, she thought he sounded interesting, but meeting him was as exciting for her as she for Jack and he had just declared an interest in her. She decided not to play her cards just yet; she did not want to make it too easy for him. She would change the subject.

"Thank you, Jack, you are very kind. What derring-do have you and my father been up to today?"

The wind had be taken from his sails. He wasn't expecting that for an answer.

"Nothing much, really, run-of-the-mill stuff, cleaning trucks and equipment, false alarms, nothing exciting, we seem to spend ninety percent of our time on routine stuff and ten percent of our time scared out of our wits."

"That's not what papa says. He told us you have literally had a baptism of fire. He thinks you'll make a good fireman."

Jack raised his eyebrows. "I hope so, I hope he's right. Anyway, enough about me. What have you been up to today?"

"Oh, just normal work stuff. I work for the Birmingham Post."

"Great, are you a reporter?"

"Not quite. I'm a cub reporter, learning my trade like you. I just get the little bits and pieces of stories that are thrown my way that no one else wants. I'm happy though, it's a start."

He was thinking how he could get the conversation around to asking Sophia out for coffee, or to a pub for drink, maybe a meal, what about a steak like Joe and Giulia were to have later. No, not a steak meal he dismissed that, too much too soon. A drink in a nice pub in the country that was the way to go, but he would have to borrow either his mother's or his father's car, no riding pillion for Sophia. He had the choice of two, his mother's Ford Escort or his father's Singer Vogue. He looked long at Sophia, the Singer Vogue was the only option for someone this beautiful. His father would be a tough nut to crack. He was not at all sure he could manage to get the keys to his father's pride and joy, but then again, perhaps it was time for Jack to buy a car. What about Harry and the E-Type, he couldn't tell Harry about Sophia, he didn't want the competition for her affections especially if Harry ended up driving an E-Type and an E-Type convertible would be even worse. Motorbike or E-type convertible, what would any girl choose; that settled it, the bike has to go, he must get a car. Jack slowly drifted back to the here and now and wondered why he was thinking about cars when in the company of Sophia.

"Where are you, Jack? You seem miles away."

Before he could speak, the front doorbell rang. Well, it didn't so much ring as play a tune. Jack recognised it instantly; 'Colonel Bogey' he had heard of these doorbells that played dozens of tunes. Apparently, you could select a tune of your choice each day if you wanted to but he had not heard one working, it sounded a bit like a stylophone to him, electronic and tinny. Sara came charging into the room.

"Your boyfriend's at the door."

Jack stood up, as a red-faced Sophia did. "Excuse me, Jack."

She left the kitchen, passing her father in the doorway.

"How's the coffee, Jack?"

"Great, it's great, it really is."

A disappointed Jack had to pull himself together.

"You look very smart, how are you and Mrs Fowles getting to town? Taxi."

"No, far too expensive. We'll go in our car. Giulia uses the car for work in the week. She's a district nurse so needs to get about. I'm happy to get the bus to work. I get to use it for work some weekends, usually if it needs cleaning, that's if Giulia is not ferrying the kids around."

"Well, I should be getting along and let you two get to town for dinner."

Giulia and Sophia came into the room together. Sophia's conversation must have been very short. They both looked beautiful, there was no doubt Sophia was her mother's daughter.

"You look lovely, Mrs Fowles. Conker, I mean Joseph is a very lucky man to have such a lovely wife and family. It has been a pleasure to meet you all, thank you for the coffee, but I should be on my way."

Sara and Alice giggled some more at the mention of the word 'Conker'; they knew their father's nickname and the reason for it but had never heard it used in the house. Sophia had her head down and seemed to be looking at the floor. Giulia had worked out what had happened. Conker was oblivious to the situation and was straightening his tie in the little circular shaving mirror that was on the windowsill above the kitchen sink.

"Sophia, would you see Jack out, and thank you, Jack, for bringing my husband home. Girls say goodbye to Jack."

The twins giggled and waved their goodbyes.

Conker watched Jack leave through the shaving mirror still adjusting his tie.

"Yes, thanks Jack. I really did enjoy the ride, we must do it again soon. Bye."

Sophia made her way out through the hall Jack followed in silence picking up his jacket from the coat hook, he slipped it on as he walked. Without turning around Sophia brought her hand up and turned the knob of the Yale lock but didn't open the door.

"It was nice to meet you, Jack. I hope to meet you again soon."

It was then she turned to face him. She seemed embarrassed to be standing at the front door again with a second young man within the space of just a few minutes. What could he say? He was just about to make a fool of himself by asking her out for a drink when luckily fate had saved him from one last embarrassment, he was thankful for that.

"That would be nice. Good evening, Sophia."

She opened the door and he was gone. He turned the bike out onto the A34 Stratford Road twisting the throttle open, he let the bike have its head, maybe a quick ride down to Stratford-upon-Avon and pint of bitter in the Dirty Duck would cheer him up; it didn't.

A Baby at Christmas

It was mid-December and Christmas was fast approaching and Sid had allowed the men of Blue Watch to put a few decorations and a small tree in the mess room of the station. They were allowed 'sensible' decorations one week before and one week after Christmas; he was very specific, he did not want his station festooned with cheap tat for weeks on end. The men were still putting up the last few fairy lights when Sid came into the room holding a twelve-inch high Santa Clause in full traditional attire red jacket and hat and little black boots.

"Who tied this to the radiator grill of the pump escape? I don't want the engines looking like dust carts. Put him on the tree or somewhere more appropriate no decorating the trucks. Am I clear?"

"Yes, SO," came the happy chorus.

Little did Sid know that Mr Claus would be making appearances throughout the festive season in lockers, peering out of crew-cab windows, probably his finest hour would ironically be at a twenty five-pump fire, one hundred feet up the turntable ladder pumping water into a furniture warehouse.

All was done and the men were admiring their work which cheered up the dowdy mess room when a short ring came on the fire bell, down the stairs they trotted chatting happily down to the watch room hallway where stood two small boys, maybe ten years old looking very sheepish as half a dozen men in uniform came towards them. Alf, the watch room attendant, stood between them, a comforting arm across on each boy's shoulder.

"These two lads have just passed a house on Witton Road, literally around the corner. They say there is smoke coming out of the windows downstairs. They didn't get a number."

"That's good enough for me," Sid said, decisively.

"Pump, and pump escape will turn-out. Alf tell control we are on our way and tell them to book us mobile to the incident."

Sid paused and looked at the lads, what was going through Sid's mind, were these two lads calling in a false alarm, he had never seen lads be this brazen, if they were, but who knows.

"And you two, jump into that fire engine there, you can show us the house. Pumps crew help them in, let's go."

Luckily, the pump was riding with four, no, fifth man this tour due to pre-Christmas leave so there was room in the back for 2 ten-year-olds, if this is all the boys wanted, a ride in a fire engine, then their wish had come true. They were both smiling from ear to ear, unfortunately for them if this was a false alarm, they would get the wrath of Screaming Sid and that could give them nightmares for years to come.

They drove the fifty yards to the end of Ettington Road at the direction of the boys, the driver of pump escape started to turn left when a small voice shouted.

"STOP, STOP."

Literally, the first house around the corner in Witton road is where the first fire engine stopped. The pump was still in Ettington Road when it pulled up at the junction. No one was dressed in fire kit, fire-boots was the most anyone had on.

"Here it is, here, look, we told you so."

The crews dismounted and still unsure, walked up to the house. Jack standing on the footpath had just pulled on his wet legs, he had his tunic in his hand, all nine firemen were in different states' of undress, no one was dressed properly. From bare-chested to working rig overalls, there was just about every permutation of clothing available, not one of the nine firemen had full fire kit on. Sid was probably the worst offender; he only had his white helmet on his head which looked weird, office trousers, white shirt and tie, the two crews walked up to the house, still getting dressed. The boys were enjoying every minute of their time in the rear of the crew cab so they decided to stay on the fire engine for as long as possible. Sid went to the front door and hammered upon it loudly with his fist to rouse the residents.

Tumble shouted, "Smoke SO, smoke from the front downstairs window. Look."

Everyone's attention turned to the window, a large Victorian four-pane sash. There it was again, a puff of smoke from around the edges. The fire was entering its pulsation phase, the firemen knew it was a job and it was cooking inside.

Sid was giving orders, high-pressure hose reels, breaking in tools, breathing apparatus, then he fell silent. Men were running left and right. Jack watched Sid in slow motion, Sid pushed at the door feeling for points of resistance, then his mind was made up. He backed up two or three short paces, stopped and took a breath. He charged at the old Victorian door, just as he got to the door, his right leg came to the height of the mortice lock, only someone that tall could have made the kick. Maybe, it was easier in office shoes, anyway it was timed to perfection. The door flew open, and a huge pulse of brown smoke belched from the open doorway. Sid dropped to the ground and started to crawl into the house. Jack moved forward, pulling on his woollen tunic, he didn't have time to button it up. Dusty Miller was at his side, dressed much the same as Jack, just tunic and leggings.

"Come on, Jack, let's follow him before he kills himself."

Sid was gone, he had disappeared into the smoke filled house. Dusty was on his stomach crawling through the doorway after his SO. Jack was so close behind that he got hit in the face by Dusty's fire boots but he wasn't going to lose contact with him, fifteen, maybe twenty feet, down the hallway, Dusty stopped.

"Doorway Jack, doorway left, going left, follow me."

Jack was crawling fast, following the boots but the smoke was getting thick; it was hard to breathe, the stinging eyes and the now familiar taste of snot was back. He could hear Dusty coughing just ahead of him but couldn't see him.

"Bedroom Jack, bedroom, going right you check the bed, okay?"

"Okay Dusty, checking the bed."

Jack realised neither of them had a torch, for all the good they were, this would have to be done by feel, even if he had a torch he wasn't sure he could have seen much with the smoke this thick and with his eyes running as bad as they were. Jack got to his knees beside the bed and started running his hands across the bed sheets of the unmade bed, nothing here.

"S-H-I-T."

As Jack heard Dusty cry out, the room lit up. It started somewhere down by the skirting board in the corner of the room. Jack looked up from the bed as the bright yellow flame raced vertically up the wall, a perfect column of flame instantly lighting the wallpaper as it went, it hit the ceiling and fanned out running slowly over the whole ceiling, the flames turning blue as it went. First, the light came then the burst of heat. Jack knew it was coming so he lay face down on the floor as the heatwave hit him, he could hear the sound of breaking glass. The pressure wave had either pushed out the windows or outside, the crews had seen what was happening and decided to ventilate the room, whichever it was, this would be only a brief respite as the fire dynamics changed the immediate heat pulse would pass but it would be back.

"Jack, Jack, here Jack."

There was urgency in Dusty's voice. Jack crawled around the foot of the bed in the light of the fire. He could see Dusty, he was holding up a small toy doll by its feet. He was offering it to Jack. Jack instinctively grabbed for it and likewise held it upside down by a leg. When he touched it with his gloveless hand, he realised, this is no toy doll. Jack pushed the limp lifeless, naked child under his tunic and fastened the bottom button just enough to stop the child falling out. He turned to crawl back towards the doorway; as he did, he shouted as loud as he could.

"Dusty, Dusty, you coming Dusty?"

A still coughing Dusty replied, "Go, go."

Jack was reluctant to leave his partner. The 'rule of two' would be broken. Firemen are always in twos or more and no one is ever left alone in a fire. Jack hesitated but Dusty was right, he was only in the back room of a terraced house and the room had been vented. He knew where he was, he would come back for him, and the child, if it was possible to save its life, it needed to be outside, now. Jack crawled through the bedroom doorway and was hit full in the face by a high-pressure hose reel spray. The two breathing apparatus wearers acknowledged him by patting him on the head as they passed.

"Get out, out."

The first one shouted through his full-face mask. It was Conker, Jack recognised the voice. He had no idea of the precious bundle hidden beneath Jack's tunic. Jack rolled onto his side and pointed at the doorway.

"DUSTY-DUSTY."

"Okay, Jack, okay."

Jack crawled along the linoleum-covered hallway, following the small black hose-reel tubing out towards the front door. He could see the hose jump and squirm as if it were alive as the water jet was turned off and on, off and on by Conker, pushing the smoke and flame before him. Jack made his way along the wet hallway floor; he could now see daylight and the outline of figures crouching low in the doorway, ducking down, trying to see underneath the smoke layer which was pushing out above their heads, at a distance of just ten feet. He still couldn't recognise anybody and they were as yet unaware of him, he crawled on, just a few more feet, then he heard Tumble's voice.

"Jack, Jack. Come on, Jack."

Tumble ran in, grabbing Jack and lifting him to his feet by his tunic shoulders, he walked him out of the building.

"Where's the SO and Dusty?"

Ignoring the question and opening his tunic, he showed Tumble the lifeless child.

"Get on the back of the pump escape; do what you can, give him some oxygen." Jack moved towards the escape but was still engaged with Tumble.

"Dusty's in the back room, left. Conker is there. I don't know where the SO went."

Tumble nodded an acknowledgement.

Jack opened the rear door of the crew cab and climbed in, he laid the lifeless child gently on the black plastic bench seating and knelt on the fire engines aluminium floor beside him. Reaching into a compartment behind the seats, he grabbed the oxygen cylinder and mask, for some unknown reason the two pieces were kept separate and had to be joined together with a large valve before they could be used. The chrome connecting wheel was always tricky to get lined up straight at the best of times, he took a piece in each hand and offered them up to each other, but his hands were shaking uncontrollably, he couldn't get the threads to line up.

"You awkward bastard," he shouted.

Looking at the lifeless child, he threw the oxygen mask down. He took the child's head in his left hand and tilted the child's head back. He ran his right forearm across the little face, moving the child's vomit and snot, taking a deep breath he placed his mouth over the little nose and mouth and gently blew, as he pulled away, the child's chest fell a little, he repeated the breath trying to put life back into the little fella, but nothing, a third breath, a fourth, a fifth, still nothing. The sound of the fire engine's engine racing to power the pump was as loud as he had ever heard. It filled his head and the cab, what now? What do I do now? The whole engine shook as the water pressure changed, it brought him back to his senses. Placing his mouth once more over the little nose and mouth, he blew, he pulled back just a little, through the din of the racing engine came a little cough, and the little body twitched, convulsed and shook, then another cough and another, the arms came to life in unison and started waving up and down, then a cry, the sweetest of cries. Jack picked up the oxygen valve and mask, brought the two halves together; without a trace of shaking, he easily connected the two and calmly turned on the flow of oxygen placing the mask over the child's face. As he did, he heard the sound of breaking glass and looked out of the crew cab side window firemen were moving away from the front doorway as window glass rained down on them. Above the front door was a small four-pane sash window, no more than two feet wide, being destroyed by a wooden chair from the inside. As Jack watched, heavy brown smoke belched readily from the newly made exit closely followed by the white station officer's helmet. Sid dragged himself half out of the window and bent downward gasping for fresh air he managed to shout, "Ladder, ladder, fetch a ladder!"

Sid had somehow got himself trapped upstairs, not good for someone who is supposed to be in charge of the fire. Tumble casually turned to Will Shakeshaft.

"Get the short extensions and get the silly bugger down," he said lowering his voice.

"Don't rush, let him suffer a bit longer." Will nodded and smiled an acknowledgement.

Back inside the pump escape, Jack was listening to the screaming child cradled in his arms. *Screaming Sid is trapped up in a bedroom and I've got a screaming child here, ironic in a way,* he thought. All of a sudden, the pavement side rear door next to him flew open. It was Dusty, his black smoke stained face was lit with a wide smile, the sooty face made his teeth look strangely white.

"How's the little chap, Jack."

"Great Dusty, no burns, just smoke."

"Well done, Jack, your first rescue."

"Not me, Dusty, you found him."

"No, you got him out, that's what counts."

Looking over Dusty's shoulder, Jack could see Sid coming down the ladder. Just as Sid reached the ground, Smudger and Conker came through the front doorway taking off their breathing apparatus masks as they made their way out. The three had a quick conversation and then came to the pump escape door to join Dusty. Sid seemed none the worse for getting himself trapped on the first floor. He was taking it in his stride and everyone else was ignoring the station officer's basic error.

"Well done, you two, well done! The ambulance has just pulled up behind, give the lad to them, he needs to be checked over, then lend a hand making the gear up."

Sid turned away to carry on with leading the last of the fire-fighting action, the others turned and followed him. Jack was alone with the crying child for only a minute when an ambulance woman appeared at the doorway.

"I hear you have a casualty."

"Yes, here he is," Jack said proudly still cradling the naked child in his arms.

"Hand him over then."

Jack knew he had to hand the child over but felt a bond with him. Surely, he was responsible for him, just handing him over didn't seem right, if he gave him up, he would have nothing to show for his first rescue. Who would protect him? Yet, he must give him up, it had to be done; he placed his black sooty hands under the little chap's armpits and held him up to look at his face one last time, then he held him forward offering him to the ambulance woman, as he did the child pissed on him. Jack extended his outstretched arms holding him out at full arms' length but the little ones peeing reach was impressive for his size, Jack got it all.

"Oh, I'm glad that was you and not me."

She said, laughing; she took hold of the child and turned away.

"Thanks, fireman and a merry pissing Christmas."

"Yes, and a Merry Christmas to you too."

The task of making up all the gear they had used had begun and the two lads who had raised the alarm were keenly helping where they could. Conker had walked down the Witton Road to a newsagent just fifty yards or so away and returned with a brown paper bag in one hand and two small bottles of ginger beer in the other. He called the two young lads to the back of the pump where they stood side by side, their smiles beaming, this was their best day ever, and they were having the time of their lives. Conker called to the available firemen to come over, a very oddly dressed group of firemen formed a small semicircle on the pavement beside the engine. Conker called for silence.

"What are your names boys?"

"I'm Daniel, an 'ees Malcom, we supports the Villa."

The young Brummie had a strong accent and obviously enjoyed his football.

"Well, Danny and Malcom, the men of Blue Watch would like to thank you for raising the alarm and calling us to this fire. We are very grateful to you, and in recognition of your bravery and service to the fire brigade we have decided to award you the order of 'The Flame'. This makes you…"

He paused, thinking on his feet, he had only got as far as 'The Order of the Flame'. Conker searched his lexicon for some more appropriate words, he carried on.

"This makes you, 'Official Blue Watch Fruit and Nutters'. Hold out your hands boys." Each boy received his ginger beer and bar of fruit and nut chocolate. The eight firemen cheered and applauded when the applause had died away, Danny looked up at Conker.

"Doe's we get a medal?"

"No, no medal, just the ginger beer and chocolate."

"Oh, okay, if that's it. We're going to the park now, come on Malc, let's go, bye firemen."

The boys seemed to take the whole event in their stride and walked off in the direction of Aston Hall Park the firemen smiled and chatted.

"Nice-one Conker," someone said as they got back to making up their gear.

A loud scream broke the air and the group turned to see a young woman struggling with Tumble on the doorstep of the house.

"Let me in, let me in. My baby, my baby, let go of me."

Tumble was having trouble restraining her without getting too physical; luckily, Harry was on hand to help calm her down. Harry decided a firm strong voice was called for.

"Come madam, calm down, you can't go in there, it's very smoky, everything's okay, the fire's out, your baby's fine."

Harry grasped her right wrist to pull her from the doorstep, which by sheer coincidence was the wrong thing to do to a left-handed mother who is not listening and thinks her child is still in the house. Not for the first time, he never saw it coming. The fist that hit him on the side of the nose was quite small but, traveling at speed, it did pretty much what a larger, slower fist would have done; not a nose broken, but a nose bloodied. After much shouting and some apologies, a tearful woman, a fireman with a good nosebleed and a screaming child could be found inside the back of the ambulance. Jack watched the scene through the ambulance rear doors.

"I'm so sorry. I'm so sorry. Is your nose okay? Is it broken?"

Harry was sitting on the gurney with his head tilted back and a cotton wool ball packed into each nostril; he gave a very nasal reply.

"No, I'm fine, I'm getting used to being hit in the face."

"I'm so, so sorry. Look what I've done and you saved my little boy as well."

"Well yes, well no, we, the crew did it."

"I don't understand it. I was only gone a few minutes, I only popped down the shops."

"You did what? You went down the shops and left him alone?"

"Come on out of there Aitch before you get punched again." Jack helped Harry from the ambulance.

The end of the shift had come and the two short rings on the station fire-bell announced that it was 1800 hours; Jack was making his way across the yard when he noticed Conkers car parked by the tower at the bottom of the yard, a rare event indeed. He could see the outline of someone in the driver's seat, surely it must be Mrs Fowles. She needed to know that Conker was out on a shout riding the pump escape over on Central's ground and it maybe some time before they got back. Walking over to the car, his heart jumped as he recognised the driver; Sophia.

"Hi Sophia, your dad's going to be some time, he's out on a shout."

"Hi Jack, how long will he be?"

"At least half an hour I reckon, probably more."

"Can I wait in the station and maybe have a coffee."

Was Jack reading this right, was she throwing him a lifeline? Was she inviting him for coffee? The options raced through Jack's mind. Red Watch had taken over, they were all animals. He couldn't put Sophia amongst them. Then there was Harry, he hadn't seen him come out of the station yet and he didn't want Harry, even with the disfiguring remnants of a black eye and a swollen nose to get a look in with Sophia. There was only one thing for it.

"I tell you what, lets pop a note on the steering wheel and tell your dad we're in the coffee house at the end of the road. Geovanni's, he knows it, he'll find us when he's finished his shift."

Inside Geovanni's was warm and welcoming. With just a few tables down one side of what was once the front room of a Victorian house, it was now reborn as an Italian Café a grand espresso machine hissed and spluttered on the top of the counter that sat against the back wall. Jack knew she would appreciate this little piece of Italy.

They sat close to the window and looked out onto the dark streets; Aston, in December, seemed at odds with the Italian surroundings. Waiting for their drinks they passed the time of day, the conversation mainly about the weather and the fast approaching Christmas holidays, only a few minutes had passed when the waitress arrived with their drinks.

"One Americano and one Breakfast coffee."

"Grazie."

"Prego."

As Jack looked down at his drink, he decided he liked Sophia speaking Italian. It somehow sounded sweet and melodic, not bad considering she had only said one word.

"Pick a letter between A and M," said Sophia.

"Why, what does that do?"

"Juke box roulette, I'm paying." Sophia flashed a mischievous smile at Jack.

"Okay, I'll choose J."

"Great and I choose the number 21; J21 it is then. I'll go and claim our prize."

Sophia walked over to the jukebox and dropped the five pence coin into the slot and pressed the keys, J and 21, the machine sprang into life. Jack instantly recognised the song, (Sitting on) The Dock of the Bay.

"Otis Reading, how did you do that? How did you know he is one of my favourites?"

"I didn't, its juke box roulette, don't you see? The gods of chance have to decide."

Jack was listening to Otis and thinking of San Francisco and the warm evening sun when Sophia cut into his thoughts.

"Jack, what's going on with all these garage fires?"

"What do you mean going on?"

"Well, I've been listening to Papa, I think there's a story to be told here, I've just started a little digging into the fires, looking at different pieces from Post and Mail reporters and others and there's a connection, I'm sure of it, too many garage and workshop fires like the ones in Ladywood, Handsworth, and the one you went to here in Aston and maybe a small fire at a Jaguar spray shop in town. They all have something in common, they all seem to be independent traders and have shady characters running them. The two injured firemen were bad enough. I do worry so about Papa, but then the shooting that has taken it up to another level, this is murder, an execution. Then remember the cop you and Papa were interviewed by, it seems the Met-Police have become involved."

"Wow Sophia, you have been doing your homework, haven't you? How far have you got?"

"Not very far but I have this, each workshop dealt in motor related crime of some description, stolen cars, some dealt in parts, engines, gearboxes that sort of stuff, all had their offices totally destroyed in the fire, therefore no records, but who keeps records of stolen stuff? There is also some evidence that stolen cars are coming up from London, to a connection here in the city, hence the Met Police."

"A connection, what sort of connection?"

"Well, it seems these shady characters are disappearing cars, you know, removing or changing their identity and selling them on, but their 'suppliers' could be from London."

"So this is not a London gang working up here then?"

"Well, I'm not sure, a lot of these cars come up the M1 motorway from London, I know that. But if it's a London gang expanding its empire then why burn out their own businesses? It doesn't make sense and you don't execute a worker that isn't on the police radar which I'm pretty sure he wasn't. But if it's a new Birmingham firm starting up and crowding out an established firm then, perhaps the old firm is getting pissed off."

"A turf war, you think. Your dad said there could be a turf war."

"Yes, but who? We have a family history that includes things that we are not proud of, you may not know Jack but way back my mother's family were not all angels. We may have a little insight but I have no clue to what's going on, I did think I had a lead but it was a dead-end."

Jack decided to ignore the reference to Giulia and the Sabini but the dead-end lead interested him.

"What did you have, maybe it wasn't a dead-end, or a *cul-de-*, it's just a mere narrowing of the road."

"Jack, don't get fancy with words, leave that to me, you're the fireman, I'm the writer."

Sophia said it with a smile, Jack knew he was being played with and he liked it.

"Oh, that's me told off, well, miss writer, tell me about your dead end."

"Okay, but this is just between me and you, nobody else, not even Papa, agreed?"

"Hold on a minute, Sophia, we are not talking about petty crime here, we are talking arson and murder. If it is a firm as you put it, they may not be happy with you poking around in their business. What if they decide you're a nuisance that needs to be made quiet? I think we should include your dad. After all, he kindled your interest in these fires."

"Jack, you're wandering into my territory again and with bad puns, but I know what you mean, but let's not say anything just yet, let's wait until we have something more concrete."

"We, what's this we? When did I sign up for this investigative journalism stuff. I'm a fireman, remember?"

"Yes, and a very pretty fireman, but two heads are better than one and FIRE is the common thread running through our investigation. What a team we make."

Jack knew she was flirting with him but wasn't sure if he liked being called pretty, but as long as Sophia thought it was the one thing it was fine with him, otherwise everything was going really well and the 'our investigation' and team reference meant future meetings, hopefully many.

"So just going back to 'our investigations' and the dead end. What was your dead end? Where are we?"

"Well, do you by any chance know a fireman called Bianchi?"

"Yes, of course, he's the station officer in charge of training school."

"Well he's also got a second-hand car business going. When I talk to people involved in these fires his name keeps cropping up but I can't make a connection."

"In what respect?"

"It's difficult to say but, he sells cars, second-hand cars, on a lot, an old bomb site down the Moseley Road. He was fined for selling a car that was made from two cars; a 'shut and cut' they call them. Apparently, the car wasn't legal as it made two insurance write offs. It was unsafe in the way it was done, apparently you can restore a write off as long as you do it correctly, just welding any two halves together isn't good. I don't really understand the mechanical stuff. There was also the story of his cars having their speedo's turned back. One guy, a Mr Leonard, complained that a car he bought of Bianchi had had its speedo turned back and threatened Bianchi with court unless he got his money back. By sheer coincidence, he was beaten up by a stranger in a fight outside a pub in Aston within a week, the 'stranger' was never caught. I managed to find Leonard and he is scared stiff. He's saying nothing, and not complaining about his car anymore, the guy is a bag of nerves."

"Wait, I think you've the wrong Bianchi. I'm talking of Tony, the fireman, you are talking of Franc, the car dealer."

"What, there's two Bianchis?"

"Yes, Tony, the station officer, and Franc, the car dealer, who was a fireman. There was a piece in the Evening Mail called 'At the double' apparently, when they joined the fire brigade together, some ten years ago. Surely, you've seen that?"

"No. How the hell? I've been chasing recent fires and dodgy cars. I've not looked back at Bianchis' history, how the hell did I miss that? What a rookie mistake; that explains why he shows up during the day down the Moseley Road, when I thought he should be at Central Station. How come people mistake them for each other? They're not?"

"Yep, identical twins."

"Why didn't I work that out either? Twins, oh my god. Oh Jack, I could kiss you. It's brilliant, that answers so many questions, that's why I have him all over the city at the wrong time. It is just Franc going about his business, I thought it was Tony who was somehow out when he should be at Central but it's not, it's just Franc being Franc. That's opened my dead-end, but not really sorted anything out. So, Franc's a dodgy car dealer, but no evidence of involvement in the fires and his brother, Tony is not a bad guy. He's a straight up fireman. Anyway, thinking about it, Franc wouldn't set fires and endanger his brother, would he?"

"Could we talk about the kiss now?"

"No, pay attention Jack, this is important. I think we have something but I'm not sure what."

"This is just a thought, a longshot. But you mentioned a pub in Aston where Leonard was beaten up. What pub in Aston?"

"The Bartons Arms. High Street Aston, why?"

"Well, there is a connection, it's not much but, that's where the twins drink. Both are well known there. Maybe Franc arranged to meet Leonard there so he could point him out to a hired thug as he approached the pub, then Frank could go into the bar, nobody would suspect him when a fight starts outside. It would be highly risky for Franc though, bringing a disgruntled customer to his own drinking haunt, but it gives him the perfect alibi, him being known in the pub and if Franc is setting fires he's not really endangering his brother because he is on the training staff, he runs the fire school he doesn't turnout operationally."

"And who's the best person to set a fire? A fireman, and a bitter ex-fireman at that, as Franc was sacked by the brigade for theft, maybe in his mind he has an axe to grind."

"This just gets better and better. So, Franc could be our man, involved not only with arson but also murder!"

"Yes, he could be, but this isn't much to go on, there is absolutely no proof of his involvement in anything."

"But if he's a dodgy car dealer that gets people beaten up, and he knows how to start fires that look right after the event or at least thinks he does, he has to be considered, don't you think?"

"Okay, now we need to talk to your dad, this is getting serious."

"Yes, I suppose you're right, we should talk to Papa."

A Hare-Brained Scheme

In the kitchen of the Fowles house sat Joseph, Giulia, Sophia and Jack. In the centre of the kitchen table, sat a pile of press cuttings. Conker had just finished sifting through them.

"Well, Papa, what do you think?"

"Well, you may have something, but can you put Franc at any fire scene just before or during the fire? Most arsonists like to see the product of their work. They often hang around to watch the fire develop, the spectacle of the fire engines arriving and firefighting operations. It is, for them, just too exciting to miss. The temptation to gloat is too much, they are often seen at multiple fires and usually very early on in the fires development."

"When I was checking Tony out, thinking he had something to do with the Aston Lane fire, I did check his whereabouts that day because it was the only fire in the morning, the others were either when the business concerned was closed, late evening or at night. Anyway, he was definitely at the fire school that day, but if we think it's Franc then I need to start again. Shall I just concentrate on the four fires we know of?"

"Okay, Sophia, but be careful, if word gets out that you're digging around, it could get nasty. Tell nobody what we're up to."

"What do we do? We have nothing, just you and me fighting one of the fires, not that I was much help there, being my first shout."

"Don't put yourself down, Jack, even the chief had to go to his first fire and you did well at yours, trust me. Talking of the chief, that gives me an idea, if we had an ally, somebody high up that knows what we are doing and who's higher up than the chief, and if it is an ex-fireman setting these fires, the chief should know about it. We can't really afford to take the chance by telling anybody else at HQ as the Bianchis have many 'friends' who may tip them off. HQ is a rumour mill at the best of times, someone could even do it unintentionally. However, the good news is the chief and I go way back, in fact we joined the brigade at the same time, we were firemen together at Central back when Adam was a lad, he's an old friend. Consider this my young investigators, if he, the guy at the top of the tree is the only one in the job who knows what we are up to, there would be no chance of a leak. If I can get him to give me his permission for us to dig in the records, then we get access to all the incident reports and talk unofficially to all the officers in charge and even the crews who were at the fires then. If we find something solid, we can hand it over to him and he can call in the cops. He gets the credit for finding a rotten apple, the cops get their man. That's my job then, getting the chief up to speed and on-board."

"Now you and Sophia both have a job, what's my role in all this."

"I don't know yet, Jack how you would do it but, we need to find a way into Franc's world without him suspecting anything. We need a way in, if we approach him, he will see us coming from a mile off, especially you, Sophia being a reporter from the Evening Mail, that's two reasons why you must stay away from the Bianchi brothers."

"Two? How is that two reasons, Papa."

"One, you are a reporter, just sniffing around would tip him off that he is a suspect. Two, it's far too dangerous for you; if our suspicions are right, if Franc is setting these fires he doesn't mind hurting people, he doesn't even mind hurting firemen, possible ex-colleagues, he may know the gunman, he may even be the gunman, this is no place for my daughter."

"Oh, Papa, don't be silly, I can look after myself."

Giulia had sat quietly through the conversation listening intently to the unfolding story but this was now her daughter under possible threat, she could stay quiet no longer.

"Sophia, listen to your father. I don't want you caught up in gang warfare. When you said you wanted to be a reporter, I never imagined this. I thought you would cover Christenings, bat mitzvahs, nice stories, maybe the social events page; you are not getting anywhere near gangs or murders."

"Mamma, I'll be fine."

"Sophia, your mother and I have spoken, that's final, you just dig into the Bianchi brother's history, both of them this time and if there is substance to our suspicions then, when we have the full story, if there is one, you can write it up and take it to your editor. This is what you do best, research and writing. I'll do my bit, I'll talk to the chief and get the ball rolling."

"I've got it, I've got a way in," Jack blurted out just as things were getting a bit tense in the Fowles' household.

"How Jack?"

"Well you said we need a way into Franc's world."

"Yes, so what."

"What about we buy a car from him, not just any car, we specify a particular car, the make, the model, we could even ask for a specific colour so he has to go out and source it, like say, an E-type Jaguar convertible."

Jack was talking and at the same time mulling over in his mind the permutations of what he was saying. He was suggesting involving Harry, who by his own admission, was a friend of Franc and may not be inclined to take part in a scheme to bring him down. It would also mean involving another person, another person at risk and another potential for a leak, and lastly Harry would probably get to meet Sophia and he didn't need to attract competition in that area.

"I like it Jack, but how are you going to pull that one off?"

"I have just the man."

"Who?"

"Harry."

Jack went through the story of Harry wanting an E-type Jag and of already approaching Franc to find him one and the possibility of working for him to pay it off. Sophia jumped in.

"Jack this is just what we need. Not only would he be ordering a car from Franc as you suggest but he could be working for him as well. It's brilliant, we would get all the inside information we need via Harry."

"Whoa, slow down you two, this would be extremely dangerous for Harry. We would have to be very careful. I need time to think. Jack, arrange a meeting, just you and me, with Harry."

'The Tavern in the town' is a small, door in the wall basement pub on New Street in the centre of town, the smoky cigarette stained bar, where Conker, Jack and Harry met one cold January afternoon. They had been together for the best part of an hour with Conker detailing the story so far and then expanding it into the role Harry was to play in the next chapter, Conker's briefing wound to a close. Harry was stunned into silence, Jack looked Harry square in the face.

"Well, Harry, say something, what do you think?"

"Oh, to hell with this, are you two mad? If you're right Franc is an arsonist, a gangster, a racketeer, a possible murderer, an executioner a…a…I don't know what else and you want me to trap him in your hare-brained scheme where I am the guy casted as bait. I would take the fall if it goes wrong, you two would be tucked up in bed safe and sound while he is pulling out my fingernails or cutting my balls off and feeding them to me, all to find out what I know. Err, let me think it over for a minute. Okay, I've thought it through. No way, Jose."

Conker laid his hands palm down on the pub table and gently patted the beer stained top and in a low controlled reassuring voice that commanded attention said, "Easy Harry, easy. Think about it, you have already made the contact, you have asked him for a car, he has offered you a job that means you are on Franc's radar. If we go digging around without you on board and he gets wind of it you'll be 'suspect *numero uno*' anyway, and what's even worse is, we won't be around to protect you. But if you join us, we can work together, the team is bigger than you think. I have contacts high up, I'm talking principle management here, they know what we are up to, you would be looked after at all times."

"Conker, you're still asking an awful lot of me, I'd be the guy at the pointed end, I'd be cannon fodder, because when it comes down to it, if it all went tits up, Franc would come looking for me and I know it's the infantry that gets killed and Generals that get the honours."

"I know, but think on this, which of the principle officers knows who 1797 Fireman Wilson is or 1834 Fireman Wolf, for that matter? Answer. None of them, not one. There are almost a thousand of us fighting fires in Brum, you and Jack are just two more recruits with less service than the station mice. Nobody knows who you are, you may not even make it through your probationary period; at the moment you are but a mere footnote in the fire brigade in this town. But, if you were instrumental in catching an arsonist, a gangster who is prepared to burn, injure and maybe kill people, even brother firemen, just so he can make a few quid on a stolen Jaguar, think of what that would bring you. You would be feted by the highest in the city, you would be in the local papers as the young fireman that risked all to bring a villain to justice, it may even go national! You would have to fight off the women looking for your attention with a stick."

Jack looked at Conker, he was working Harry, he wasn't just laying the charm on thick, he was putting it on in with a shovel, but the bit about the mice and the women was uncalled for, he would protect Sophia from Harry at all costs. Jack watched as Harry's demeanour changed he was holding himself somehow differently now, no more closed and guarded with arms folded, he was sitting upright with a straight back, his head held high and proud. Conker had turned Harry, it took less than five minutes.

"Conker, you're right, I'll do it."

Conker's deeply tanned right hand came across the table to shake Harry's hand, as their hands met Conker's left hand grasped the locked hands, so surrounding Harry's smaller whiter hand, Conker eyes engaged Harry's.

"Don't worry son, to get to you, he would have to come through me and that ain't going to happen."

Jack offered his hand and a smiling Harry shook it cheerfully. Jack was not as comfortable as Conker. Harry was turned so quickly it made him uneasy. He had gone from unwilling castrated bait to a babe magnet fire-hero in less than five minutes. It was his suggestion that was putting Harry in danger, it would be his fault if Harry got hurt, Jack looked across at Conker with a question in his eyes, Conker knew, the unsaid gestures were working again, Conker pursed his lips and nodded a little, 'yes, yes, I know, I'll look after him'.

Harry sprang into life like a man on a mission. "Right, if I am to buy an E-type we need a hundred pounds for the deposit. Where do we get that? I don't have that sort of money, do you Jack?"

Before Jack could speak Conker was back in.

"Don't worry about that I have a little put to one side. When we are on station tomorrow, I'll give you the money." Conker paused, he was deep in thought.

"Harry, when you meet up with Franc, I want you to start bargaining. This is what I want you to do. Firstly, flash the money then put it away, he must see the wad. I'll make sure you have lots of small notes so a fat wad, but you must put it away in a pocket out of sight, that's important. Don't make it easy for Franc, he must think this is a fortune for you to be handing over, it's your savings or part of an inheritance or something, but it means a lot to you. He will suspect something is up if you just suddenly turn up with the money and are prepared to hand it over with no explanation of where it came from, when last week you didn't have it. Now, here's the next bit, tell him you really want a red convertible with a black soft top a roadster, or whatever they are called, you don't want the saloon, hard top version. Tell him if he can get one you would be prepared to give him one hundred and fifty pounds deposit, but only when you've seen it. Remember don't make it easy for him, be reluctant, make him work for the money. Then be sure to ask about your part-time job, as you will need it to pay off any balance after the car is sourced, ask for an early start date so you can work up some credit with him. Tell him, this has to be part of the deal or you won't be able to afford to pay it off. We have to draw him in with a convincing story, lots of detail, do you understand?"

"Okay, I see where you're going, I think," came the long drawn out reply.

"Now, he probably won't go for that, he's going to want a deposit up front. You have to stay focused, now the bargaining continues, you offer him fifty quid up front and a hundred when you've seen the car. Remember, we need to know where the car is before you go to see it, so I can get it watched. Anyway, this deal gives him fifty quid more than he's asked for. We are appealing to his greed. The hook and the bait are set. You have to be firm at this point, that's the deal. The money and the job or you walk away, no matter what else he says. You really have to walk away, if he won't take the bait, the story has to remain convincing, we walk but leave the door open. Do you understand?"

"Okay, Conker, I understand, you don't have to paint me a picture."

"Harry, listen, this is it, it's our best shot, even with the door open we may not get two goes at this. It's important you understand and stay focused."

"Okay, Conker, how many times, okay, give me a break I've got it. Just one question though."

"What!" came Conkers irritated reply.

"You know when this is all over and Franc is behind bars, presuming its Franc doing this shit that is, then when we have had the piss-up to celebrate, pictures in the paper, beating girls off with sticks and all that, could I?"

"Could you what?"

"Well, can I keep the car?"

"For Christ's sake, Harry, have you been listening to anything Conkers been telling you. This guy may have put a bullet in someone's head, he isn't a good guy. Five minutes ago, in your mind he was going to be feeding you your own balls, now your only concern is, if you can keep a stolen car? Harry, you're such an idiot. Conker, we can't let Harry loose, he'll get himself killed. We'll have to come up with another plan. He just ain't getting it."

"Oh, listen to you; it isn't you taking the risk, is it? No, it's me. I'm the one doing the dirty work, you're just setting me up, you're making the bullets but I'm the one firing them, it's easy for you. If, for my services, I get a little reward, a little something on the side, what's wrong with that? What's it to you? Jack you are such an uptight, miserable little shit."

"You two boys, calm down, enough of calling each other names, this is getting us nowhere. Harry go home, think through what we have been talking about, if you're still up for it then rehearse how the meeting with Franc will play out, you have to play him like an instrument, and if he takes charge of the conversation, you're in trouble. And NO, you can't keep the car. Got it?"

Harry stood up from the table and went to move away.

"Wait, Jack, Harry, shake hands, we are brothers, we rely on each other daily, our lives depend on it, nobody leaves this table with ill will for a brother fireman, do you two get it? You are as bad as each other."

"Sorry, Harry."

"Yes, I'm sorry too, mate. It's not the first time I've said this Jack, but no hard feelings from me, just a bit of banter. See you tomorrow at the fire station." Harry finished the last few drops of his beer smiled at Conker, then turned and left.

"Are you sure about this, Conker."

"Yep, he'll be fine, I'm sure. Right then, it's your round. I'll have another Mild, please, Jack."

As Jack approached the bar for another round of drinks, he looked in the mirror behind the optics fixed to the back wall. In the mirror, he watched Conker cross himself and silently say a prayer.

Jack placed a pint of Mild on the table in front of Conker. Conker was staring down at the floor, deep in thought. He ignored him. Jack made his way around the small table, placing his pint of bitter down he sat beside him, Jack said nothing, then slowly and with purpose, he picked up his pint and took a long steady pull on the beer, as he finished his first mouthful he held the glass up to the ceiling light to check the clarity of the pint, then he broke the silence.

"Where are you going to get one hundred and fifty pounds from, by tomorrow? And how come you can afford to risk it? That's a lot of money and a lot of risk."

Conker looked up from the floor. "Oh Jack, you really are easy to read, never play cards for money, you'll lose. Did you forget I have two hundred pounds in used notes in my locker? No, you didn't, you're not stupid. What you're asking me is where it came from and how come I can afford to lose one hundred and fifty pounds on our little scheme."

"No, no, it's none of my business, I know that, but two hundred quid, Conker, just sitting in your locker. That's a fortune, well, to me it's a fortune. I could only dream of having three months' wages sitting in my locker doing nothing."

"It isn't doing nothing, Jack, what you don't know is, I run a book. Not a big book, just the lads on the station and some friends down my local, maybe there's a few old lads at HQ who have a flutter now and then. I have run one for years, just horses, no dogs or anything else, I have to cover bets, I have to be ready for the unexpected win and I have to pay out immediately. I do lay bets off, but I try to cover them on my own if I can. Admittedly, I'm well up at the moment but that can change with a couple of races. I don't make a fortune but usually enough to pay for a good family Christmas each year and my stake to start me off the following year. Giulia is always happy when I turn up with a wedge and hand it over to her to pay for Christmas, she knows how it works."

"Wow, I never knew you sly old fox, but you're risking one-fifty of it on a maybe, a maybe that Harry is handling, is that a good bet?"

"It's not one-fifty though, is it? Franc will never get the one-fifty. He's seen it and he will think it's his, but in reality he will only ever have fifty, half what he asked for. In his mind, he will be getting fifty quid more than he asked for, to get the remaining hundred he has to get the right car, so I'm only risking fifty quid up-front to get a car sourced. Hopefully, we can nail Franc before Harry has to produce any more money."

At 0845 hours, in the locker room at Aston, Blue Watch were making ready for their day shift while the off going crew added to the hubbub as they prepared to go home. The locker room was alive with happy friendly banter and conversation, the huddle with their backs to the room had their wet civvy coats drying on the old cast iron radiator under the window at the far end of the room, but drying coats wasn't the real purpose of the huddle. Conker had just handed one hundred and fifty one pound notes to Harry in a large white envelope, none of Blue Watch took any notice of the three men. Most chatted about the weather, and their two days off-duty which had passed so quickly, nobody saw the fat wad changing hands.

One hundred and fifty one pound notes were not hard for Conker to get together, when running his 'book' he didn't take shrapnel, only folding. "If you can't afford a note don't bother me with small change, you can't afford to gamble," he would often tell would-be punters. Harry turned to the wall of lockers and placed the envelope on the top shelf of his locker.

"I've arranged to meet him, at his local after work this evening. Do you two want to be there to make sure it goes well?" Harry was talking into his locker.

"Not me. Franc would suspect something if I turned up, but Jack could go with you. What would be more normal than two mates having a pint after work. You okay with that, Jack?"

"Yes, fine with me, I take it, it's the Bartons Arms?"

"It sure is, it's as good a place as any to get beaten up and robbed of one fifty, don't you think."

"I don't think Franc would risk having someone else beaten up at his local and certainly not two of us. Even Franc isn't that stupid, well, I hope not."

"Have you rehearsed what you are going to say to him?"

"Don't start, Conker, it's all sorted, now no more questions, no more reassurance, no more nothing. Let's get on with the day and I'll take this evenings meeting as it comes."

Conker looked at Jack and raised his eyebrows. "Okay, Harry, it's all yours, it's up to you now."

The day was slow to pass, just routines and false alarms. To Jack, it seemed to drag on deliberately to frustrate him, not one decent shout all day.

Just before 1900 hours in the Bartons Arms, Harry and Jack watched Franc complete with Fedora come into the bar. He saw the two young firemen seated under the window and made his way over to them, without stopping at the bar to get himself a drink.

Jack rose to his feet and offered Franc his hand, Franc ignored the offered hand and sat down.

"What's the sprog doing here, Harry? Who invited him into our bit of business?"

"This is Jack. You remember Jack, he was here with me last time, he's all right Franc."

"He's got nothing to do with this, what we're doing is private just me and you, the sprog can piss off out of it."

Jack looked at Harry. Harry was frozen to the spot, the silence was deafening. This is just what Conker had warned against, Franc was in control and the conversation was all his.

"Go on sprog, take a walk we have business to do."

Harry was dumbstruck. Jack willed him to speak but nothing, just plain nothing. Jack knew he had to act, he had to take charge of the situation.

90

"Harry, Harry, give me my fifty quid back, I'm not staying here, I know when I'm not wanted."

Things were happening far too fast for Harry. He looked first at Franc and then back to Jack, still he said nothing.

"Harry, my fifty quid. Give me my fifty quid back, I'm not staying here to be insulted."

Harry still didn't know what was happening but was sure that Jack was telegraphing something to him, he reached to the inside pocket of his coat and pulled out the white envelope. As he did, Jack nodded a 'yes' to him. Jack flashed a look across to Franc whose eyes lit up at the sight of the envelope full of money. Jack didn't want to give Harry instructions, he didn't want to say it out loud but Harry was not catching on at all.

"Count my fifty out, Harry, I'm not leaving without it, give me my money back and I'll walk."

"Hold the phone, hold on, let's not get too hasty here. Harry put that bloody money away before everybody in the bar sees it. What's your part in this sprog, how come you have fifty quid in?"

Harry looked at Jack and seemed to be more interested in the answer than Franc.

"Not that it's any of your business, Bianchi, but I've offered to lend Harry fifty quid towards this car, the rest he got from his grandma or somewhere or other. I told him not to buy a heap of shit that will cost him more to keep on the road than it's worth, but Harry knows nothing about cars so I am going to give it the once over for him. You know, the things to look for, don't you Bianchi? You're in the trade, good bodywork, nice shut lines, no blue smoke when you rev the engine, no nasty rattles from bearings, tight gearbox, sharp steering, all run of the mill stuff. Unless you have something to hide, something you don't want us to see."

"It's Mr Bianchi to you, don't run your mouth off with me you little shit, you ain't mechanic of the year, you ain't even a real fireman."

Jack had hoped that calling Franc by his surname would wind him up and he was right. So he would keep using it.

"Fine with me, Bianchi, if I'm pissing on your parade, I'll leave, I'll take my money and I'm out of here."

"He gets to see the car when I get my hundred upfront and not before, and you, you little shit with your smart mouth can piss off."

"A hundred? Wow, that's a lot. I'm not sure about that. What do you say Harry?"

Harry was like a person watching tennis, his head swung from side to side in admiration of the match performance.

"Sprog, are you trying to piss me off or what?"

Jack looked at Harry and waited, his hopes were not high.

"Harry, we don't need this, let's leave Bianchi here with his foul mouth. Let's go where the air is fresher."

Jack and Franc stared at each other.

"I've been thinking it through, Franc, I would like a convertible, a red convertible with a black hood."

"What! Where did that come from? A red convertible! You must be joking, I tell you what you're gonna get, what's available, that's what. White, blue, green, who gives a monkey's about colour?"

"I'm prepared to go to say, fifty down now for a convertible in red and another hundred when I see it. I have all the money here in readies if we can do the deal now. Oh, and I almost forgot, we also need to discuss the start date for my little driving job."

"Are you pair winding me up or what?"

Harry drew the envelope from his pocket and dropped it on the table. It landed with a hefty thud. "Franc, it's make your mind up time. Fifty pounds deposit, for a red convertible, another hundred when Jack says it's kosher, one fifty total, balance to be agreed and paid off in cash and or kind. That's the deal, the money and the job, or we walk away no matter what else you say. We really have to walk away if you won't take the deal."

Jack looked across at Harry; this wasn't Harry it was an automaton, that last bit Harry said, sounded almost as if Conker were talking but it seemed to have caught Franc's attention.

"Give me a minute, let me think." Franc looked at the cash on the table. How good was Conker at setting a trap? Nothing had gone to plan so far and from the look on Harry's face there was nothing left in the tank. He couldn't freestyle, if the negotiations were to continue, Jack would be alone.

"Okay, Harry. Now put the bloody money away, you can have it your way, I can work with that, just one thing, keep this annoying little shit away from me. I don't want to see him again."

Jack's heart was racing, he was scared stiff of Bianchi, but he kept going.

"Don't worry, Bianchi, the feeling's mutual. I want to see the car, not you."

Harry had three bundles of fifty notes, each held together by an elastic band. He pulled one bundle from the envelope and handed it to Franc, the other two went back in his pocket. Harry having found his voice asked, "Can I have a receipt for that, please?"

"Don't be a prat, Harry." Franc flicked through the notes, stood and put the bundle in his left trouser pocket. "I'll call you at the station when I have some news." He didn't say goodbye, he just turned and left.

"Well, Jack, I thought that went well, we played him, got him hook line and sinker."

"Harry, you were amazing it was pretty to watch." Harry didn't hear the irony in Jack's voice.

Three long weeks had passed since the boys had given Franc the fifty pounds deposit when Harry got a phone call on the station payphone which hung on the wall just along from the mess room. As Harry came up the stairs towards the mess, he saw Jones 600 offering him the receiver.

"Some bloke called Franc it is, says he's a friend of yours."

Harry took the phone from 600. "Hello, Franc?"

A beaming Harry burst into the locker room. Instantly he spotted Jack and Conker standing at their usual place by the radiator at the far end of the room.

"He's got one, a red one," he announced loudly to the room. Nobody took any notice as Harry shouting in the locker room was not a strange event and Harry shouting something nonsensical was also nothing new, nevertheless Conker's head dropped as he heard Harry spread the news.

"Okay, Harry, keep it down. No need to broadcast it to everyone, what do you know?" Conker said in a lowered voice as Harry drew near.

"Franc's done it, he's got a red E-Type convertible. Can you believe it? It's in town being worked on. He says I can see it next week, he'll let me know when, isn't that great. He wouldn't tell me exactly where it was though, just told me to get the money together."

"That's all right, I know where it is. It's in a lock-up in Inge Street, in town." Both Harry and Jack turned and looked at Conker in amazement.

"What are you two staring at? I haven't been asleep you know. I have been working on our little project while we waited. I arranged for Franc to be watched."

"Come on, Conker, what have you been up to? You can arrange to have people watched? WOW, that's fab, tell all, tell us what's been going on," Harry said, excitedly.

"Never you mind, my impatient friend; you don't need to know all the details yet. But I can tell you this. Franc has had a stolen Jag driven up from London on false plates, a group of bad lads from the smoke dropped it off a week ago, it's being worked on right now."

Jack could stay quiet no longer.

"Conker how come you know all this stuff? You know it's stolen, you know when it arrived, you know 'bad lads' from the smoke are involved, and you know it's being worked on in Inge Street. How come you know all this?"

"All in due time Jack, first things first; we must stick to the plan. Now, remember it's stolen so probably no damage, it's only two years old so it should be in good nick, my guess is they're changing the numbers so check the chassis and engine numbers."

600 shouted through the open locker room door, "Harry you in here?"

"Yes, Jonesy what do you want?"

"Your boyfriend 'Franc' is on the payphone again, he's waiting for you."

Everybody in the locker room heard the boyfriend remark loud and clear, it prompted a chorus of 'Oooh Harry', then a cheer.

A few minutes later, Harry returned to the locker room. "We're on. Tomorrow at 1200 hours, Inge Street. I've told him I'd be taking Jack. He wasn't best pleased but he said okay."

"Right lads, that doesn't give us much time. This is what you have to do, he has the car and it's nicked, as apparently are the others in the same lock-up. Jack, you have to subtly let him know you have concerns about its authenticity. Harry has asked for a legitimate car, a repaired accident damaged car, that's what you are looking for, a bargain from a friend in the trade. Appear naïve, don't tell him you think it's nicked, just be concerned about the numbers or something but lay it on thick, casually drop into the conversation that you have a mate in the Police at Steelhouse Lane who can check the details out for you. Say he's a junior on a special project, to do with stolen cars and London, but be vague, pad it out if you want, I'll leave it to you."

"Harry, you refuse to pay the hundred until Jack has had the car checked out. Do not take the money with you, we only give him that if we have to later, if this drags out. We need to rattle him, we need to push him into making a stupid move so, you both have to piss him off, you have to make him mad and most of all he has to feel he and his dodgy business is under threat, but do it quick and get out, don't give him time to think."

"Oh great, this sounds as good as one of Jack's plans, getting Franc Bianchi mad with me doesn't sound like a good idea."

Inge Street is a nondescript side street off of the horse fair in the city, a mixture of garages, lock ups and small warehouses typical of any inner city street. Jack and Harry had walked across town having met in the Gunmakers Arms for a liquid lunch. Harry had decided he needed a little drink before facing Franc. They were to meet Conker in the same pub later.

Conker was waiting in the Gunmakers Arms, sat at the table closest to the fireplace as a serious looking Jack and an ashen faced Harry approached with their drinks. "How did it go?"

Jack breathed out a huge sigh as he sat down. "The meeting with Franc didn't really go to plan."

"What happened?"

"Well, we looked at the car. Harry just saw a bright red E-type convertible and promptly forgot what we were there for; he just sat in the driving seat and started making weird engine noises while I checked it over."

Harry's head dropped and he seemed even paler now, his shaking hand reached forward for his drink.

"No, I wasn't, I was checking the interior, the leatherwork, the mileage and stuff."

"Yeah right, anyway. I couldn't find an engine number. I think it may have been ground off, and the chassis plate has been replaced and not very well. I think there is a donor car somewhere, another E-type that has been wrecked and the one we saw has taken its identity. So I thought it would be a good idea to tell Franc that he may have been the unsuspecting purchaser/restorer of a motor that might not be 100% kosher and that I would have it checked out by a mate at Steelhouse Lane.

"Well, that's as far as I got when Franc went ballistic, all hell broke loose, the air turned blue, and Franc picked up a crowbar or whatever it was and started swinging and demanding Harry gets out of the car. When he does, Franc sticks the bar under his chin and told him in no uncertain terms that the deal was off and if he breathed a word of any of their dealings to anyone, he would insert the bar where the sun don't shine. He then jabbed the end of the bar up and gave Harry a kiss on the side of the head with it."

Harry slowly turned his head to the left, showing Conker a rapidly growing bruise down the side of his face.

"I went over to assist Harry and Franc swung at me but missed. Luckily, we weren't far from the small side door where we went in so we managed to back out as Franc kept swinging while calling us every name under the sun. Harry was first out, then just as I was ducking to back out, Franc grabbed me by my jacket lapels and pulled me towards his face saying, any word of this gets out, any poking around by anyone and I'd wake up like Hattie.

"And he's been mumbling about it all across town, Conker, no concern for my head, the head that keeps getting hit every time I get near you two, no concern for me! No concern that Franc has me top of his list of people to get beaten up. No, just the 'Hattie' remark that's all he talked about on the way back. 'Hattie bloody Jacques' which makes no sense to anyone but Jack."

"It does, Harry, Jacques Garage was Jack's first fire on Aston lane. Hattie must have been the owner's nickname."

"I need another pint, my head is starting to ache." Harry grabbed the three empty glasses and went to the bar.

"It's him Conker, isn't it? It's Franc."

"Well, we don't know that he pulled the trigger, but he was surely involved, yet I think he's working for someone, he's part of a bigger picture."

"What happens next? Do you think he will try and torch his own stock in Inge Street?"

As Harry came back from the bar with three fresh pints the door of the pub swung open. A tall London police officer walked confidently in and over to the table where the three firemen sat. Jack instantly recognised him, he was one of the two at Aston Lane and later at the station.

"May I join you?" Before the reply came he sat down. "Well you boys have been busy haven't you, time for you to step away, you're messing with things you don't understand."

Harry looked at the guy in amazement. "Who the hell are you?"

The cop looked at all three men. He had to make a decision, did he warn them off or, did he tell them what he knew. He decided on the latter.

He offered his hand out to Harry first. "DC Thomas, David Thomas, Met Police. Get me a beer and I'll tell you what I know."

The lunchtime trade at the Gunmakers Arms had made their way back to work, the bar was almost deserted as David Thomas told his story. Conker and Jack had their serious faces firmly fixed on Thomas, Harry was starting to slur his words from too much beer and a swollen face, but he was full of enthusiasm and somehow reassured that the police were involved.

"Well, Joe, can I call you Joe?" Conker nodded yes. A slurred voice said, "Joe, who's Joe?"

"Harry, just listen you may learn something."

"Joe, you went to the fire chief with your suspicions of Franc Bianchi being involved in the fires and maybe more, and your plan with a bit of entrapment involved. You wanted to know what we knew, so you got your chief on board, knowing he would call in a favour and ask the police chief for help. You also knew I was up from London on the case so I would probably get the call, you got me working for you, very clever, my hat comes off to you, good contacts at a high level, can anybody say no to their chief. But we had a meeting this morning at Fire HQ. We think its best if you stop now, Joe you got us watching Franc but we've also been watching you three and Sophia, we know she's been digging around. But Joe, the boys from London use shooters; this is no local fire bombing, no local turf war."

"Well, what is it."

"We think Franc is trying to take over the Birmingham trade and he's pushing out people who don't dance to his tune, torching the one man bands that won't co-operate, he seems to be working with a known London gang. He's had a few motors off them and they have become interested in his growing business."

"So Franc is torching these places and shooting people."

"No Harry, we think Franc's got in over his head, he was putting the frighteners on people that wouldn't co-operate with his little schemes and torching them if they didn't toe the line. It was all going well for Franc until he started to deal with London when he was moving stuff for them, they saw an opportunity. So a few lads came up from south of the river, Franc was showing them around when the Aston Lane incident got out of hand. We think one of the London lads got carried away and topped Jacques, maybe it was to show Franc they meant business. Franc, probably in haste, and without thinking it through, set the fire to cover for them, hoping the fire would be big enough to get rid of Jacques completely, well the bit with the hole in it, but you boys did too good a job and got the fire out real quick."

"I've been through the fire reports, I reckon there are at least six fires that could be down to Franc, with one dead that's Jacques in Aston, plus the two injured firemen in Ladywood. This is getting rough, they don't care who they hurt."

"Eight Joe, we reckon we have him down for eight arson jobs, but he's always got a rock solid alibi, he's in his local getting pissed and buying everyone drinks."

"But is he? You know he has a twin, Tony."

"Joe we thought of that, but he looks clean. It's hard to work out how they do it if they do, we've watched him we've got nothing on him. So we want you and your crew, including Sophia, to back off and give us some room, I know you'd love to catch a bent fireman but this is our job."

"Ex-fireman, he's a bent ex-fireman."

"Okay, Jack, ex-fireman, but we really do have this covered. Franc has to make a move soon, I reckon he knows somethings happening, you and Harry have become a thorn in his side and the London boys are putting on the pressure, now we will lean on him a little, let's see what he does. If he or the London boys get nasty, we don't want you in the firing line. Your chief is happy with everyone present here and knows the whole story. So, will you leave it alone and give us room to do our job? As a courtesy you will be the first to know when we have someone in custody."

"Yes, of course, we will, as you don't fight fires, I guess we shouldn't play cops. I'll let my daughter know, she will be disappointed though, she's been working on the outline of the story for weeks, I'm sure she would love to break the story when this is over, if that's possible."

Rising to his feet he shook each hand in turn. "I'll see what I can do, but mum's the word until you hear from me again." He turned and left through the front door leaving a good half pint still in his glass.

"All that work, Conker, all that trouble and we just leave it alone, we just drop it? We have a battered and bruised Harry, you've lost fifty quid and no story for Sophia, we haven't got much to show for our efforts have we, Conker?"

"No, no we haven't. I know it's a bit of an anti-climax, but at least we know Franc's bent and the cops are on his trail. So at least we have achieved something. Thomas is right we should leave it to them, let's see what they come up with."

"Conker, I have just one question."

"What?"

"Who's Hattie Jacques?"

"Harry, you're a star."

Twenty-Five Pumps

The winter was drawing to a close and giving way to spring, the days started to get longer rather than shorter. The three boys from Blue Watch had heard nothing about Franc Bianchi and the London firm from anyone, even Conker's 'Principle' officers had heard nothing.

At Aston, the shift started much the same as any other day apart from it being Sunday which meant relaxed weekend routines and more stand-down time for the firemen. The roll was called, the runners and riders were announced for the day. Riding the pump had now become routine for Jack, usually as fifth man, as he hadn't been in service the twelve months minimum required before he could attend the two week breathing apparatus school training course. Breathing apparatus was always referred to simply as BA which is the way firemen manage to shorten most words involving their officers, fire engines and equipment. He was expected to eat smoke and learn the art of firefighting without BA for the first year at least, riding the back of the pump is certainly the best place to for that.

Today was no exception, he was fifth man, with Conker on his left as number one BA and Fatal to his right as number two, Jones 600 was driver, pump operator and the Sub-Officer Dwyer was riding in the front passenger seat as OiC. The crew chatted happily as they went through their checks and routines. 600 checked the fire engine was full of fuel, that the engine oil and engine coolant water were topped up and the fire pump and power take off all worked as they should, the main one thousand gallon tank was also to be kept full.

The two BA men checked their sets as they had done hundreds of times before, they went through a strict procedure testing every aspect of the set and that the cylinders were full, lastly the distress signal units horns would sound out loudly as they were deliberately actuated to make sure they worked correctly. Jack had checked the outside locker stowage and everything was present and working, he sat in the centre of the bench seat playing with a reluctant right

100

angled torch trying to decide if new batteries would improve the feeble light it shone, perhaps a sharp rap on the walkie-talkie carrier in front of him might make it better, he gave it a good whack on the wooden carrier, the feeble light went out and refused all Jack's attempts to get it working again.

"I reckon I've broken it," he said, looking into the little round reflector.

A short ring on the fire bell brought everyone's attention towards the watch room.

"Make pumps five, Lawley Street, junction Lister Street City. Full house, Aces and Queens, everybody goes." Toot Taylor the TLs driver shouted into the engine house.

Toot had been chatting with the watch room attendant when the bright red fire control tablet dropped on the ancient wooden switchboard. To the right of the switchboard, an A5 sized message pad was prepared with two sheets of blue carbon paper separating three leaves of paper, one for the officer in charge of each Fire Engine. He had seen the attendant write the first line then reach forward to press the fire bell push to give the short ring. He left the small watch room to give the officers who would be there in second's space to pick up their messages.

As Tumble climbed into his seat, he switched on the brigade wide radio, called up the control room and booked all three fire engines' mobile.

"Warehouse boys, no BA, let's see what they want us for, it's a 'five' shout so the control unit will be set up when we get there. The job's right behind Central. Looks like we might be relaying them water."

Jack and the crew knew that if an assistance call came from the fire ground for five pumps or more, the mobile control unit and other resources would arrive automatically the mobile control would take the incident radio traffic away from fire control which would help them get on with running the rest of the brigades logistics. The three fire engines blue lights flashing and two tones blaring, they made their way into town, turning off Sixways, they sped down high street Aston. Jack looked out of the left crew cab window as they passed the Bartons Arms, he wondered if Franc would be drinking cold beer and eating a roast beef lunch later, while they were fighting the fire growing ahead, he pushed the thought from his mind.

The brigade wide radio crackled to life. "Assistance message from station one PE, over."

Centrals pump escape was calling for more help. "Go ahead station, one PE."

"Make pumps fifteen, Ariel's three."

The OiC at Lawley Street, had decided after his initial observation of five, probably made en-route to get things rolling, that he would need at least fifteen, one thousand gallon a minute pumps to bring the fire under control. This fire was big if it needed over sixty tons of water a minute pumped onto it.

"Bloody hell it's going." 600 was pointing at a huge column of smoke rising above the city skyline.

Aston's three engines rounded Masshouse Circus and onto the southbound carriageway of Lawley Street, towards the traffic lights at the junction of Lister Street. As the sound of fire engine's two-tone horns filled the city streets, the huge column of smoke grew, rising hundreds of feet into the air, it was now drifting at an angle of maybe forty-five degrees as the wind caught hold of it, pushing it over the Duddeston district. Centrals' two trucks had pulled up short of the warehouse to give room for their turntable ladder to get to the buildings face where it would be used as a water tower. Aston's pump crew watched Central's turntable being manoeuvred into place, the crew were positioning the turntable out of the debris 'fall zone' just in case the brick façade gave way.

As they watched, Central's TL, the huge column of smoke lowered to almost horizontal with a heart of flame, fanned by a strong westerly wind. The flames once maybe a hundred feet high were lowering towards Central's Turntable. The Pump escape ahead of them was still accelerating hard but 600 slowed their approach as the curtain of smoke and flame crossed the roadway. Screaming's driver had decided to power through the lowering smoke column, the pumps crew watched the spectacle in silence as the smoke started to change to flame, now it was more flame than smoke, the flame crossed the dual carriageway and hit the ground on the opposite side of the road, some eighty feet from the warehouse roof, where it's heart lay, but it was not done, the roll was not complete, the flames seemed glued to the ground, the force of the wind and the nearby buildings had caused a fluke, the wind at ground level blew back towards the warehouse.

The flames raced across the roadway back towards Centrals trucks, ahead of them the pump escape drove on regardless, they were committed. 600 was still slowing the pump bringing it short of the wall of flame, but the pump escape was powering through, a perfect circle of fire now surrounded the truck just a few yards in front of them, it had reached down across the roof of the truck, then curled to run underneath, encapsulating the whole engine in flame, then up again to re-join itself in one burning mass, the circle was complete. The two wooden carriage wheels of the fifty-foot escape ladder mounted on the back of the truck, disappeared into the growing ball of flame the lead truck was gone from sight, gone into the inferno.

"Hells gates," 600 shouted out loud.

Astons pump and turntable were now separated from their pump escape by a wall of flame that crossed the whole of Lawley Street. Jack could feel the radiated heat coming through the windscreen even from the backseat. Rolling almost to a stop at the crossroads, 600 looked around weighing up his options.

"There," Tumble shouted, pointing to the opposite carriageway.

"Cross onto the wrong side of the road and we'll get this side of it, we can put the turntable on the corner."

Tumble's instinct was good, surrounding this fire was the first priority. If they just pumped water into its heart it would probably spread to the warehouse next door before they could bring it under control. They would, if they weren't careful, end up chasing it from building to building until it got to the end of the street a natural firebreak. The pump pulled across the middle of the roadway, Central's trucks were facing them just fifty yards ahead but separated by a wall of flame and smoke the only thing they could see was Central's turntable, the ladder raised but it's head disappeared into the darkening smoke column. The turntable crew were taking the worst of the punishment, but at least it was just a water tower, no one was at the top directing its powerful one and a half inch jet putting five tons of water into the building each minute.

As the pump crew dismounted they looked for a white helmet, Central's station officer must surely be close by giving out his orders, directing how this fire was to be fought. As they took in the grand spectacle before them, a tall white helmeted apparition came walking calmly through the smoke from the direction of Centrals trucks. Screaming Sid, helmet tilted back on his head, his woollen tunic buttoned to the collar but no wet legs, once again, just his officer trousers and fire-boots, by his side was Fireman Harrison fully kitted.

"Well done, Tumble, good positioning, we got a bit bloody warm getting to the other side but, hey Ho." He pointed up Lister Street towards a canal bridge which had a small red access door cut into it.

"The Birmingham navigation canal runs at the back of this lot, set into it on the bridge and supply our turntable ladder. When you've done that, make an entry through this end of the warehouse, I'll get you some help when I can. George you stay here and give them a hand."

As he spoke, a huge explosion shook the ground they stood on, large pieces of wired glass started to rain down on them from a section of Northlight roof which had been sent dozens of feet into the air by the force of the explosion. Then came the lighter corrugated asbestos roof sheeting, large pieces, some three feet long and six inches wide smashed on the road amongst the crews, no one moved, no one looked up, Jack had learnt that at Sapphire Tower, don't look up if things are falling.

"Probably an acetylene cylinder or the gas main," Sid said nonchalantly turning to go back the way he came.

Tumble started giving his orders to get the pump drawing water from the canal and supplying the turntable ladder, the crew had already started gathering the equipment together before he had finished speaking, they knew what Sid wanted and they were practiced at their tasks. Little was said as Aston's water tower was made ready.

Jack, like the other firemen had been connecting the eight foot lengths of big six inch suction hose together and then running delivery hose out to supply the turntable, the whole operation probably took less than five minutes but to Jack things seemed to be happening far too slowly. While concentrating on the task at hand to him there was no sound; he was oblivious to anything around him other than getting the water tower working. Burning debris, some weighing pounds from the fire fell around him; it was the contents of the warehouse that the beast was spitting out of its smoke column using its huge thermal force. It flew high into the air where it would slow then hold station for a split second before raining down and tormenting the men fighting the fire below.

It was done, two loud retorts of compressed air from the turntable ladder monitor jet announced the arrival of another five tons of water to be directed into the fire each minute. Tumble shouting as loud as he could above the din called to the only four men left without tasks to him, Jack, Conker, George and Fatal came running. Toot and 600 would work their trucks alone.

"This is our way in." He stood by a heavy single doorway which was covered in sheet steel secured by eight large coach bolts, the doorway sat deep in a recess in the end wall of the warehouse.

"George, Fatal, take this door out. Conker, Jack, run out a main jet, you're going in boys."

It was then Jack realised the noise, its why Tumble was shouting every order, he hadn't heard the roar at all, the roar of the beast, it was as if an express train was hurtling past them, a never ending train of noise that resonated in his chest, a sound like he had never heard, loud cracks and bangs were coming from inside the building, then a large piece of brickwork fell, just along from where they stood, the five firemen looked at the end wall, a rolled steel joist had punched its way through the two foot thick brick wall pushing a square yard of bricks before it.

Tumble looked with fresh eyes at the building; he checked the end wall for movement. "It's on the move boys, be careful when you get water on those RSJ's. When they cool they could pull the wall back in on you."

Tumble knew a two hundred foot long RSJ heated to over a thousand degrees would easily grow four feet in length and would push anything out of its way. A two-foot thick wall was nothing to an expanding beam, but when you cool it, the joist returns to its original length that's what may pull the sixty-foot high wall in on the men. The crews nodded their understanding and went about their allotted tasks. Conker and Jack ran out their jet, they had several figure of eights flaked behind them so they could go deep inside without needing to extend the hose. With excellent timing, the canvas hose snaked into life as it was charged by 600 back at the pump, it became solid with water.

The re-enforced doorway gave way to the efforts of George and Fatal, heavy fire axes, pry bars, and sledgehammers had all played their part, the doorway at last gave up its resistance, it came away from its fixings. George and Fatal put their arms around each other's shoulders and in unison kicked the door inward, frame and all. All four men looked into the opening and wondered at the spectacle before them, just twenty yards away through giant stacks of household furniture, chairs and settees, lay the heart of the inferno swirling flame, a hundred feet wide and ten stories high.

It roared through the now giant hole in the roof, heat so intense the skin on their faces and hands was reddening. Looking into its heart dried the very water in their eyes, all blinked unconsciously to keep their eyes lubricated. As a group, the four men stepped to the side shielding themselves from the furnace heat, just a short step, a few feet but a different world, nobody could stand that amount of heat for long. As he moved, Jack's hand brushed against his fire tunic, flinching, he pulled it away, his tunic was too hot to the touch. Conker picked up the hose that lay by the doorway and shouted through the ever-increasing din.

"Come on, Fatal, let's do this."

Conker would be first in, followed by Fatal; turning to Jack he pointed at the flaked hose and called out.

"Jack, feed us the hose until we stop moving forward then come and join us, George, then you stay in the doorway feeding the hose, when the three of us are working the jet you keep an eye out for us, and watch that bloody wall."

Jack nodded his acknowledgement; George also nodded and waived them forward.

Conker opened up the one inch jet of water that shot rope like into the building, he lent into it to take the weight of the jet reaction, Fatal stood the opposite side of the hose holding it waist high he put his shoulder against Conkers back and helped take the weight.

With the jet of water being directed straight forward they edged through the doorway and into the fire. As they entered the building, Conker turned the large wheel around the branch and a cone shaped curtain of water burst into life in front of them. This would give some protection from the intense heat. Jack fed the hose into the doorway, a foot at a time, he counted each foot off as he did, twelve, thirteen, fourteen, fifteen, when he got to twenty-five the hose stopped, it was his turn to go in. George looked him in the eye.

"In you go, lad."

Jack hadn't realised but Conker and Fatal were gone from sight, no more bright fire now, a wall of rolling sucking smoke, a straight line of canvas hose leading through the doorway and into the blackness. Jack moved towards the doorway, at the threshold a new sensation took hold of him, the wind, the draft caused by the fire pulled him through the doorway and off his feet. He landed face first across the hose, realising what had happened, he wondered at the force of the draft feeding the flames, now the beast had the building it would claim anything loose to fuel itself. The smoke was thick and tasted of wood. Jack's smoke eating apprenticeship was educating his palate, and he could recognise what was burning from the smell and taste of the smoke.

Lying on the hose, he noticed the smoke was a foot or so off the floor, the coldest air was running across the floor to feed the fire he would crawl the rest of the way. Just twenty-five feet, it might as well be twenty-five miles. He thought he knew fear but this was fear on another scale, the heat, the stinging eyes, the snotty nose he knew, but the sheer scale of this fire created awe in him, the constant fear of imminent death was something he had not felt before, he had been in house fires which were usually one room fires but in the back of his mind he always had an escape plan, a window, a doorway. But this was new, this was fire on a huge scale, it was causing flukes of wind, it was raining debris down upon them, it could pull a grown man off his feet and into the building.

It could drop iron beams weighing tons upon the crew, it could topple stacks of furniture fifty feet high, anyway it chose. Jack kept crawling, a small explosion off to his left which on another day would have been an event in itself, was now his new normal. The water he was crawling in was almost too hot to put his hands in, surely it must be close to boiling. At last, he came upon the kneeling Conker and Fatal in the fog of smoke, he couldn't make out features of faces but he knew which was which. He tapped Fatal on his back, Fatal turned and nodded, turning back he leant forward and shouted in Conker's ear. Conker nodded and looked back at Jack, his outstretched arm pointed forward, the roar of the fire and the noise of the jet of water made communicating other than by shouting at the top of your voice impossible, so Conker shouted just one word.

"Forward."

The three firemen shuffled forward on their knees with their jet directed at the heart of the fire. Little did they know at that moment they were the only fire crew in the biggest furniture depository in the country, having crews inside a fire when you have water towers working outside can be dangerous, it can only be done on the largest of buildings where there is no chance of the water tower hitting the men inside or pushing debris onto them. Conker waived the jet from side to side listening constantly to the reaction of the fire, they would then shuffle a few more feet into the building, again Conker waived the jet from side to side; no change they shuffled once more as they pulled on the hose, they could feel it ease as George fed more hose in for them.

The smoke was thick, every few minutes, he would bend double like Conker and Fatal then take a few deep breaths of the cold fresh air that swirled around them just inches from the floor of boiling water.

As his head came up from one such grab of fresh air, Jack looked through the smoke to his right, through the thick brown smoke he could just make out the outline of a little truck, fully engulfed in fire. Looking closer, he realised what it was, the forks were unmistakable, the little solid wheels, a forklift truck, but that was not what caught his attention it was the LPG cylinder clamped to the back behind the driver's seat, it was a gas-powered truck he reached forward past Fatal tapping Conker on the shoulder who looked around, Jack pointed and shouted.

"Cylinder."

Conker and Fatal looked across in the direction Jack was pointing, turning the jet ninety degrees was not an easy task. Conker shut the jet down so they could re-position themselves, as they did, they saw a tower of large sofas that was stacked on purpose built racking some fifty feet high start to move, it leant toward the burning forklift, the heat was weakening the lower metal struts that supported the tower, it was giving way, as they pulled in more hose and swung around to take up the new position, the tower began to fall in earnest.

The fall was now so quick, the top half could not keep up with the rate of fall, the furniture tower broke in the centre, the top half still falling but now falling almost backwards, the top would land at its own base. The first half of the tower hit the forklift burying it in sofas, the second half followed to land more or less in the same place creating a huge ball of fire that rose lazily, making its way skyward staying as a rolling ball in the smoke column rising out through the roof, the shower of sparks and debris that shot towards the men made them huddle together, with eyes closed they pointed the jet in the general direction of the newly created bonfire, now just ahead of them.

Thirty seconds passed, nobody moved, the huddle was tight, they just waited and breathed the smoke laden air, Fatal opened his tunic and buried his face into the opening, trying to filter some clean air from the crap that swirled around them. Still they waited, in the heat, and smoke while burning debris rained down, perhaps it was wood ash, perhaps it was bits of roof, none of the three moved to look and see what was pelting them, they just pulled together tighter and waited for it to end.

Two short tugs came on the hose, it was a signal from George he had seen the fire-ball and huge shower of sparks enter the smoke column from outside while pulling more hose nearer the doorway, he knew something had collapsed inside so he was checking the guys were okay. The huddle broke, Conker and Fatal together pulled on the hose and returned the two tugs. The guys looked across to the forklift; it was gone, buried in a mass of burning furniture. They pulled more hose around so it was laid out straight behind them.

As Conker opened up the branch, Fatal and Jack felt the jet-reaction push them back, once more they leant forward to counter the force allowing Conker to work the jet; the one-inch rope of water played upon the huge bonfire of furniture, the fire was so intense it made little difference. Conker worked the branch left, right, trying to get a foothold, a point in the mass of fire which was put out, once he had made his foothold he could expand it, he was working it where he had last seen the fork lift.

Fatal and Jack backed him up, they watched wondering what was happening beneath the pile, minutes passed, the jet seemed to be having no effect. Then they saw it, an area of black just off centre to the left of the main body of fire. Conker saw it appear at the same time, this is where he would concentrate his attack. As the jet played on the blackness, it started to grow, they were at last having an effect, the fire was being knocked down. As he worked the jet, Conker looked around, unbelievably there were stacks of furniture, wardrobes, beds, tables and chairs, that were as yet unaffected by the fire. This store was huge, it must cover three or four acres and it's full to the roof, this was a fire waiting to happen.

Outside, Horace and Smudger had arrived at the doorway. "How's it going, George?"

"Where have you two been? Where is everybody?"

"Had to run in a short supply relay in from the canal bridge on Heneage Street for Central's trucks they were over-drawing the town's mains, not enough water to go around. They're trying to save the office block on the front. The SO is piling BA men in there, they reckon the warehouse is pretty much lost, the white hats are like a snowstorm around that side, you've never seen so many divisional officers, they're throwing everything in the other end to stop it before it gets to the offices."

"How many have they made it?"

"It's now a twenty-five pumper, it sounds like chaos on the radio. Anyway, what do you want us to do, George?"

"600's got enough water for another jet, if you run one out, you can go in and join them."

As they talked, three fire engines pulled up behind Aston's pump, the crews dismounted fourteen fresh firemen, ready to go. The station officer in charge of the three trucks walked up to Aston's crew, George didn't recognise him. There was no time for pleasantries.

"Who's in there?"

"Three Aston guys; SO been in about half an hour, I think they're taking some punishment, we were just going to run in another jet."

"Are you Aston men as well?"

"Yes, SO."

"Okay, you three go and relieve your mates. I'll get a BA crew to relieve you as soon as I can."

"Yes, Sir."

Horace, Smudger and George didn't need telling twice; they were on the knees and into the smoke and gone before the station officer had time to speak again, or change his mind.

The station officer looked up at the water tower and the wall with a piece of masonry hanging on the end of an eighteen-inch steel beam.

"Right, one man up on that TL and keep that bloody monitor away from these men. Have I got a BA entry control man here?"

"Yes, sir," someone called.

"Right, set up an entry control point here. Only BA men inside from now on, you six get rigged in BA. Let's go, boys."

The men scattered and went about their tasks, leaving just the station officer at the doorway, he looked into the blackness and weighed his options. Was it worth putting men into the building that was pretty much totally involved? Once more he looked up at the TL monitor, why not pull everyone out and set up ground monitors and flood the place? There were no reports of people trapped inside, so why risk men's lives to save a building that would probably be demolished. The sound of bricks hitting the ground made the station officer spin around, another beam was making its way through the wall. His decision was made.

The BA entry point was set up at the doorway and six firemen in BA were going through their final checks.

Inside, Conker and the lads were making good progress. They seemed to be knocking the fire down, it was still an inferno but there was definitely an area which had been put out. The fire was no longer advancing towards them, it was not in retreat yet but it was being held, the conditions were tolerable now. They were just one length of hose into the building, just seventy-five feet, having crawled and dragged the charged hose through the labyrinth of racking and debris. Jack still felt a long way inside, he was still not as happy as he would be in a house fire but he was getting used to it. Conker called for more hose so he could move forward, as they began to move the LPG cylinder beneath the furniture pile exploded.

One hundred pounds of liquid petroleum gas had been heated to a point where the pressure inside the cylinder was sufficient to tear it apart; as it did, the liquid instantly turned to vapour and ignited. Sublimation was the name for it in fire school but firemen as usual had given it their own name, a 'BLEVE' a boiling liquid expanding vapour explosion.

The whole building shook as the blast wave instantly forced smoke and flame from every opening in the building, then pieces of heavy roofing fell inwards. The explosion was just fifty or so feet in front of them, the radiated heat from the rolling ball of fire instantly reddened their exposed skin, the eruption of the bonfire of furniture sent whole tables and settees flying through the air, table legs and steel racking pieces became missiles, all three men were blown in different directions, twenty or so feet across the floor.

Conker lost control of the jet, he let it go, part by accident, part by design, as he was now the only one still holding it. It was better to let it go than be dragged around and possibly thrown into the fire by the out of control and madly snaking loose hose.

Jack rolled unconscious to a stop against a section of tall racking; he would lay there on his side for two or three minutes before slowly consciousness returned.

For him, it was the headache that he was first aware of, then the light, things were bright, unnaturally bright, he tried to work out what had happened. He wasn't sure where he was, he had no idea of what had happened.

Then he remembered that he was with Conker and Fatal, realising his senses had been knocked out of him, he tried to pull them back together but the lack of sound made it difficult, being that close to an explosion had temporarily deafened him. He rolled onto his back and looked up, a stack of wooden tables forty feet high were burning, but only at the top. Jack looked at the tower and wondered why just the top was burning. He was lying in hot water next to undamaged furniture, yet forty or fifty feet above him a fire raged from furniture stack to furniture stack.

His mind wandered as he watched the fire, slowly his senses returned, this fire should not be allowed to get behind them, if it went over their heads and dropped down, it could cut off their only escape route. He lowered his eyes to the floor, he surveyed his new surroundings, where was he? He recognised nothing.

He watched, mesmerised, as the now loose jet snaked from side to side in a huge arc, the jet of water now useless except for powering the thrashing thing. The side-to-side motion stopped and slowly it reared up twenty feet into the air like a giant snake preparing to strike, then flicked forward in an almost mock attack, only to go through the same routine once more. He watched it perform this dance two or three times.

Then he realised he was lying in hot water without a care in the world, as chaos reigned around him, the panic was gone the feeling was strange. He felt nothing, no fear, yet he knew he had to get himself out, he had no conception of time but now he could hear sounds, he had to find Conker and Fatal. Rolling onto his stomach in the hot black water, he looked around for the other two firemen.

"Jack, Jack. Where are you Jack?" Conker was calling him, his hearing was returning.

"Here, Conker, I'm here. I'm okay."

Jack looked in the direction of Conker's voice just a short distance away in the smoke he could just make out Conker kneeling over what surely must be the point where Fatal was lying unmoving underneath a pile of wooden pallets and furniture.

"Give me a hand, Jack. Fatal is out cold."

Jack gave a quick look at the snaking hose still going through the same dance, from side to side, when it seemed to be most dangerous, so he waited until it reared once more, then he made his move. He crawled as fast as he could over to Conker.

"I was getting worried about you Jack, been calling you for ages."

"Yes, I'm not really sure what happened over there myself."

"Give me a hand, Jack, get this stuff off Fatal."

Together they pulled at the pallets and pieces of furniture that covered Fatal. Every time they moved a piece of furniture it seemed that another fell to replace it, Jack looked up at a stack of what looked like bedside tables that was leaning at a precarious angle threatening to fall upon not only them but would bury Fatal even deeper in debris and like the stack Jack had landed by it was only on fire at the top.

"Give me a hand with this sofa, Jack. I can't move it myself."

Jack slipped his left hand under the heavy chesterfield sofa his right grabbed the top corner of the back, together they threw the sofa forward as far as they could. Jack looked down to where Fatal was on the floor all he could see was yellow leggings nothing else he was under a good six feet of furniture and pallets and he wasn't moving Jack called out his name "Fatal, Fatal are you okay, Fatal?" But nothing, not a movement not a murmur.

"You hurt, Jack?"

"No, no, I'm fine."

"Where's all the blood coming from then? Your right hand's covered in it."

Jack hadn't seen his right hand. He felt no pain, and it was a mystery to him where this blood came from. Jack carried on moving pallets.

"Bloody hell, are you two all right?" Horace Smudger and George had arrived to find Conker and Jack pulling at twisted metal, trying to dig Fatal out.

"Give a hand, lads. Fatal's under all this shit."

The five firemen dug amongst the twisted metal and furniture some of it still burning with their bare hands, in silence they worked as a team helping each other move the larger more awkward pieces of furniture and debris, no one spoke of the fire that raged so close by threatening to engulf them, the fire was working to cut them off from their escape route, they all knew deep down that they were moments away from being trapped, cut off, with no way out, all six could be burned to death in this fire yet without discussion they accepted that risk to save their colleague, their mate, their Fatal, they would not leave without him, they dug and dug.

"Heads up, lads," Smudger shouted.

The five watched as the next tower of furniture in line stacked with bedside tables prepared itself for a fall, it started to move and was heading their way just as it did a large steel beam still anchored to the roof at one end, swung from its anchor point like a giant pendulum, swinging to the ground, it hit the corner of the stack on its way down. The five men cowered over the place where Fatal was buried, the two forces were immense, the roof beam, probably weighed two thousand pounds the stack of furniture probably half that weight.

The beam struck the ground with a tremendous thud and dug itself deep into the concrete floor just feet from the huddled group. The falling stack of furniture seemed to hesitate on being hit and it's unstoppable fall resumed, but now the beam was in its fall path. As the stack hit the beam it performed a delicate yet mechanical pirouette, the sound of metal on metal called out loud of the immense forces involved, the tower twisted and turned to the right, its fall was now just a few degrees off line and away from its original drop zone, it missed the men by a good ten feet.

The stack landed with a tremendous crash, scattering furniture in all directions, another fireball rose through the roof in a giant shower of sparks. The unburnt furniture buried their hose line but by sheer chance it had missed them;

without saying a word they looked at each other then carried on digging, digging like men possessed, shrouded in smoke the eerie glow of the fire made a scene akin to Dante's inferno complete with an evil snake writhing close by waiting to strike the innocent that came close enough. Jack looked around briefly and muttered. "If there is a hell, it should look like this."

The chaos inside was almost matched by that outside, the explosion had pushed at a large section of wall that hesitated in its fall, then almost in slow motion, crashed into the street. It had missed the BA crews but several tons had been flung across the road, Astons pump and TL were now surrounded by a debris field of bricks and mortar. The one hose line into the building burst instantly on being hit sending a plume of water skyward, a chunk of masonry had cut it almost in two. Inside, the evil snake jerked on being mortally wounded. Then it reared in its death throw one last time to fall limp and lifeless on the ground; nobody noticed.

600 looked at the burst, he stretched forward and put his hand on the delivery valve of the pump that controlled the burst hose line. He was reluctant to close it down the men inside would lose any water they may have, and losing water in a fire was never a good thing, he looked again at the burst length, it was bad, they were probably getting nothing inside but if they were he was about to shut it down, he turned the valve. The thought of six men in a burning building without water sent a cold shiver trough him. He looked at the doorway, he would not take his eyes off it until he saw them come out.

"Right, are you three ready?" the station officer pointed to the first three in the line.

"Yes, Sir."

"Right, hand your entry tallies in to the entry control officer, couple-up and in you go. Find Astons crew, six strong and bring them out. Go."

He emphasised the six, there was to be no doubt how many should come out.

"Yes, sir."

The clack of demand valves, the release of compressed air into the masks was a familiar sound as they tightened their facemasks, they each put on their helmets fastening them tightly, tapping each other, they nodded their joint readiness and made their way into the burning building following the flat lifeless hose line; it was not only their way in, but like Theseus' thread it would show their way out.

114

Fatal murmured, as the last piece of wood was pulled off his legs, five firemen looked down into the pit they had dug in the debris, down upon their bedraggled colleague. George spoke first.

"Fatal, you okay?"

"What the hell happened? Where am I? Shit, my leg, I think it's broken, shit, shit."

"Oh good, as long as you're not hurt," Conker replied.

"Jack find a piece of wood to put the moaning bugger on, we'll carry him out."

"A piece of burning roof some twenty foot square crashed to the ground beside them. They all automatically crouched down waiting to be hit by bits of roof."

"Time to go, lads."

Fatal was loaded onto a smouldering piece of headboard Jack had found. Horace, Smudger, and George would carry him out. Conker and Jack would clear the way through the debris following the hose line. They had only gone ten feet or so when they met the three BA men on their way in.

"Hooray, the cavalry," Fatal shouted from the lying position on the headboard, this was not really news; he was the last to see them as they approached the exiting group.

"The governor's decided he wants everyone out," a fireman in BA shouted through the din of the fire.

All Fatal's senses were now back to full working order, even the sense of humour had returned.

"You'll get no argument from me. I've got to cancel my dancing lessons."

600 was looking at the doorway when, one, two, three, BA men came out through the opening. They stopped at entry control and picked up their tallies. Just a few steps behind came a smoke blackened Conker and Jack, then Horace, Smudger, and George carrying Fatal on the makeshift stretcher. The station officer asked how Fatal was, then pointed to an ambulance parked at the Lawley Street, traffic lights just a hundred yards away, the ambulance was part of the automatic resources ordered on at five pumps or more. The Aston boys stayed together while they loaded Fatal into the ambulance.

The five looked through the ambulance rear doors while the medic checked Fatal over, as he lay on the gurney.

"Yep, that leg's broken plus a few burns and your left wrist is also broken, matey."

"Oh, no, not my wrist. Will I be able to play the piano when it heals?"

"It's just a simple fracture, it will heal fine, there's no reason why you shouldn't be able to play the piano."

"That's amazing."

"Why is it amazing?"

"I couldn't play the piano before."

The five men turned and walked away smiling and shaking their heads, making their way back up to the entry point. Fatal would be fine, he had found new friends in an ambulance crew that would play along with his terrible jokes. Jack looked back at the ambulance, he was going to mention his finger, but when he heard of Fatal's broken bones and burns, a mere cut finger did seem a bit paltry, he would get it seen to later.

The five Aston firemen looked at the scene around their trucks. The TL at one hundred feet extension had a man at its head, directing the monitor, as they watched it working, Toot waived a greeting to them from the deck controls. Jack waived a tired bloodied hand back in acknowledgement. The street was covered in hose lines and fallen masonry, ground monitors had been placed every forty or so feet along the road and giant jets of water arched over the remaining wall which now lent outward at a precarious angle. Nobody was near the doorway, their doorway, the flat lifeless hose the only indication that anybody had been fighting the fire inside the building.

The station officer was now on the opposite side of the road with a group of clean fresh firemen, watching the ground monitors flood the place. The five smoke-stained soaking-wet Aston men walked up to the group.

"Where do you want us, boss?"

The station officer turned and looked at the sorry looking bunch. Conker's eyes seemed extra bright as they shone defiantly out of his smoke blackened face. Jack's face was much the same. By comparison, Horace, Smudger and George were relatively clean, just wet and covered in ash but they all looked battle weary. The SO noticed the blood dripping from Jack's right hand.

"You're the Aston boys, aren't you? Take a break, men, take the weight of your feet, sit against the wall here. You lot look like drowned rats." The SO pointed at Jack's hand. "Get somebody to look at that."

116

Jack looked at his hand, for the first time his forefinger was split from the first knuckle through the second knuckle up to the fingernail, which was slowly turning black. Now, it hurt, the nail especially started to throb. Jack looked back to where the ambulance was parked but it was gone, it had taken Fatal to hospital, he looked down again at the finger.

"Come on, Jack, let's get you a bandage off the truck for that, at least we can stop its bleeding until you can get it stitched."

They walked to the rear locker of the nearest pump where the first aid kit was carried. Pulling out the box Conker found a roll of bandage and started to unwrap it from the cellophane wrapper.

"Hey, what are you two up to? The pump's driver was asking what was being taken off his truck."

"Just grabbing a bandage for the lad."

"Is he okay? Need any help?" the driver asked, while walking up to them.

"He's fine just a cut."

"You two been inside, what's it like?"

"Yes, indeed, it got a little warm."

Conker replied while he wound the bandage around Jack's index finger and his middle finger; the middle finger gave support.

"How many did they make it in the end?" Conker asked looking around the immediate fire ground.

"Stayed at twenty five, with three TLs, they stopped it at the offices and they reckon this end has some unaffected stuff left in it. They say it was stopped before it got all the way to this end, perhaps you saw that from inside."

"Yes, you could say we had a ringside seat."

"The warehouse is pretty much buggered though, isn't it? Our governor reckons it's a total loss."

"Where the hell are you guys from? Calling your station officer 'governor' is a London thing."

"We're from Lichfield. Our SO is a Londoner though, he likes to be called 'Governor'."

"Lichfield, Staffordshire! How come you got called into the city? We don't usually need over the border assistance for a twenty five pumper."

"You've got another, a fifteen pumper on at the same time, so running low on resources I guess."

"A fifteen pumper as well, where's that?"

"Don't know Brum that well, but its' here in town somewhere." The pump operator called over to a Staffordshire fireman leaning on the wall, smoking a cigarette.

"Stan, where in town is that fifteen pumper?"

"Stan blew blue tobacco smoke high into the air. Just off 'The Horse fair', Inge Street."

Conker stopped winding bandage and looked at Jack's face. "Bianchi."

"Do you reckon he's torched it, Conker?"

Conker turned back to the Lichfield Fireman. "Do you know anything more about the fifteen pumper?"

"Nope, just that there's another big job on, that's all."

"Come on, Jack. Let's take a walk and look for the Con-Unit, we can find out what's happening."

Conker called to the other three and told them where they were going.

"Wait for us, there may be a canteen wagon, we can have a cuppa."

The station officer waived them off as they let him know where they were going. He seemed more interested in chatting and smoking cigarettes than the Aston rats' whereabouts.

Lawley Street was a sea of fire engines and specialist fire trucks charged lines of hose made up a spaghettini that locked them all into place. Firemen were everywhere, over a hundred and forty, now all outside, nobody was inside the building. At the end of the mass of men and equipment, they could just make out the red and white chequered band that wound its way around the roofline of the control-unit and beside it, the canteen wagon.

They picked their way through the mass of hose and equipment, steaming water ran from the warehouse doorways and roller shuttered loading bays, across the empty carpark and footpath down over the kerbs edge, running in steaming rivers to cast iron slotted drain covers which gurgled with delight as the water thundered in. Further down the road, the drains were blocked with debris, a natural dip in the dual carriageway had slowly become a steaming lake of black run-off water from the fire.

As they made their way along the street, they greeted old friends and the men they knew with a wave, a rude comment or sometimes a two-fingered salute. Jack didn't know many of the characters so he was just looking around trying to make sense of this organised chaos. Looking up at the smoke column, Jack was impressed with its size. It was huge and rose hundreds of feet into the midday sky but it had changed, it was no longer the angry roaring beast that consumed all before it. It was a passive thing, a eunuch, it was no longer threatening, it was grey and streaked with snow white steam, it was as if it had grown old. Its life was drawing to a close.

Jack saw Harry, not too far ahead of them. He was drinking from a branch, he had his cupped hand trying to catch water from the jet but it was being knocked away by the pressure of the water, yet he was managing to get enough to drink. He and another unknown fireman were directing the jet through a ground floor doorway, it was doing absolutely nothing but adding to the water damage. Jack pointed him out to Conker, the group made their way over to him stepping over more hose lines. Harry didn't recognise them until they were just a few feet away, his face lit up in a huge grin.

"Hey guys, where have you been? All the action has been around this side, you should have seen it, me and Dave here have been taking it in turns up the TL. You can see the lot from up there, explosions, fireballs, everything, isn't it fantastic?"

Conker looked at the clean dry Harry and his new found friend, then he turned to the rats who had, as one, decided in their tired state to ignore him, he turned back to give Harry a dressing down, then he looked again at the beaming Harry. Was it Harry's fault he had spent his time upwind in clean air at the head of a TL? Or here, just standing in the road like a ground monitor? No, not really, everybody did their bit.

"Must have been quite a spectacle, Harry. But now you need to come with us, knock that jet off and stop drinking the water. It'll make you ill, we'll get a drink at the canteen wagon." Harry closed the jet down and placed it on the ground. He and Dave joined the little group that headed off up the street.

"Conker?"

"What?"

"Why will the water make me ill?"

"Do you normally drink canal water, which has piss and all types of shit in it, because that's what you've been doing. Ever heard of Weils disease?"

"Oh my god, will it kill me?"

"Hopefully, then we will all have some peace."

The drowned rats and Dave arrived at the canteen wagon; all but Conker and Jack headed straight for the drinks and free cigarettes, one cigarette only with each fresh tea was the rule no one stuck to. At the control-unit, Conker and Jack waited in turn by the dispatch window, from behind the sliding glass a station officer in shirtsleeves was sending away a runner, Conker got his attention.

"Can't tell you a lot. I've been far too busy running this job to worry about Inge Street."

"Mike, here's my main scheme radio-man. He may have heard something, one of you can come in and have a word with him, just one of you mind, I don't want this place full of chatter."

Jack nodded his acceptance to stay outside as Conker turned to him. "I'll wait here."

"Pretty straight forward from what I can make out."

Mike, a portly ageing fireman who was happy with his less physical role had been listening in to all the radio traffic and sending periodic updates to HQ Fire Control.

"Fifteen pumps, one hydraulic platform, water from street mains, no relaying. But they have just found two stiffs according to their last message. The first half-dozen or so calls said it was an explosion followed by a fire. That's about it mate. I've got nothing else, it sounds a bit boring to be honest. Oh, there is one more thing."

"What's that?"

"Well, it's a bit strange really the chief was in here running the show, it being a twenty five pumper and all, then this copper comes in and talks to him. I thought it was just a liaison officer, for road closures, key-holders and stuff, but after their chat, the chief puts the deputy in charge here and goes on to Inge Street, a fifteen pumper, how strange is that? The deputy in charge of the big job and the chief in charge of the smaller one, don't make sense, does it?"

"Thanks, Mike. Great name for someone who works the radio by the way."

Conker waived as he made his way out of the Con-unit. "Thanks SO."

"No problem, wait, were you on the first attendance?"

"Sort of, we came on five, at 0930 hours, the three trucks from Aston."

The SO spun around and looked at his disposition board. He had every fire engine and specialist vehicle listed on the board, how many riders each had, including their names and where they were on the fire ground. Each officer also had his own tally. Nobody would be missed if they needed to take a roll call.

"Yes, Central then Aston here at 0923 hours. Right you've done your bit. Find your officer, he flicked through the crew boards station officer? Station Officer Jackson? Ah, Sid Jackson, yes, find your SO and tell him if he can get his equipment stowed and get his trucks out. He will be relieved by fresh crews at 1430 hours. He needs to be released in person by us here though, not just driving off, okay?"

"Yes, SO, thanks," Conker shouted as he walked away. As they walked to the canteen wagon, Conker brought Jack up to speed telling him of the two stiffs found at Inge Street.

The canteen wagon buzzed with the chatter and laughter of firemen who were fresh from the fight, each had a story to tell of his part in the downfall of the beast. The canteen wagon was a big red, slab-sided aluminium trailer towed by a Land Rover, on one side there was a flap window some six feet long, that opened up supported on metal stays providing a little shelter and access to the serving hatch, behind which two firemen in tee shirts were constantly boiling water in huge gas powered urns that spluttered into giant tea pots, each holding two gallons or more of tea. They provided an endless supply for the thirsty men, coffee was available and Jack's drink of choice but the instant coffee they offered was only marginally better than the liquid variety in the station mess, but he drank it. It was welcomed for all it was.

Harry turned to Jack. "Ask for your cigarette."

"I don't want a cigarette."

"No, but I do, get me some more."

"They'll kill you, Harry."

"Yes, you're probably right, and you think with all the shit we have to breathe, this little coffin nail is gonna make a big difference?"

"It's up to you, Harry."

"Good man, ask for a few."

"Harry, Jack, come over here." Conker stood alone just to the side of the canteen wagon with a large mug of tea in one hand and a capstan full strength in the other. They looked around to see who was within earshot, nobody.

Conker told Harry of the events on Inge Street. "Now the question is, is it Bianchi's garage? Sounds a bit big to me to be Bianchi's, but if it is, who are the two stiffs? Do you two fancy a pint in town after the shift ends tonight? We could take a look down Inge Street and see who's there; the lads might have some info. Then we can visit Fatal in the general."

"A nice pint on a Sunday evening after a job to wash away the soot, sounds good to me."

By the time the shift had ended and the three had showered and changed clothes, it was coming up to 1900 hours when they got to Inge Street. Red and white barrier tape blocked off the street to stop cars and pedestrians going down towards the fire. Four pumps with just hazard lights flashing, were parked neatly down the centre of the road, a few firemen could be seen milling about in the fading light, like Lawley Street just a mile or so away, a column of steam rose lazily into the evening sky.

Rolling Thunder

"That's it, that's Bianchi's lock up, that's where Bianchi thumped Harry with the iron bar."

"Are you sure?"

"Well, if Jack ain't sure, I am. I'm not forgetting that in a hurry, the bastard."

"Let's take a walk down and see who we can see."

All three ducked under the barrier tape and walked down the street towards the fire ground. As they approached the building, a voice called out to them.

"Whoa, wait up there, where do you three think you're going?"

A portly older fireman approached them as they walked closer to the building.

"Conker, is that you?"

"Bubbles, Bubbles, you old dog. What the hell you doing here? It's a three-day camel ride from Northfield; you boys on the frilly edge of the brigade shouldn't be out in the big bad city at night. It's dangerous for you bumpkins, you know."

"Bollocks to you, Fowles. Anyway, haven't you got anything better to do than wander around fires when you're off duty?"

Conker had to work out how to get his old friend to tell all he knew without arousing suspicion. If Bubbles thought he was being questioned or giving away sensitive information, he may clam up.

"Not really, Bubbles, me and the lads here, Jack and Harry." Nods were exchanged as greetings.

"We're out for a few beers, after the Lawley Street job, we heard of this one on the radio earlier. Trouble is Bubbles, Harry here has a car inside. We came down to see what's happening, see if it survived before we have a pint, what can you tell us?"

Bubbles looked around; he drew them to the side of the footpath under a streetlight.

"Your cars had it, mate, there ain't nothing in there that isn't a burnout wreck, but that ain't it, Conker. There's a rumour buzzing around. One of the stiffs is Franc Bianchi, can you believe it? They reckon it was arson, looks like someone torched all three garages, lots of cops showing an interest and interviewing witnesses, forensics, digging in the ashes and stuff."

Harry spoke up. "Three? I thought there was one."

"No mate, this goes way back, almost to Bromsgrove Street, there must be, I guess forty fifty cars inside trucks, motorbikes to anything and everything with wheels by the look of it."

"Well, well, well, why isn't this a surprise?" A London accented voice came from behind them.

"Mr Fowles."

"Mr Thomas."

They turned to see the tall London cop behind them, smiling. Bubbles turned and wandered into the background then disappeared behind a truck.

"It's been a while boys. How have you been?"

"Good, thank you, we heard the news so me and the lads thought we would come and take a look. Was one of the stiffs Bianchi?" Conker had decided not to play games.

"Let's take a walk to the end of the street."

As they walked, Thomas told the three how the weekend had played out.

"Bianchi met with two, 'known' guys up from London, midday yesterday, they spent most of the afternoon drinking in a strip joint. Meeting up again, early today in a little café in town, before driving around here to Inge Street, Franc and one went inside. If the one that went in with Franc is who I think it is, he was probably the trigger man at the Aston Lane job, the other man stayed outside, just sitting in his car as lookout. Within minutes of them going in, the whole place went up with a huge explosion, like thunder. The lookout drove off straight after it went up, unfortunately we lost him in the confusion. Hopefully, we can locate him before he goes to ground in London."

"Did they carry anything in with them?"

"No, Joe, why do you ask?"

"Just an idea."

It was not Thomas's intention to involve the firemen any further in the investigation but Franc was dead and if the other body was who he thought it

124

was, the Birmingham end of the investigation was pretty much over. If the firemen had some insight into what happened, they may be useful one last time.

"I tell you what, Joe, I'm meeting one of my men in The Shakespeare on Lower Temple Street. Would you boys like to come along, see what he's dug up."

"Yes, if it's all right with you, it's all right with me. What do you say lads?"

Harry, as enthusiastic as ever, said, "Yeah, it's just like being in an episode of Softly, Softly and I could do with a beer after today."

"Well, you've changed your tune; not long ago you asked us to 'leave it alone and give you room to do your job'. Months and not a word, nothing, even Conker with his contacts has nothing. Now you're being all friendly and asking us to join you and meet one of your men. I take it 'dug-up' means a forensics man?"

"Yes, Jack you're right, but Joe and I have been chatting all along, he asked for favours at the beginning and I've helped out where I can, I also made sure none of you four came to any harm. But it's been really quiet, nothing has been happening at all, my boss was about to pull me off this job and leave it to the locals, it was a close run thing."

"I reckon Franc was lying low just keeping his head down, then when he thought the coast was clear, he got back to business."

"So you've been following him all this time."

"Yep, and you and the others, on and off, especially if we thought he was getting close to one of you. And you must slowdown on that motorbike of yours, it's hard to follow the way you ride it."

"So you're Conker's contact." Conker smiled.

"The card...the card, you gave him your card."

"If you remember anything, give me a call. That was a special number, just for you at Lloyd house."

"Nice one, Jack, you do catch on quick, don't you? Even the dug-up shot. But there really has been nothing worth talking about so far, well, until the fire."

"So Franc and this guy walked in and within minutes it just blew-up?" Conker asked.

"Yep, pretty much, they could only have been in there three or four minutes then all the windows blew out and the place went up in a huge fire-ball."

"You said like thunder. What did you mean like thunder?"

"Well, it didn't go bang, as a single explosion, it rolled like thunder, a rolling bang, then flames shot out the windows if that makes sense."

125

"Yes, it does, it certainly does." Conker looked up Hurst Street toward the Hippodrome Theatre and mused aloud.

"So close to the theatre. Franc had set the stage for the last act. He had pre-prepared the garage ready to burn. They wouldn't have had the time to set the fire the way you describe it, to get the right effect it would take time to set-up. It's ironic either one or both of them were Jacques killers and they die in their own fire. But I care not; a man can die but once, they owed God a death."

Inside The Shakespeare, sat at a large oak table, holding court was a respectable middle-aged man, a pint glass of tap water was placed in front of him by Harry. He looked so normal, he disappeared into the furniture, he could probably walk unnoticed anywhere. His spectacles were maybe a little thick, his clothes maybe a little old-fashioned, he was average height, and average built, he was unremarkable in just about every way possible. He spoke softly and deliberately and the one quality that Jack quickly grew to like was the accuracy with which he spoke. There was no use of nonsense words nothing was 'like' anything, every sentence did not end with. Do you know what I mean? He was very specific, no thingummies' or whatsits, just plain English.

The four men sipped their beer while he finished his 'initial observations'.

"In summation, my initial observations are that there are at least six seats of fire starting at the south end of the main building where I recovered these from, a two gallon metal oil can with the side cut out, it was situated close to a 13 amp socket outlet, we shall call that site one."

He pointed to a clear plastic evidence bag on the table. Inside were some little pieces of metal, a lump of melted plastic with a piece of light bulb imbedded in it, a tiny motor, and a few other bits and pieces. Conker picked them up and checked them out without removing them from the bag he passed them to Jack.

"Sites two through six were evenly spaced northward, down the central walkway of the building terminating close to the entrance door furthermore at each site I believe there is residue of petroleum spirit. It would appear there was a pool of petroleum at each seat of fire that is of course pending laboratory verification of the samples I've taken. After ignition, the pursuant explosion blew out the windows, outward opening doors and a section of roof thus venting the fire, the following conflagration destroying the entire contents of the building."

He paused and looked at the group buttoning his jacket as he did so.

"If that is all gentlemen, I would bid you good evening, I have a cat to get home to."

He rose to his feet, put on a flat cap, picked up the evidence bag and dropped it into his battered black briefcase and made his way out of the pub. The two young firemen looked towards a thoughtful Conker.

"Jack, do I look like that in my flat cap?"

"Pretty much."

"I'm throwing it, don't let me wear it again."

"Good idea."

"Anyway, Jack what did you make of those bits in the evidence bag?"

"A weird assortment micro switches, tiny motors, a block of something, that could be a receiver but I'm not sure. I thought it was the workings of a radio control for a model at first but then there was the 240 volt light bulb stem and lamp holder, it's all a bit weird, really."

"Well, lads, you are the experts in fire. What do you think?"

Harry decided, as he had been called an expert, he should give his vast knowledge of fire scene investigation gained in his whole year of firefighting an airing, he should let the Copper wonder at the magnitude of his talent, he went to speak. But Jack had seen Harry preparing himself, instinctively he knew Harry was about to let forth another gem of wisdom, so he decided to stop him.

"Conker is the one who has the experience. He's probably seen most of the ways arsonists set fires. We are newbies, we are still learning. What do you think, Conker?"

Harry looked at Jack, crestfallen but relieved, as he had no idea what any of this meant, so he turned to Conker with interest.

Just as Conker went to speak, a man walked up to the table. "Can I have a word?"

There were no ranks mentioned, no sir, no mister Thomas, he was a copper that knew not to announce their presence. The two walked toward the doorway; as they did, the unknown cop handed Thomas another clear plastic bag, they chatted for a few minutes and the unknown cop left. Thomas returned to the table. Putting the evidence bag on the tabletop, he spoke in a hushed voice.

"We have the driver, short chase down the Coventry Road but he's back here in custody, stolen car of course, false plates absolutely nothing in the car but this."

Harry looked at it. "What is it?"

"It's a model airplane control box, apparently."

Conker picked up the little plastic box with two joysticks on the front and a little toggle switch on the top. "That's it, the final piece of the jigsaw, that's how they did it."

"You reckon you've worked it out without even going into the building, Joe."

"Well, it's got all the right pieces of a simple but effective arson job that's hard to spot at first glance. Your forensics guy still has lots of work to do, fingerprints from inside of this would be a good start, the batteries are your best bet, and a real close look at the fire scene, because it's clever."

"Come on, Joe, help us out, point us in a direction. What do you think happened in there."

"Well, you have a problem. The guy you have in custody is either an idiot or a murderer, that's up to you to work out."

"Okay, how do you come to that conclusion, Joe?"

"Well, firstly if you want to torch the place you have to make it look like a genuine accident, so you mustn't use anything that shouldn't be normally found in the premises. You wouldn't find petrol in a fruit and vegetable shop, for instance, but you would in a garage or workshop where finding an accelerant like petrol is normal, that's a good start for Franc, when he gets this fire going with petrol there's so much petrol around anyway, it's nothing unusual.

"But your forensic guy said six seats of fire that was his first mistake. The temptation to start more than one fire to make sure the whole lot goes up is irresistible for your average arsonist, but Franc's ego got in the way, he thought he had a way of fooling forensics. He had almost certainly prepared things in advance and was waiting for his moment in time.

"Franc would have probably preferred a night-time fire, it always takes longer for a fire to be spotted at night, but then he had a stroke of luck, the twenty five pumper, local radio were there in minutes, reporting live so he must have known of the Lawley Street job. He also knew getting enough resources to another large fire in the city would be difficult and would take time. For Franc, the timing couldn't be better, but was there another deadly agenda at work that Franc knew nothing of?"

"What do you mean, Joe, another agenda?"

"A moment, dear Sir, I'll come to that."

"Fire seat number one was the mother fire, she would spawn the rest. It was an oil can full of petrol a couple of gallons maybe, nobody would think it odd, an oil can in a garage, but your forensic man is good, he noticed the wall socket and the jumble of electrical bits and pieces, a lightbulb filament stem intact in the can. That's mistake two, it left non-combustible evidence; he should have used a mechanism that would be destroyed early on in the fire's development. The lump of melted plastic is, as Jack thought, a model airplane receiver that had the little electric motor attached to it that would actuate the switch for the light bulb filament which would burn white hot and light the petrol in the oil can, all done by radio from the model airplane control box a short distance away outside."

"Like, outside in a parked car, you mean the lookouts' car," Harry said excitedly.

"Exactly."

"But surely, Joe, model airplane controls work on little, low volt batteries, not mains electricity."

"Yes, but as I'm sure Jack will agree, it only has to work for a split second, if all the tiny wiring is overloaded and bursts into flames, so much the better. Is that right, Jack?"

"Conker's right, once the radio signal was received, he probably didn't need the light bulb filament, just the overload would have done the job."

"Okay, Joe. If that's the case, if that's how he started it, why and how did it spread so quickly, why did it roll like thunder?"

"That's when he makes mistake number three; he has to spread the fire so he uses the old balloon trick. A large good quality balloon will hold over a gallon of petrol, he fills five with petrol and hangs them from the roof beams by thin cord or string spaced evenly down the Central walkway. That's why your man found pool marks and residue where there were no cars; why petrol and no cars?"

"He should have hung them over the rear of a few cars where the petrol tanks are, that's where you would expect to find petrol residue. So, actuated from the control box outside, up goes the petrol he's just put in the open oil can, the fire quickly reaches the first balloon hanging from the ceiling. It instantly melts the balloon whoosh, the petrol drops to the floor in a fire-ball which gets to the next balloon and so on, whoosh and whoosh and whoosh, the rolling thunder worked its way down the centre of the garage blowing out doors and windows as it goes, the whole place is now on fire."

"Your man is going to have a hard job finding a few feet of string and what's left of five balloons in that lot and it is possible there were more dotted around."

"So, Joe, that's why it went up so quick, rolled like thunder and flames shot out the windows."

Harry thought it was time he joined in the conversation.

"Yes, that's pretty much how we think it happened. It's a clever, but not an unusual ploy used by the, the err, underworld fraternity."

"Yes, thanks Harry. Get your guy to check the windows and doors of the cars, he probably went around the garage opening them up to make sure the fire could get in. He may even have been stupid enough to have doused the interiors of a few with petrol for good measure."

Jack came into the conversation.

"I see where you're going, Conker. If Franc and the other guy were becoming a liability for the London firm, maybe he stepped out of line when he shot Jacques in Aston, this was an easy way to get rid of them both, no shooter and no witness."

"I'm lost Joe, why would Franc be stupid enough to set up a fire in which he and his Aston accomplice are to be killed."

"He didn't, well not knowingly, let's say he was boasting of how he could torch the place remotely from way down the road or maybe even in a pub around the corner, he showed them the remote control and explained how it works, then later the two go inside to check all is ready, they put the petrol in the open can for the mother fire, leaving an open can of petrol would have been way too risky to be in the building with for long even for Franc, then they turn on the power, the plan was then to come out and light it up."

"But what if 'Brutus', the lookout, has worked out a way to get rid of them both? As soon as they go in, he turns on the radio control by the little toggle switch, actuates the joysticks and waits. As soon as Franc flicks the wall socket switch on, they're both instantly engulfed in the mother fire. '*Et tu, Brute.* Or there is another possibility."

"We call it the idiot theory, it's a technical term."

"Yes, thanks Harry, anyway, let's say he is an idiot that got bored and had no idea what he was doing? He picks up the control box and starts playing with it, he flicks the toggle switch and starts playing with the joysticks. To him, it was harmless, it did nothing, but it was only a matter of time until Franc, not knowing that someone had armed the system, turned on the wall socket. The result was the same, instant fireball. That's what I meant when I said, a murderer or an idiot."

"Clever. It's very clever, murderer or idiot? I have work to do. Can I get you boys another beer?"

"Two pints of Mild and a pint of Bitter, please."

The four men moved to the bar and started chatting about the events of the past few months while the drinks were poured, Conker asked if Sophia could now have an exclusive and break the story. They had been chatting for less than a couple of minutes when a familiar face walked towards them again. This time he didn't speak, he just looked at Thomas, turned and walked back to the entrance door. Thomas followed his lead, it was a very short conversation. Thomas returned to the bar while the unknown cop waited at the doorway.

"Apparently, we have arrested Franc in the Bartons Arms, he's in custody."

"What! That's impossible?" Harry was the only one to speak. Conker and Jack just looked at Thomas hardly believing what they had just heard.

"Can't tell you any more, I'll be in touch." He threw a fifty pence piece on the bar top. The two Cops left the pub together.

"What the hell is going on Conker, Franc's been cooked alive, in Inge Street, hasn't he? They had him there, they saw him, they watched him go into the building for Christ's sake. How the hell did Franc get out of that?"

"Harry's right, Conker. The cops had the two London men and Franc at Inge Street, they have the lookout in custody, what better witnesses than a bunch of cops covertly watching as Franc and the other one are killed in the fire. As far as I can see, there is only one plausible explanation. It's Tony."

"You're right Jack, they think they have Franc because he's told them he's Franc but they actually have Tony playing the part of Franc. That's what he does, he has to give Franc his alibi, and he's still playing his part, I bet he doesn't know his brother is dead, so the show must go on."

"Oh, I don't believe it. Sherlock bloody Holmes and Doctor bleeding Watson are on the case. Will you two ever give this up? I think you two make it up as you go along. Every time you two get involved in anything other than sleeping, shit happens; this has been one long cock-up after another, now it's happened again. Are you saying Tony is involved in all this after all?"

"Up to his neck. Hang on here a minute."

Conker caught the attention of the barman. "Have you got a payphone mate?"

"Yes, in the corridor." He pointed towards the back of the pub.

"Wait here, I'll just be a minute. The answer is at hand."

"What the hell's going on, Jack? I thought Tony was in the clear, the cops had nothing on him."

"I'm not sure, Conker has always been suspicious of the twins, let's see what he's got when he gets back, but if Tony and Franc have been in it together all along, they could easily have given each other alibis, they probably always have, they're that identical their mother can't tell them apart. They could change places anytime, maybe even when they were firemen if one wanted a shift off, if so, who stole petrol? And who took the fall? It's possible they changed places a lot."

"What, even with their wives. Wow, you mean…you mean, wife swapping?"

"Harry, try and concentrate."

Conker returned to the bar and picked up his drink. "Let's grab a table and sit down."

"What's going on, Conker? Is Tony involved? Is Franc dead? Jack's completely lost, he has no clue."

Jack looked across at Harry and smiled. "Thanks Harry."

"Well, I haven't got the entire story. Thomas didn't go into detail but in a nutshell this is where we are. Franc and Tony move from pukka car sales and start selling a few stolen cars, then somehow get involved with a bigger gang from London that move them around the country.

"The twins get little one man bands to do the dirty work for them, changing vehicle identities, resprays, new plates, that sort of stuff, it keeps the workshops at arm's length and let's say they have a disagreement, the little man won't play ball, he needs to be sent a message, so he gets the frighteners put on him. He's warned but still won't play ball, that's when they torch the place, that's their specialty and the word travels.

"The next person thinking of not playing ball or even worse, double crossing them knows the consequences. But as the business grew they were noticed by a London mob that came north to take over the business. Little did the twins know but they would have the frighteners put on them.

"The London gang started to play rough at Jacques, one of the London gang goes in with Franc but instead of roughing him up, he is shot, and Franc is told he's next if he doesn't play their game, their way. Franc hastily torches the place but cannot hide the bullet hole in the head in that short space of time, the fire didn't get chance to do its job.

"Thomas won't admit it but he thinks they were rumbled, the London lads had a tip off that they were being watched. So, on the orders of the Londoners,

Franc and Tony run around town trying to get rid of any evidence of their involvement. The final act was to be burning of Inge Street.

"But what Thomas still doesn't know is, was it an accident by the idiot with the control box? Or was it murder to get rid of two liabilities? He's pissed off that after all their work they only have a dumb driver who didn't have the common sense to throw the control out the window of the car, the idiot kept it with him, so perhaps we should go with the idiot theory."

"Hang-on, Conker. Are you saying that I was talking with Tony about an E-Type, not Franc?"

"You were talking to them both at different times."

"Harry, do you remember when there was just you and me left in the Bartons Arms before we went to the Longboat, remember the flash clothes complete with Fedora, he made a grand entrance making sure he's noticed. He had to, they were creating an alibi."

"Who was?"

Conker drank the last of his drink. "Never mind, Harry. Let's go home. I'll see you two at the station Wednesday."

At Steelhouse Lane Police Station in a small, windowless, dimly lit basement room, lined with white enamelled bricks, Tony Bianchi sat at a tiny wooden table facing DC David Thomas, the only other person in the room was a police constable who stood in silence by the closed entrance door.

"Constable, was it you that took this statement of Mister Bianchi?"

"Yes, Sir."

"Is that Mister Bianchi's signature?"

"Yes, Sir."

Thomas stood and walked over to the constable, dropped his mouth to the constable's ear and whispered something unheard by Tony. A one-word reply also went unheard. Thomas returned to his seat.

"So, Tony why were you in the Bartons Arms impersonating Franc."

"*Non sono, Toni.*"

"Why the attitude, Tony? Why the Italian? Does it make you feel tough? Are you a hard man, Tony? Let's try again. Why are you impersonating Franc?"

His chin came up, as he curled his lips, his mouth seemed to droop downwards at the edges, slowly he looked down his nose with heavy lidded eyes at DC Thomas, the gaze held nothing but disdain for the man in front of him.

"That's because I am Franc, *Sono Franco*. I'm not impersonating him. You pigs have got nothing on us, you've got shit for brains, we have a way with dealing with *pene piccolo* like you. You really shouldn't mess with us copper or our business if you know what's good for you. You should look after your own business at home. My brother Tony is with your wife again now. I know how she likes an Italian now and then. *Bastardi della polizia*."

Thomas looked him in the eye, he may have a Welsh surname but he could speak Italian and French fluently and the swearing in Italian was pissing him off. Tony Bianchi looked straight back and smirked, nodding a yes to his accuser and muttering, "*Pene piccolo*."

Tony, Tony, you have got attitude, haven't you? How hard are you, Tony? Is the Italian supposed to scare me?

"*Tutti i Poliziotta sono idiotic*."

Thomas waited a few seconds, watching the smirking Tony Bianchi sitting before him, so cocky. He'd had enough. Thomas smiled a smile of acceptance; for Bianchi the writing was on the wall. He struck, his right fist flew with a speed that caught Tony Bianchi completely off guard. It hit him just in front of his left ear, close to the temple. As it landed there was a sharp snap that only Tony heard. Tony's head spun around with the sheer force of the impact, his body tried to follow and twisted on the metal seat. With the suddenness of the move, Tony lost his balance, the chair flipped from under him in a metallic clatter, he landed on the cold concrete floor clutching his face. Thomas looked over at the constable standing at the doorway, the stony-faced constable did not move a muscle, yet his eyes looked down to the floor where Tony lay moaning in agony, then up again to Thomas.

"Two milky teas, then Sir, one with sugar and one without, I won't be long."

The constable turned and left the room. Thomas walked over to a whimpering Tony.

"Get up, you little shit, and start talking and talk English." He grabbed the chair and slammed it back into place. "SIT!"

Tony was in shock, he didn't for one moment think the attack was coming, he had just been punched by the mild mannered copper and more could be coming his way. The Italian language was gone, he was back to brummie.

"You've broken my jaw, my jaw's broke."

134

"That's just the start, your fingers are next. I'll snap them like twigs, just you and me in here now, just you and me. *Capisci*? Let's see your wallet, empty you pockets before I brain you."

"I ain't got no wallet, they had all my stuff at the front desk. Look." His hands pulled out both trouser pocket linings then his right hand went to his trouser back pocket. Turning, he showed Thomas another empty pocket.

Thomas had the reaction he wanted but best to be doubly sure. While Tony watched, he clenched his fist once more and motioned that he was about to strike. Tony's right hand came up palm forward.

"Whoa, whoa, you can't hit me, I have rights. This is police brutality."

"You're right, Tony, but you have just told me who you are."

"Yes, I'm Franc Bianchi and when my lawyer has finished with you you'll be collecting cans in the street, copper."

"Well I think you are Tony Bianchi and you are an accessory to murder, probably an arsonist and a receiver of stolen goods. I may even think of more charges."

The constable came through the door with two teas.

"Oh, you actually got tea, good for you constable. Would you take Mister Bianchi to the desk sergeant and have him charged with…shall I make you the principle or the accessory? For now, I'll call you an accessory. The charge is accessory to the murder of Pierre Jacques on 28 October and make sure he signs the charge sheet with his right hand as before."

"What about my jaw, it's busted you broke it, I need to go to hospital."

"Good point, Tony. Constable get the desk sergeant to note Mister Bianchi's injuries in the station log, sustained while resisting arrest and also note that despite our best efforts he fell down the basement steps on the way to the interview room. Then take him around to the general hospital. We wouldn't want you to suffer needlessly, would we?"

"You wait until my brother finds out, copper, you ain't seen nothing yet. You wait till he gets here with our lawyer then you'll be in the shit, be lucky to keep your job."

"Oh, Tony, I'm so sorry. I forgot to tell you, Franc's dead, at your lock-up in Inge Street, burnt to death in his own fire. Bit of a cock-up with the ignition sequence apparently, but you know how easy that is. I don't really understand that fire stuff myself but he's dead all right, burnt to a crisp, a right mess. And you know how bad burnt bodies look, don't you? You being a fireman and all, can you picture your dead brother, Tony? Can you smell your dead brother? Can you smell him? I bet you can. Perhaps you know how Jacques' wife feels now. Take him away, constable. I've had enough of him."

As the constable led a muttering Tony Bianchi through the door, Thomas called out, "Tony, remember, *Per te l'odore della morte rimarra sempre.*"

Looking back the constable asked, "What's that mean, boss?"

"For you, the smell of death will remain always."

At the general hospital, Tony Bianchi sat on a small plastic chair in the waiting room of the accident and emergency department, beside him and handcuffed together, sat a very bored constable who watched while a young doctor made a cursory examination of Tony's Jaw.

"It's not broken, constable, it's dislocated. Just clench your teeth and tilt your head back for me to have a look."

Tony obliged and winced as his teeth met, but happy to be away from the torment of Steelhouse Lane Police Station. The longer he could spin this out the better. Was Thomas thinking of meting out some more punishment. Is that why he had logged him falling down the basement stairs? Was that fall still to come?

"Just a little further, right back, there's a good fellow."

Tony's head was back pretty much as far as it would go, he was now looking at the ceiling lights. Out of Tony's line of sight, the upper-cut of the doctors hand was moving with some force, with his fingers rolled back the ball of his right hand hit the underside of Tony's chin with a hard but controlled thud. Tony cried out in pain as the dislocated jaw went back into place. Once more, it was only Tony that heard the snap, but most heard him yelp.

"There you are, easy, wasn't it? Now, no eating hard or chewy food for a few weeks just let the joint settle down."

The copper laughed out loud. "That's no problem, Doc he's got lots of porridge coming his way."

The doctor looked at Tony's face and the alignment of his jaw whilst checking the joints on either side; he noticed the tears of pain rolling down Tony's cheeks.

"Would you like some pain killers to get you over the next few days?"

Nursing his jaw in his cupped hands, Tony spoke through gritted teeth.

"Yes, please Doc, the stronger the better."

"No, he's all right Doc, no need for that. He can't have any drugs in the cells, far too dangerous. He'll be fine, thanks Doc. We don't want to spoil him, do we?"

"Let's go, Bianchi."

Dinner with Sophia

In the locker room at Aston, Blue Watch were chatting as usual at the beginning of their shift, men were putting on their undress uniform and polishing their shoes, the final act of this beginning of shift ritual would be checking their fire-kit, helmet, tunic, axe belt and pouch then boots and leggings. The boots and leggings were always kept together with the leggings rolled down over the boots so when you stepped into them, it was just a straight pull-up on the elasticated braces, the woollen double breasted tunics with the six rows of chrome buttons was kept folded in a particular way so the outside did not come into contact with the inside, but could be flicked out and slipped on quickly, then the belt and axe, the black fire helmet would go on last. The fire-kit would be placed on the fire engine in the rider's position at the beginning of each shift. Jack had his routine down to an art, he could now do it without thinking, as the older men did.

The runners and riders were detailed as usual by the sub-officer as the station officer casually looked over at his men and their personal protective equipment. The new standing orders and technical bulletins were read, then lastly the hatched, matched and dispatched. Without too much ceremony, the men were brought to attention and dismissed. The eleven men of Blue Watch moved around the engine house going about their daily checks and routines. Once more, Jack was fifth man, but on the back of the pump escape this time, Conker was to his left as number one BA. The escape had oxygen BA with a one-hour duration, which could be dragged out to double that time or maybe more if the wearer became trapped or immobile, compressed air BA was short duration and only on the pump. The oxygen used by this crew would only be worn for deep penetration into a building fire. Only the most experienced men would wear these sets.

"I've been thinking Jack, we ought to have a get together. Sophia has almost finished her Bianchi story, she is hoping it will be published in instalments when the trial ends, which should be Friday. So what about us all getting together at my house for dinner Sunday evening. Giulia and I will cook for you?"

"That's very kind, Conker. I'd love to come over. Do you really cook or is it Misses F that does it all."

"I'll have you know I make my own pasta and Arancini, maybe I will make some Cannoli for afters."

"I have no idea what you're talking about but, if it tastes half as good as it sounds then I'll be a happy man."

"Don't you usually eat Italian food then, Jack?"

"No, not really. I'm more of an Indian or Bangladeshi food type of guy if I eat out. There are some great places around town, my dad spent some time in Chittagong and Burma during the war so I grew up eating spicy food, everything else seems a little tame to me."

"Maybe we can convert you to be a lover of Italian food but to help get you started I may have to get some bomba Calabrese, it's an Italian hot vegetable and chili sauce, Italians can do spicy too, you know."

The two day shifts Wednesday and Thursday from 0900 hours until 1800 hours and the two night shifts 1800 hours to 0900 hours. Friday and Saturday passed with nothing more than alarms, minor road traffic accidents and car fires. This was a slow tour of duty which gave firemen time to bring their equipment up to a shiny readiness rarely seen on busy fire stations. Everything was spotless, the trucks gleamed with a fresh coat of wax, ladders had been scraped and varnished, they positively glistened in the sunlight, even the steel tyres of the big, six foot diameter escape wheels had boot black applied to them to pick them out against the bright red of the wheels felloes.

Anything that could be taken apart was, then greased or oiled. They had done all that was possible to do, their trucks would more than just pass muster, they were show standard, they were ready for whatever would be asked of them. As Saturday evening slowly became night, firemen began drifting off to the dormitory in groups as tiredness overtook them, all were asleep by midnight.

The night passed as the rest of the tour had, easy, not one call. When roused from their sleep by two short rings on the fire bell at 0630 hours, they slowly in dribs and drabs got out of bed, some mumbling, some grumbling a bit of coughing and a lot of scratching was around the dormitory then. One by one they started making up their bedrolls and stowing them in the wooden racks by the side of the fire pole-drop door. All agreed that it had been a good sleep, apart from 600's snoring.

"A quiet night has to be paid for with many sleepless nights, you know that boys," came the Welshman's prophetic retort.

A breakfast of soggy toast from the plate warmer and liquid chicory coffee was now Jack's normal. He was accustomed to the food and drink served up on station but would sometimes give a miss to unpalatable meals that were created for war veterans with delicate stomachs. There would not be any spices used in the Blue Watch mess, most dishes were bland and over cooked, mashed and pureed vegetables seemed Horace's specialty. Jack thought his reputation as a good cook a little overrated.

The fire bell announced 0900 hours and the end of the shift, so back to the locker room. Jack took his fire-kit, it was cleaner than when it came out, the tunic had been washed and dried in the basement drying room, the leggings scrubbed back to bright yellow and the boots shone with boot black as good as any day on training school parade. He had even found time to sharpen and clean the steel of his personal fire-axe. It had been a slow tour of duty for Jack.

Conker walked past Jack's locker and slapped him on the shoulder. "See you later Jack 1930 hours eating at 2000 hours."

"Yes, cheers Conker, see you later."

Harry turned to Jack. "Are you taking flowers or booze, Jack?"

"Flowers, I think flowers."

Jack had no idea where that reply came from, it just seemed right to take the ladies flowers. "Great, see you there Jack." Harry was waving his hand as he walked out through the locker room door.

Jack didn't know why but he hadn't thought of Harry going to Conker's for dinner. He had imagined himself sitting across from Sophia, filling her glass with red wine and what small talk he would make. He had, at no time, put Harry in the picture. Shit, Harry could be a problem, but then at least he wouldn't be turning up in an E-type convertible, but should he go to Conker's house on his motorbike?

If it was to rain, he would look like Scott of the Antarctic on arrival, not very suave and sophisticated. Harry probably has an Italian bespoke suit. Jack went through in his mind what he would wear, which wasn't really a problem and didn't take long as he only had one suit which he had bought for a friends' wedding. It was a mud brown two piece suit with a thin orange stripe running vertically through the weave, single breasted with a tight waist, sporting extra wide lapels and a fashionable double vent at the rear. The trousers were high-waisted and skin-tight to the knee where the twelve-inch flair began. He was offered a fifteen-inch option by the man at Burtons tailors but he thought twelve inches was enough of a flair for anyone. He had also purchased a bright yellow floral shirt with matching floral tie at the suggestion of the salesman, brown Cuban-heeled calf-length boots would complete the look. He was proud of his trendy suit and boots, this was bound to impress Sophia.

Jack changed his uniform for his motorbike riding gear complete with flying jacket and made his way out onto the drill yard. Jack watched as the crew drove out of the car park one by one. Jack thought of buying a car but, what type of car? He loved riding motorbikes and his gold flash but they had their drawbacks, the biggest drawback being the English weather. It was no fun riding in the rain and in a snowstorm was a complete no, no, a motorbike no matter what colour, was not really going to help him win the heart of Sophia.

He should find a car that suited his personality. Harry was talking of buying a Triumph Spitfire getting one the same as much as he liked spitfires was out of the question. No, he would think of something else. He decided to have a ride around town, it was a beautiful morning he would visit a few second hand dealers perhaps giving a miss to the Moseley Road dealership of the Bianchi family.

He headed out of the yard and into town. Down the Bristol Road, he cruised toward a Ford dealership, he stopped his bike by a line of highly polished, very cool Capris' the prices on the screens prevented him from dismounting but maybe one day he could afford one.

Twisting the throttle, he headed off, leaving a salesman who was heading his way standing on the footpath. Selly Oak was his next stop, a little forecourt second hand place, just down from the university entrance. Jack kicked the stand down and lent his bike onto it, he started to walk amongst the reasonably priced cars, an Austin A40 black with a white roof? No, that would not do. A Wolseley 1500, no, that's a car your uncle would drive, then past a Hillman imp; that's a maybe, he thought, then a row of three minis' although looking again, one had a boot, it was a Wolseley Hornet. Sophia would like that, it had a cheeky friendly appeal.

"Can I help you, Sir?" A forty-year-old, very well-dressed salesman, in a brown three-piece suit that bore remarkable similarities to his own Burton special, approached him.

Jack didn't really like the piece of theatre that was to play out, he would be happy left alone, perhaps look over the engine bay, have a good look at the car

141

before being badgered into a purchase, the over-keen salesman was not really what he wanted.

"No. No, just looking."

"I see, you're looking at the lovely little Hornet, a low mileage example of this very popular marque and a good choice if I may say so, Sir. One lady owner from new, she had it serviced regularly. I'm sure you have noticed the new tyres on the front, in all very straight and ready to go. You'll need to snap it up quick if you want it though, Sir, it won't be around long, very popular they are. A small deposit will secure it for seven days. Shall we take it for a road test?"

It had begun; the very thing he didn't want to happen just had, a salesman who didn't have an 'off' switch and could he not keep calling him 'sir'.

"Little bit expensive for me. I don't have much money, I'm looking for something a little cheaper."

"Three hundred pounds Sir, mere bagatelle I can arrange finance for you at competitive rates and have you on the road in a week."

"Still a bit too expensive for me."

"Have you a trade-in, Sir? Perhaps that would help."

"Well, I have my bike over there, the Gold Flash."

The salesman's eyes lit up, as he looked over to the small parking area where Jack's bike gleamed in the morning sun.

"A Golden Flash. You have a Golden Flash, what year?"

"Nineteen sixty two, re-built it myself, it's like new."

The salesman almost broke into a run as he went over to it.

"Oh, she's beautiful, the chrome, look at the chrome the plungers and the beautiful A10 engine."

"Yes, when I stripped her down, I had it all re-chromed."

"My first bike was a Golden Flash but it was never as good as this. I'll take it in PX for the Hornet I'll give you fifty quid what do you say?"

"Well, I really don't think I can afford it. I fancied the hornet because it was different. Perhaps I should look for something I can work on, something I can re-build."

"Sixty quid off the Hornet for your bike."

"No, no, I really can't afford it."

"Sixty five, what do you say?"

"Honestly, I can't do it."

"Hmm, something to work on, is that what you want? I have an idea. Come with me."

The salesman led the way through a small building that housed his office and a Jensen Interceptor, the only car under cover. Past the Jensen, a white painted door led to a small workshop that held six cars, only one of which could be worked on at any time in the centre of the workshop. Directly behind a single steel roller shutter door was a four-post car lift with a Morris eleven hundred on top; underneath a very overweight middle-aged mechanic in brown oil stained overalls was fitting a new exhaust system.

Jack looked around. This seemed to be just the place the Bianchi brothers would operate from. The salesman threaded his way through the chaos of cars, gearboxes, engines and abandoned projects that littered the workshop floor. In the far corner of the workshop was a large green canvas sheet covering something. Jack had no clue what it was but the salesman was heading that way, when he reached sheet he turned to Jack and grabbing a corner he pulled the sheet off the car.

"What do you think of that?"

Underneath the canvas sheet was a dust covered 1966 MGB soft top in old English white, but with no seats or hood, sat in the corner; as it was it looked very sorry for itself.

"It's an MGB Roadster. I can't afford that."

"Well, perhaps you can, it needs some work, I know, but its only six, okay, seven years old, two hundred and seventy five and your bike makes it yours."

"What's wrong with it, that you would let it go for that price?"

"Well, I have robbed it of some bits and the hood got damaged so I threw it. I was going to replace it after I'd fixed the other bits. The seats I put in another MGB that I sold, and there is a little problem with the engine."

The smarm had gone, there was no rehearsed patter this guy at last seemed to be talking normally and hopefully honestly, this did seem a reasonable buy. But the engine!

"What's wrong with the engine? What's the little problem?"

"The head gasket's gone and I'm not sure about the head, it may not be straight."

Jack liked this sort of challenge, he had to juggle several things together and come up with an answer quickly. New soft top, replacement seats, he could probably find some second-hand ones, fix the head gasket, he may have to skim the head but, he would end up with a very desirable Old English white MGB with leather upholstery sitting on chrome wire wheels. Now that's what you call a car, but until he could get it back on the road, he would have to use the bus for work. That didn't seem too bad. The salesman was staring at Jack waiting for a response.

"That's a lot of work and cost. I'm not sure it will be worth it in the end."

"Oh, you bet it will. I'm offering you a great deal. I'll be straight with you, if I did the work and polished this up, I would easily double my money. Have you got a girl?"

Jack was not expecting that question in the middle of negotiating a price.

"Err. No, no, I haven't."

"Well, you soon will have when you start driving around in this."

He could tell Conker and the girls tonight over dinner about his fantastic new project; Sophia would surely be impressed and would want to see it. He decided he would buy it.

"What do you say? Two seven five and your bike."

"The bike, two hundred and fifty, including delivery and you have a deal."

The salesman looked long and hard at Jack. He thought of the restored Golden Flash. He really wanted the bike, this young guy was getting a good deal, yet the garage space it freed up was badly needed. He held out his hand, Jack grasped it and they exchanged a firm handshake. The salesman drew his hand back and noticed a small oily smudge mark left by Jack's thumb.

"We have a deal, you have an MGB and I have a BSA Golden Flash."

At half past seven, that evening Jack pulled up outside Conker's house in his mother's metallic green Ford Escort 1300L. He parked behind a brand new canary yellow Triumph spitfire, surely Harry's latest investment. Excited as he was, Jack would say nothing of his MGB project. This was Harry's moment, not his.

A tinny electronic Colonel Bogey still announced the arrival of visitors. Jack could hear it repeat the same few notes as he checked and buttoned his suit, looking down he checked for marks on the polished boots. The Maypole supermarket plastic carrier bag he held in his right hand detracted from the look he was going for, but liberal use of Brut aftershave was enough to grab everyone's attention.

Sara and Alice opened the front door. Who actually turned the Yale lock and physically opened the door, Jack was not sure, but as it opened, it was Sara who announced that everyone was in the kitchen. The twins turned and ran up the narrow staircase, it sounded like a herd of elephants rather than two 15-year-olds, but then the twins did nothing quietly or for that matter slowly.

Conker was at the small kitchen table pouring drinks for Giulia and Sophia. Giulia was stirring a large pot of Ragu on the small four-burner gas stove, each burner had a pot over it and was simmering something or other, the room was heavy with the smell of tomatoes and herbs but above all the dominant aroma was that of garlic, it was a heady mix that Jack liked.

In the corner of the room, standing close to the back door, was Sophia. She smiled at Jack and nodded over the shoulder of Harry, who to Jack's eyes, had her pinned in the corner. Harry still had his back to Jack but he knew it was Harry the moment he entered the room. The red and white stripped boating blazer was having another outing. Conker looked up as Jack walked in.

"Hey, Jack welcome, it's good to see you. What'll you have?"

"Same as you, please, Joseph. When in Rome…"

Giulia looked across and gave a little wave with her left hand as she carried a pan to the sink. "Hello Jack."

Jack thought maybe he should walk over to her and kiss her on the cheek, but no, maybe next time when he knows her better.

Harry didn't turn around, he was much too preoccupied.

The staircase drummed again, heralding the entrance of the twins, each wearing their best party frocks.

Sophia decided to escape the attentions of Harry with a "Hey Jack," as she squeezed past Harry in a move to escape.

"Hi Sophia," Jack replied lifting his plastic carrier bag and putting it on the table.

"First things first, gifts for the ladies."

From the supermarket carrier bag, he pulled two small bunches of pink Oleander flowers, wrapped in light hessian and tied with light brown twine that a little booklet hung from in which, on the small white pages a sentiment could be written. The posies had obviously been individually made by a good florist, they were beautiful. These were not cheap petrol station flowers. He handed each woman her present.

"Giulia, Sophia, ladies these are for you."

Giulia looked at her flowers with the widest smile on her face. "Jack, they are lovely."

Giulia opened her little book attached to the twine, it simply said, 'For Giulia'.

Sophia opened her little book, smiled and closed the pages tightly together. Giulia leaned forward and kissed him on the cheek. Sophia watched her mother; as she did she gently tugged the little book free from its twine fastening and slid it unnoticed into her skirt pocket, then in turn she leant forward and kissed him but she held the kiss just a second longer than needed.

"Thank you so much, Jack."

Jack's pulse raced, he was sure he was turning scarlet but he kept going, trying his hardest to ignore his feeling of excitement.

He realised that if he had got these two posies mixed up it would have been a disaster, but he hadn't, all was well. Giulia looked at him just for a second, she knew.

"And these are for you two young ladies, one for you, Sara and one for you, Alice."

Jack handed over two little brightly coloured cardboard boxes they were no more than four-inch cubes, each one identical to the other. The girls looked at them quizzically, then at each other then back to the boxes. They flipped open the cardboard lids, pulling out the little glass jar that was held inside, each of the twins let out a little sigh as the small spray of pink orchids was revealed. Next it was Conker's turn.

"And for you, Joseph a bottle of Grappa."

"Thank you, Jack, that's very kind."

"Wait, hold on. I forgot my present, its outside in the car. Give me a moment, I'll go and get it."

Harry rushed out of the house and out to his car, he was back in the room in no time at all holding a large bumper of beer.

"There you go girls, Watney's Party Seven, how fab is that? We'll need a screwdriver and a hammer to open it."

"That's very kind of you Harry. Would you do the honours and open it for me. I think we three should have a pint, but if you would do it outside as they can make a mess when opened, you won't need a screwdriver. There's a can opener in the drawer by the sink."

"Sure, no problem. It's the way you open them, if you don't know what you're doing they erupt and cover you in beer, I never have problems with 'em."

Harry took the Party Seven outside. The twins were admiring their orchids, Giulia and Sophia had turned their attentions back to the cooking when, following a whooshing noise from outside, a beer soaked Harry appeared at the back door.

From the top of his head to the hem of his boating blazer, he was soaked in Watney's bitter, it was dripping from him onto the kitchen floor as he came in. Everyone laughed out loud as he came to a halt just inside the doorway.

"Have you got a towel, Conker?"

The twins laughed a bit louder and a bit longer than the others. Conker threw a hand towel to him. Harry started by drying his hair and worked his way down. Was it the use of Joseph's nickname or the dripping beer soaked Harry that made the girls laugh? Either way they were having fun and they had a lovely present each, the evening had begun.

In the dining room, just off the kitchen, Joseph, the twins, along with Jack and Harry sat tightly packed into the small space leaving just enough room for Sophia and Giulia. Harry was no longer wet with beer but still a little damp, the smell of stale beer was now competing for dominance with that of Brut aftershave, however this changed instantly to the smells of Italy as Giulia and Sophia started arriving with steaming bowls and plates. The table was quickly loaded with food and breads, Sophia placed her last bowl down and took up her seat. Giulia remained standing and removing her apron pointed to each dish in turn.

"There you are, shredded beef Ragu with Pappardelle and Pasta alla Norma with Bucatini, Caprese salad and Cipollini in agrodolce. You have to make your own choice. Sophia has made the bread. That one is Pane Toscano; this one is Pane di Segale." Sophia smiled coyly at the mention of her baking. "Please don't wait to be served, do help yourselves."

"No starters' boys but leave a little room, there's a pudding which I may have had a hand in making."

"I'll look forward to that but before we do can I just say thank you for inviting Harry and I to your lovely home and for going to all this trouble just for us."

"Well said Jack, this looks like a feast, thank you. May I propose a toast? To the Fowles, may all their troubles be little ones."

Beer, wine, and lime cordial were sipped in celebration.

"Enough speech making, let's eat." Conker led the way, the clatter of spoons on crockery and the passing of plates, bowls and the grating of parmesan cheese soon got into a rhythm all of its own. The twins were engrossed in the food and had no intention of talking, the food was their priority. Giulia looked to Joseph to create some small talk but he was breaking a piece of Toscano bread and checking the texture. Harry was the first to speak.

"This bread is delicious, do you like making bread, Sophia?"

"Yes, it's a hobby of mine baking, making bread is my favourite though. You may not believe it but there are hundreds of Italian breads, so many, I may be baking for a number of years just to try them all. How's about you, Harry, we don't know much about you and your hobbies, what do you do in your spare time?"

"Nothing much to tell really. I haven't got a hobby as such, I like cars though. I've just bought a new car that's my Spitfire outside. I'll have to take you for a spin whenever you want. I'm single and available."

Harry didn't do subtle. "I live at home with Mom. She doesn't enjoy the best of health though, she had a stroke at twenty-four and my father upped and left her, well us. We've never heard from him, I was only a year old so I don't remember him at all. It's been just me and Mom and she needs help with things about the house so shift work has been a godsend to us, I can leave her in the evening, work a night shift and be back by half past nine in the morning to help her through the day. She thinks it's great, out of every week I'm home four days."

"Oh, well done, Harry, your mother must be proud of you. You'll have to take Mamma for a spin too."

"And us, can we go for a spin?" Alice chipped in excitedly.

"Well, it's only a two seater but I'm sure we can arrange something soon."

"Oh great, when?"

"Alice, leave Harry alone, he has said he will take you out for a ride in his new car, be patient."

"How come you haven't brought the car to the station Harry, so the boys can have a look over it?"

"I only picked it up this afternoon; it's only got twenty miles on the clock."

"Nice one, Harry, much better than an E-type, it looks great. I parked right behind it out front. The chrome boot rack really suits it."

"Thanks Jack, you'll have to get a motor, then we could go on days out together and trips to the seaside. I could take Mom she would love that."

The meal was accompanied by lively chatter from the twins regarding school and exams.

The topic then turned to the making of the Ragu and Giulia's passion for all things Italian and her dream of one day visiting Venice, but it was just a dream as it was so expensive and not possible on firemen's and nurse's wages, but maybe when they retire it might be a present for them both.

"Papa, I've finished, please. May I leave the table?"

"And me, Papa."

"Yes, girls you may, but there is still pudding so don't go far."

Everyone shuffled their seats around to let the two girls out from behind the table, the run upstairs was heard once again. Jack thought it was time to mention the purpose of the dinner.

"How is the Bianchi story coming along, Sophia? I saw you got the front page on the arrest day edition, what's to come when we have a verdict?"

"Well, we should have had the verdict on Friday as you know, hopefully it will be Monday or maybe Tuesday now. I was hoping to do the story in instalments, my editor's not keen on that though, he wants it done in one. But he has contacts at BBC Pebble Mill. They are showing interest in the story, they have their own people but they want to talk to me as I've been in from the beginning."

"That sounds great; you may be breaking into Television then!"

"Well I wouldn't go that far, I've got the whole story on paper, you and Papa even get a mention and I've sat in the Victoria law courts for the past fortnight listening to Bianchi's feeble denial. All I need now is the verdict and it's done."

"Well, now it's time for me to make a toast," Giulia said rising to her feet.

"To three brave firemen and my lovely daughter, the writer, well done all of you."

"Cheers." The Fowles family Brierley Crystal clinked above the table.

"Now it must be time for pudding, my specialty. Wait till you taste this."

Conker got to his feet and was out through the doorway and into the kitchen, from the dining room they heard him calling the twins down for their pudding, once more they thundered down the stairs following their father into the room.

"Here we are, my favourite, Cannoli. I made them myself, well almost, we used to make the dough and deep fry the shells but we have found a little Italian pastry shop in town that makes them, so a bit of a cheat but the filling is all mine. Please, help yourselves."

The twins were obviously relishing the imminent treat but waited until the guests had taken their pastry from the doily-lined plate. Jack had never seen

Cannoli before and looked at his quizzically, they were the size of brandy snaps and looked similar with the white creamy filling but then again they were different, unknowingly he lifted the pastry to his nose and smelt it, lowering it to look upon it once more.

"I have never seen these before Conker, what exactly is it made of?"

"Favourite of mine, Jack from Sicily, deep fried dough in the form of a shell, filled with sweetened ricotta cheese, I have also put in little pieces of dark chocolate. It's the way I like them but you can make up your own taste, there are no rules, go on try it."

Jack took a bite, he didn't realise he had a sweet tooth but these little pastries were a delight. He also now had a favourite pudding.

The evening was drawing to a close, the twins once more had retired to their room. Little tulip shaped glasses had been brought to the table by Conker along with the bottle of Grappa Jack had brought. A digestive, for the last time glasses clinked over the table.

The Fowles family stood in the doorway of their little semi-detached house as the yellow Spitfire roared off from the cul-de-sac followed by the more sedate Ford Escort. From inside the Ford, Jack looked to the doorway and Sophia, he wished he had said more, he wished to the bottom of his heart he could be alone with her and tell her of his feelings but she was with someone, the boyfriend at the door. He had never seen him but he was jealous of him he would be holding her, he would be kissing her. Life was not fair, why tease him so, why show him something he cannot have?

This was a hurt like no other hurt, this was an ache that got worse whenever he saw her. Yet, deep down, deep in his subconscious something was telling him there was hope, the words softly spoken. The hardly noticeable lingering kiss. Was she telegraphing a message to him? He would wait, his day would come.

In the doorway of the Fowles house, the family were now waving goodbye to their guests. At the back of the group, Sophia stood quietly, she took the little book from her pocket and opened it once more, inside the sentiment read, 'Somewhere in my heart there is a fire that burns for you.' She kissed the little book and slipped it back into her pocket.

Expressway RTA

Jack was in the backwash of Aston coiling canvas hose that he, Nobby and Toot had just hauled down from drying in the drill tower when the fire-bell let out a short ring. They both dropped everything and made their way to the engine house waiting for the small coloured light that hung over each engine to light up, when the watch room attendant knew what was to be sent, he would flick the corresponding switch on his console and the coloured light above the responding engine lit up, first to light was the red globe above the pump escape then the green for the pump, the yellow the turntable ladder stayed unlit, from the watch room doorway and unseen by Jack, someone shouted.

"Pump and pump escape, Road Traffic Accident, Aston expressway."

Jack jumped on the back of the pump; not surprisingly Jack was in his usual position as number five in the back, he had started getting dressed when Tumble climbed into the front passenger seat just after the fire-bell sounded the full alarm. Tumble turned to his crew.

"RTA Aston expressway, two Lorries involved, persons trapped, access via Park Circus, northbound carriageway, don't forget your fluorescent jackets."

The rhythm of staccato speech that firemen used when giving information, Jack was getting used to, usually just four or five pieces of information put together so the listener has all the information he needs, no preamble, no pleasantries just pure information. They all now knew what was coming.

As the engines roared into life, the twin blue lights on the roof of each engine could be seen reflected in the windows of the houses opposite the station, they came on more or less together then the headlights lit up like eyes as the sleeping giants awoke.

The drivers were going through a rehearsed set of switches and levers which was breathing life into their machines. The big wooden sectional engine house doors rolled across the ceiling once more in a clatter that was now familiar to Jack. As always, the pump escape with Sid in charge was leading the way, it swung out left from the engine house pushing out a plume of blue smoke from its exhaust as the Rolls Royce engine was called upon to release all its power within seconds of starting. The pump followed with an identical pulse of blue smoke now hanging in the air as the engine house doors clattered once more while making their way down to the ground, leaving the station strangely silent.

Nobby was driving the pump hard, he would keep pace with the lead engine, as drivers know it is easier to follow than to lead, perhaps that could be said of all things but, when driving heavy vehicles in fast convoy the first truck has to be noticed and part the traffic, the second just slots in behind in a game of 'follow my leader' played with twenty ton fire engines flying along as fast as possible.

Nobby's foot, when it wasn't pressing hard on the accelerator, would hover over the brake pedal, he had to make sure he didn't run into the back of the pump escape, he wouldn't be the first in the brigade to do so, or probably the last but the ignominy of it would last years, if it happened it would probably spawn a new nickname, 'Shunter' Or 'Ramrod' had been taken by two such unfortunates, but his crew would be sure to find an alternative should it be required.

Powering along the Victoria road then onto Park Circus just ahead, Nobby didn't take his foot off the gas, this shout was persons trapped, speed was of the essence. They swung an inertia inducing left turn, the right-side suspension sagged under the induced transfer of weight, the fire engines body rolled gently dipping to the right which sent unrestrained equipment sliding across the crew cab floor.

Nobby held his line, correcting his chosen line now would be a catastrophe the fire engine was like a ship under sail, a perfectly balanced piece of engineering that good drivers can feel through the steering and the seat of their pants.

The thousand gallons of water in the tank behind the crew cab started to move, powered by the centrifugal force, it climbed the side walls of the tank reaching the overflow pipe down it went to pour out of the back of the truck by the gallon leaving a watery arc on the roads surface, every fireman that followed would recognise the tell-tale mark.

From the Circus they gathered more speed as they raced down the on ramp to the A38(M) the Aston Expressway as they did Jack looked through the gap between Nobby and Tumble through the windscreen he could see two articulated lorries hard against the Armco barriers on the left just five hundred yards after the on-ramp merging lane finished, there were two Police cars both in front of the accident. They were affectionately known as 'Jam sandwiches' to firemen as they were all white with a single red stripe along each side, it ran the length of the car from boot to bonnet.

The Pump escape went past the two Lorries and police cars pulling up tight to the Armco, Nobby pulled up short but bringing the front of the engine out to block lanes one and two, this would protect all the emergency workers from being hit by someone driving into the accident scene. To get to rescuers they would have to hit a twenty-ton fire Engine first.

The ten firemen were out of their engines Sid had ordered his crew their task when he first saw the scene from the top of the ramp, they were putting out accident signs he was looking at the lorries talking to a police officer as the pumps crew got the cutting gear ready, Jack looked at the two lorries which on the face of things looked quite unremarkable, one flat bed articulated lorry had run into the back of another flatbed not much to see really he thought. On the bed of the lead artic two police officers stood looking through the smashed windscreen into the cab of the artic that had run into the back of the other. Sid's high-pitched voice came to life.

"Nobby, Jack, get up there and tell me what you can see."

Nobby was first onto the flatbed with the cops, quickly followed by Jack with the first aid bag.

"Hi guys, how's the driver?"

"Think he's dead mate, he's crushed and trapped from the waist down and from the waist up he ain't pretty."

The older cop had made his mind up, this was body retrieval. Nobby lay on the flatbed face to bloody disfigured face with the unconscious driver slumped over the misshapen steering wheel he pressed the tips of his fingers against the drivers carotid artery, everyone stayed silent for a few seconds.

"He's alive, not very, but he's still alive."

"What's going on up there Nobby?"

"He's still alive SO we need a doctor sharpish, he's slipping away fast and we need to get this truck out of the way so we can cut him out, but slow SO, don't just drive it out."

"Okay, Nobby, you and Jack stay with him, callout what you need and I'll see you get it."

"Have you got a pulse, mate? I could feel nothing, I thought he was dead."

"It's weak but it's there."

"The ambulance is on its way, the general hospital is only a mile away I'll get a doctor."

The Cop jumped down from the flat bed and ran to his car which lit up like a Christmas tree all lights and sirens, as the crews watched he performed a dangerous but well executed 'U' turn on a seven lane section of motorway, he was either foolhardy or good but whatever he was it worked, blue smoke rolled off the tyres and he was gone.

Jack climbed off the trailer bed through the shattered windscreen of the truck and onto the bench style passenger seat beside the unconscious driver. The dashboard had been pushed back so far that there was hardly any room now between it and the seat squab. Nobby was already in the cab he had climbed behind the driver and was pulling him back and into the upright position by the shoulders while gently supporting his head this would keep his airway open the driver made no sound but there was a feint gurgle of blood in the mans' throat.

"Great Jack he's breathing. Can you get to his legs?"

Jack tried to get between the seat and the dash but that was impossible, he looked around for a way to get to his legs, the whole front of the truck had caved in, the driver's door which before the impact was over three feet wide was now only a twelve inch piece of concertinaed metal and broken glass, he looked to the passenger door it was gone ripped off by a stanchion or the Armco as the truck ran along the wall of the motorway Jack wondered if he could crawl under the dashboard to get to the mans' legs.

"Nobby, I'll see if I can get under the dash from this side, when they've pulled the other truck away see if they can get the driver's door off and work on him from that side it would be easier."

"Do what you can from that side, Jack, we need to roll the dash back first then we can work on the driver's door."

Jack was aware of orders being given and heavy equipment being laid out for his world was all-consuming he had his task and he had to play his part. This was a rescue team of police, fire, and ambulance twenty strong, each person had a task. As Jack moved position to get out of the cab through the passenger side, he looked to the bed of the first truck. There he saw Bert and George helping two ambulance men onto the flat bed, green medical bags were being thrown up to them by other ambulance crews. Jack turned away and looking out of the doorway he saw the expressway's concrete barrier wall. The wall was about the same height as the dashboard of the truck, it had a double layer of Armco some

154

two feet in front of it but this was now imbedded in the side of the truck the concrete wall was now only a foot away. As Jack pulled his weight onto it, he realised what he was doing and pulled himself back, he had forgotten that sections of the expressway are elevated. As it passes through Aston, it is seventy feet or so above the normal roadway below, the wall he was about to step on was not four feet off the ground it was seventy-four feet off the ground. He looked over the edge and watched the traffic moving below oblivious to what was happening overhead, he carefully made his way out onto the wall and then back in beneath the dash, he crawled on the floor of the truck until just his leather fire boots were showing outside, as he did two ambulance crew took his place in the cab.

Nobby was now cornered in the cab by the injured driver and two ambulance guys. Below them, Jack looked at the driver's legs, both were broken, not that he could see breaks or much blood for that matter but from the shape and position they were in, there could be no doubt, but it was the feet that concerned him most, both were totally wrapped in twisted metal that had folded around and through them.

A shout of 'we're pulling the truck out boys' was quickly followed by the screeching and grinding of metal as the first truck was winched out of the front of the truck that had run into it. Three crews had been working with the heavy recovery vehicle crew from Central that Jack did not even see or hear arrive to separate the two trucks. Specks of light now shone through the mangled cab. Jack heard the thud of short extension ladders being placed against the front of the truck which was now separated from its tormentor with fire and ambulance crews all around and inside swarming like ants in a joint attempt at freeing and saving the unconscious driver.

"How's it looking down there, Jack?" He could hear the station officer's voice calling to him. Sid and Nobby must have had a conversation that went unheard by Jack.

"Good SO, if I could have the hydraulic small wedge I may be able to free his feet."

"Okay Jack, on its way. Stay with him."

Sid turned and gave the order to set the hydraulic wedge up and passed to Jack, as he did a jam sandwich pulled up in the lane next to the truck the policeman had brought a doctor from the general hospital, an ambulance man finished fitting a cervical collar then gave up his position in the cab allowing the doctor to make his assessment of the casualty. The doctor went about his work with some urgency within minutes the casualty had an airway and a drip in his arm, the doctor talked to no one in particular but gave a running commentary of what he wanted and what he was doing.

"I want him out lads as soon as possible, please, we've ten, perhaps fifteen minutes at the most."

"Heads up Jack," was followed by a metallic clunk above his head as a small hydraulic wedge no more than six inches long was lowered to him through a small gap by its black hydraulic hose tubing, he would push this into the gaps around the casualties feet where it would be opened like a crocodile's jaws on his command, by an operator somewhere above, who? Jack had no idea until they spoke. No one spoke unnecessarily at RTA's; essential information only passed between rescuers. Jack pushed the wedge into a gap just to the side of casualty's left foot, as he did, he heard the sound of heavy chains being passed over the dashboard and through the floor but he could not see anything, his world was a twelve inch cube of air directly in front of him, in that cube wall just inches away, were two mangled legs and somewhere, as yet unseen, two crushed feet.

"Open," Jack called out loud and strong.

Harry's voice came back, "Open."

The little six inch jaws of the wedge slowly opened pushing twisted metal before them.

Jack held it in place as it did its work freeing the driver's left foot, at the end of its travel, Jack gave the command 'close'. As the jaws closed, the wedge became free. Jack, lying on his belly and taking his weight on his elbows, tried to lift his head to find another position for the wedge but his helmet stopped him raising his head. Placing the wedge down on the cab floor, he unclipped his helmet chin strap, he tried to take the helmet off but there was no room to raise it from his head, Jack lowered his head to the cab floor and lay the right side of his face on the rubber floor mat, his cheek was in some fluid that he could not see, probably engine coolant or engine oil or both. He tugged at the helmet, it came off his head but there was no room to put it anywhere. Reaching over his shoulders with his right hand he managed to push the helmet between his shoulder blades and down his back. Rolling onto his right side, he managed to bring his left arm up behind his back and grab the helmet and pull it down to the top of his legs where it was to stay for the time being. Jack could now lift his head up much further; as he did, he selected a new place for the wedge.

"Open."

Harry's voice came back. "Open."

This exchange carried on six or seven times slowly and methodically a space was made for the foot to be released. Jack laid the wedge on the rubber mat, pushed both hands forward getting hold of the driver's foot, shod in a cheap trainer, he gave a short tug and it came free of its bindings in one smooth move. As it did, Jack noticed the movement of the leg and foot was not natural, legs and feet don't move in the way he had pulled them but the left leg and foot were now free. He looked past the newly freed leg and looked for the right leg; he could just make out the leg but from the ankle down he could only see twisted metal, the foot was there somewhere.

"Harry, tell the Doc left leg and foot are free, working on the right."

"Open."

Harry's voice came back. "Wait Jack. Jack, can you hear me?"

Jack hadn't realised but he was sweating, the salty water ran into his eyes and stung, wiping his eyes with his tunic sleeve, he saw his gloveless hands, they were both covered in blood then he realised it was sticky, his fingers felt as if he had been working with glue, he wiped them on his tunic sleeves; as he did, he replied to Harry.

"Yes, Harry I can hear you."

"We're going to roll the dashboard off of him, might get noisy, watch out for metal flicking out in your direction and Doc says he wants him out as soon as the dash is off him. Will you be ready?"

As he spoke, there was a tremendous sound of squealing brakes followed by the explosive sound of impact, the sound of cars crashing head-on into each other then, a split second later, the truck jerked forward Jack rolled on the truck's floor.

"What the hell was that Harry?"

"Don't know, somethings happened behind us."

"Okay Harry, let's go again. Open."

Harry's voice came back, "Open."

Three or four times, Jack found a crevice to put the wedge in, the metal was bent away but his right foot was squashed flat but still attached to the leg. Jack kept going, still the sweat rolled down his forehead and in to his eyes.

"Open," Jack called out.

Harry's voice came back, "Wait Jack, we're rolling the dash."

As Harry spoke, a great creaking and grinding of metal started, the dash moved slowly at first and then as the weight was taken by the chains, things began to move as one, his space became slightly bigger, it was opening out, it was slow but it was moving the right way. Jack could now see more of the driver's leg but the foot was still wrapped in metal, a shaft of light fell into Jack's little space. He twisted and looked up through a little gap. There was Harry no more than two or three feet away there were other people up there too but he could not make out who they were.

"Jack, Jack, the SO is coming to talk to you, see you in a minute." Harry was gone.

Jack tugged at the driver's leg and pieces of metal, the leg seemed to be free but around the foot, nothing moved. The strain of holding his head up and back was making his neck ache. He let his head drop to lay on the rubber floor mat to give it a rest. The next thing he heard was Sid's voice.

"Jack?"

"Yes, SO."

"How long before he is free and we can lift him out?"

"Just his right foot SO, it's pretty well mangled and encased in metal, if I can have ten minutes or fifteen tops I should be able to free it."

"Wait, Jack."

Unbeknown to Jack, Sid had turned to the doctor who had been monitoring his patient. Sid looked at the doctor and awaited his decision.

"No, no more time, he has to come out now, if it's just his foot that's holding him it must come off, we will have a dead casualty with two feet or a live one with one foot. Tell your man to cut it off."

"How? We've no instruments for cutting limbs off?"

"Have you got a hacksaw?"

"Yes, but it's nowhere near sterile."

"I'm not worried about infection. I'm trying to keep this guy alive, give your man a hacksaw and cut the foot off, we have no time to discuss this."

"Sid looked at the doctor, square in the face. Okay Doc, your call."

As Sid called down to Jack, he remembered it was his new recruit, he would have preferred one of the older men be given the job of cutting off the man's foot but that was not how it had played out. He remembered Jack's face in the cellar at Victoria Road, the white-faced youth, the young man he had bought a pint in the Barton Arms. Jack was about to be given an awful job but it must be done.

"Jack."

"Yes, SO."

"This man is dying he has minutes to live, the doctor has given instructions to cut his foot off, now, do you understand?"

"Yes, yes, I do SO." Jack looked at the ankle and mentally picked a place to cut if he had to.

"Is there no other way, SO?"

"Here's a hacksaw, Jack, make it quick and make it clean, do it now, Jack."

Jack laid the hacksaw on the man's bloodied leg just above the ankle, he thought of how simple changing light bulbs in the offices of the Austin works had been and the siren suited foreman, then he cut, more light bulbs, he cut again, more light bulbs with each stroke of the saw he repeated more light bulbs, more light bulbs. It only made sense to Jack.

"He's free, SO."

No sooner had he said the words than the two legs with only one foot attached rose from his little world and were gone. Jack rested his heavy head on the rubber mat once more facing the foot he had just severed.

"Out you come, Jack, you've done your bit, I'll get somebody else to get the foot out."

"Thanks, SO."

Jack was back on the expressway in a world of his own, watching the ambulance make its way into town with the ambulance crew and doctor aboard, all trying desperately to keep the patient alive.

Conker approached Jack. "You're covered in blood, all the side of your face and look at your hands."

As Conker said the words, Jack remembered why he had sticky fingers, the wet cab floor, blood was caked on his face and hands.

"I'll have a wash under the pumps delivery valves, get this shit off me."

"Best go to the escape at the front, some bloke in a lorry came down the ramp and ran into the back of the pump, didn't you feel it? The pump was pushed into the truck you were in. Pissed as a fart he was, it's pretty much wrecked, the pump bay. We had to cut the idiot out as well, still he never hit any of us, thank the lord. But I guess you would have swapped places with any of us out here, eh, Jack?"

"Yes, my world was very small. You could say just one foot of space."

"Ha, you're a good man, Jack." Conker slapped his friend on the back.

"Enough chatting you two, lend a hand here, let's get this gear made up."

Jack had forgotten Tumble was at the job, but hey, everything was back to normal now.

All the stowed kit on the pump, even the ladders were taken off the engine and loaded onto a brigade lorry to be taken back to Aston. The recovery vehicle which had been used to free the driver was now lifting the pump's back wheels off the ground in readiness to tow it to the brigade workshop. The offside rear and pump bay was a complete mess it would be in the repair shop for months it may even be a write off Jack thought.

Firemen and Policemen were sweeping the road clean, the police would open all but lane one, a missing section of Armco barrier was all that would mark the spot where a man who was clinging to life by the merest of threads, lost his foot. The traffic had built up now and queues of slow moving traffic had formed in all lanes. Jack was sweeping glass off the roadway by a traffic cone as a car passed slowly by, the front seat passenger called out to Jack from his open window.

"Hey you, have you bastards caused all this and made us late for the match? Crashed your fire engine and now you're sweeping the streets. It's what you wooden tops deserve, what a load of wankers, I wouldn't pay you twats in washers."

The man gave Jack a two-fingered salute as the car moved off. Jack could hear the laughter of his three friends inside the car.

Jack stopped and watched the car slowly move away, he said nothing.

"Come on, Jack, don't stand around admiring your work. Let's get on."

Tumble was back.

The Examination

Lying in his little Divan bed in the small back bedroom of his parent's house just after eight o'clock on a fine Monday morning, Jack mused over the dream that had woken him in a sweat at four thirty. It was not the first time this dream had visited him, it was always the same, it was short, terrifying and always the sweats.

He shot out of bed and stripped the damp sheets from the bed, a quick shower then down the stairs into the kitchen where he made himself coffee and two rounds of white toast, it was sliced bread but at least it was crispy, not soggy station toast and the coffee was fresh, not powdered or liquid, proper coffee.

He thought again of the dream, what did it mean? And why was it re-occurring? He shrugged his shoulders. Who knows?

He decided to go out to the garage and have a look over his car to see what work was left to be done to make it roadworthy. Out through the back door with his second mug of coffee, he went to the garage by the side of the house, the fluorescent light fitting that hung on chains from the roof beam flashed once or twice then hummed into life.

There she was, his little MGB sitting under a creamy white paint-spattered dustsheet which he pulled away. He had been working on her for two months now, the mechanicals were finished, the engine was running like a sewing machine and the bodywork had cleaned up really well, the wheels had been re-chromed and two new leather seats which had been bought for him by his parents, sat proudly in position. So, there was just the hood to buy, saving for that was slow but he was getting there, maybe another month of bus journeys back and forth to the station and he would be able to afford a new black hood. Then there was the road tax and insurance, perhaps he could pay the insurance in instalments but first things first, the hood.

When he went into the garage it was his intention to do some work, no matter how trivial, on the car but, looking at it, there wasn't really anything to do until he got the hood. Another cut and polish wouldn't achieve much, it would just be hard work. Jack let out a deep sigh and pictured himself driving through the streets with Sophia by his side, get the car and the girl, how fab would that be, but at the moment he had neither. Pulling the dustsheet back over the car, he started talking to himself out loud.

"What shall I do on my day off? Nothing to do on the car, my few electrician mates are at work. I know, I'll ring Harry see if he fancies a pint in town."

Making his way back into the house, Jack left his empty coffee mug on the stainless steel draining board in the kitchen then into the hallway, where the two tone green telephone was positioned half way up the wall, on a little semi-circular glass-topped telephone table. His father had tried to spray the metalwork the same colour as the phone but had not really succeeded in a match. Jack rang Harry's number but the phone just rang out, no answer.

"Right, I'll go into town and have a pint alone then." He had started talking to himself again, but at least he was speaking into the phone. He put the handset back on its base.

"Perhaps I'll treat me to lunch."

Jack sat by a window of another of his favourite Victorian city pubs, The Old Contemptible, reading the Birmingham Post he bought from a street vendor as he walked across town at lunch-time.

Opening the broadsheet paper, there it was, on page two, Sophia's article, a full page. 'City gang busted' not the serial she had wanted but nevertheless a full page, it was undoubtedly a triumph for a cub reporter. Jack was proud of her and her great news article. Harry, Conker and Jack were not mentioned by name but firemen were mentioned quite often and Tony Bianchi was behind bars for ten years which was great news.

Jack was happy with the small part he and his friends had played in the downfall of not only the Bianchi brothers, but a larger London-based operation as well. Just as he finished reading the article for the second time, a noisy crowd of half a dozen men and women came bursting through the main entrance door, the men calling for drinks and slapping each other on the back, the women giggling and laughing out loud made a welcome change to what was a quiet afternoon. He looked over in their direction and smiled, he thought how nice it would be to have a few beers with friends at lunchtime rather than be sitting alone reading a newspaper.

As he watched the group, he realised who he was looking at, at the same time Sophia who was looking around the room realised who she was looking at. She didn't hesitate, she made her apologies to the group, which seemed to go completely unnoticed and headed straight over to Jack's table. She walked with a grace that only Sophia had, her legs glided over the floor, it was a self-conscious yet positive walk. For Jack, she would not look out of place on a catwalk, he was totally smitten, he rose to greet her.

"Jack, Jack, where have you been." She leant forward to be kissed. Jack kissed her once on each cheek, it was his turn to make the kisses linger a little longer than necessary.

"Nowhere really, just walking around town a bit of clothes shopping, but what brings you in here on lunchtime?"

"We just popped out for lunchtime drink, the guys at work offered to buy me a drink to celebrate my first article, but they seem to have decided to have a drinking session. There's whispers of taking the afternoon off to carry on drinking, I don't think I can keep up with them, they're on a roll."

"Wow, isn't that a coincidence? I just came in for a swift one, I don't know what made me come in here."

For the slightest moment, they both froze gazing into each other's eyes. Jack could not believe his luck.

"Not really, it's the Gods of chance again, they are working for us, you must believe in them Jack, we can't fight it, it's meant to be."

"Who's fighting it, I'm happy if you're happy."

"I'm very happy Jack, I loved the flowers you gave me and I still have your sweet note on my bedside table."

Jack knew he was colouring up, he must be, he was getting hot and his heart rate had just gone through the roof, but he also knew he couldn't and shouldn't stop, this was his moment this was his time.

"Sophia, I hope you know how I feel about you, you mean everything to me, but I know you are with someone and I wouldn't, for the world, come between you and your boyfriend but, if one day you are free I will be waiting, I will wait as long as it takes."

Jack stopped talking, he had just blurted out his feelings and Sophia had only been sat thirty seconds, she didn't even have a drink yet. He had done it again, started talking before he had engaged his brain, would he ever learn to keep quiet and listen rather than go charging in.

Sophia was looking at him smiling, that made him feel worse. *She thinks I'm an idiot and I am bright red, probably sweating and definitely shaking, bloody hell I've just blown any chance I may have had. Best to apologise for offending her and make a dignified and quick exit, perhaps Conker would not find out about him making a pass at his eldest and much loved, probably betrothed daughter. When Conker did find out it could be very awkward at work.*

Jack's mind was racing at a million miles an hour, he didn't want to lose Conker's friendship. Oh, the embarrassment, perhaps he could get a transfer from Aston to Central if things became really awkward. Oh, shit, best to apologise for my outburst, a good sincere apology would sort things out, he went to speak. Sophia stopped him short.

"Oh Jack, you are so silly I've been waiting for you, I've dreamed of us being together. I'm not with anyone I have no boyfriend."

"But, but, the boy at the door, the first time we met, the twins said 'your boyfriend was at the front door'."

"Oh, pay no attention to the twins Jack, he is just a neighbour I went to school with, the twins think every boy I talk to is a boyfriend, that's the twins."

"So, so there is nobody special, nobody you're walking out with?"

"Well there is someone special, someone I would like to be 'walking out with' as you put it."

"Oh. Oh. I thought there might be."

Why was it that whenever he came under pressure he repeated words? He knew he did it but it never stopped, it was automatic, it was an affliction. *I have an affliction,* he thought to himself, *and I can hear it. Probably nobody has noticed, maybe, maybe not, and why when I'm under pressure does my mind wander so, to other things?* He watched Sophia speaking, she's gorgeous.

"Yes, he's sitting in the Old Contemptible reading my article."

Jack's mind was wandering that much, he hadn't really heard what Sophia had just said, all he had heard was that there was somebody else. Crestfallen, he looked down at his newspaper. As he did, it sunk in, he realised what she had just said. Jack's face lit up like a firework, his hands shot across the table, as they did Sophia's hands did the same, mirroring his movement, they clenched hands tightly and stared deep into each other's eyes, once more in a look that lasted forever.

Slowly, Sophia lent across the table, now it was Jack's turn to follow her lead, their lips met in the sweetest of kisses, no matter what happened from now

164

on, no matter what the world would throw at them Jack would remember this day, this was the day he found his true love, his Sophia, his soul knew it, she was the one.

"Okay, you two love birds, cut it out. Sophie what are you drinking."

"Oh no more for me, Phil, you lot carry on without me. My friend Jack here is taking me out to lunch. Jack this is Phillip, my boss."

Jack rose from the table and grasped the hand offered to him.

"You're a lucky man Jack she's the toast of the newsroom and much admired. Enjoy your lunch you two. Sophie, take the afternoon off, a little present from me, see you tomorrow bright and early."

Phillip turned and went back to the oblivious group chatting loudly at the bar.

"Where are you taking me then?"

"Do you like curry?"

"Jack, you are not taking me for lunch on our first date and eating curry."

"No, you're right, what about a ploughman's in a pub by the canal side?"

"A Ploughman's lunch in a pub? With raw onions? Jack think about it."

"Oh yes, err, no, no, not Ploughman's then."

"Jack, you're hopeless. I'll have to make the decision. I know a lovely little Italian restaurant, that's not really a surprise I suppose. It's not far from here, we can have a light lunch and a glass of wine."

"Italian? Garlic? Isn't that as bad as raw onions."

"No, it's not, it's a beautiful thing, now drink up. Let's get out of here, away from prying eyes to where we can be together, but alone."

"Are you always going to tell me what to do?"

"Probably."

"Conker, can I have a word?"

Jack strolled out of the backwash of the station towards the hose-room and stopped in the open yard at the hose-room doorway. Conker, having seen Jack's serious face followed close behind.

"Yes, Jack."

"Conker, err, Joseph. I have recently become very fond of your daughter, Sophia and I would, if you and Misses Fowles have no objection, like your permission to…"

"Ah, my good fellow, you took your time, didn't you! I thought grass was growing under your feet. Giulia and I have been waiting for you two to get together, you don't need our permission, Jack we are more than happy for you to be going out with our daughter. Tell you the truth Jack, I'm looking forward to having some male company in the house, a man can only take so much female company you know, even if they are family." Conker put an arm around Jack's shoulders. "I'm going to let you take me out for a pint to celebrate, how good is that."

Jack's face broke out into a broad grin, he felt as if he were joining a new family, his friend was many years his senior and the father of his now girlfriend but it was Conker, he was more than a friend, they had in their short time of knowing each other, become very close. From dragging Jacques body from an inspection pit to digging Fatal out from under a collapsed furniture tower, a bond had been created between them, they could communicate in nods and body language. Jack felt Conker was more like a brother than a potential father-in-law; he couldn't be happier.

The Tanoy crackled into life, it was Screaming's high voice. "Fireman Wolf to the Station Office."

"Ah Jack, come in." Jack stood to attention in front of the large mahogany desk once more.

"I have here a 'billet doux' from headquarters, your six-month probationary examination is overdue, a bit of a mess at fire training school apparently, the training officer being put in prison has caused a few problems."

Sid looked up at Jack and smiled. Jack gave a little smile and a nod but said nothing, best not gloat especially in front of the station officer, he thought. Sid watched and waited for a comment but was pleased that Jack had not decided not to claim any credit for Bianchi's downfall.

"So you are booked on the next available examination at training school which is next Thursday, the nineteenth and Friday, the twentieth for your practical and your theory examination. Its short notice I know but, are you ready?"

"Yes, SO."

"Are you sure, Jack? I'm happy to let Leading Fireman Miller spend some time with you going through technical bulletins, equipment specs and station ground topography if you want."

"Thank you, SO, but I believe I'm on top of the practical stuff."

"How about your Hydraulics, Jack, have you got the relevant formulas' in your head."

"They don't come easily, but I think I'm okay, thanks SO."

"Jack, when you came on the station, your file said you were mister average, twelfth out of twenty four if I remember correctly, but you have proven the fire school wrong in many ways. You are not mister average, you are a fine young man and I'm proud to have you on my watch. You are a credit to the uniform you are wearing. You have had a rough start, Jack, yet you have come through it all with flying colours. Now you go back to the fire school and show them Jack, no more average, show them who Jack Wolf is. Off you go son, make us proud."

"Thank you SO." Jack turned smartly and made his way out of the station office with the widest grin. Things were just getting better and better.

Many wet drills had already soaked the cobbled yard at Central Station as the ten probationer firemen walked out once more onto the drill ground. Slowly they formed a squad line, Jack knew seven of them Brown, Edison, Ford, Harvey, Marchant, Nelson, and Wright from his initial training course but the other two were strangers. One of the men stood next to him in the squad line holding his fire helmet in front of him while adjusting the leather chinstrap, he turned to Jack.

"Hi, Keith Webb from Kings Norton."

"Hi, I'm Jack Wolf, Aston. How come you're here with us, Keith?"

"Call me Spider, me and Eddy got back coursed, failed our six month exam. In fact we failed both tech and theory, last chance saloon for us two, if we mess this up, we're out."

"Really you only get one more chance?"

"That's what we were told, if we fail today we will get our termination letters before we leave here Friday."

"Good grief Spider, they don't mess around here, do they? Have you been studying?"

"Yeah, we have been swatting and training on the drill ground together, both being on the same watch has helped. Looking on the bright side, at least they have had a shake-up here, changed the staff around, pretty much everyone's new so maybe they will be a bit more tolerant."

"So what happens today? You must know the score."

"Yes, they'll run us ragged the rest of the day, the instructors will try and break us, they'll push and push to see if we'll give up. At least, that bastard Bianchi's gone, he enjoyed running you until you were exhausted then making you carry someone down from the fourth floor when you could hardly stand on your own two feet, let alone carry someone down the escape. I fainted after carrying my man down and he failed me for being unfit, the bastard, you're lucky he's not here anymore."

"Yes, I heard he was some trouble."

"You probably don't know, Jack but he's inside for stealing cars or something, the best place for him, perhaps me and little Ed will get a fair go this time." Spider decided the chinstrap was adjusted properly and put his helmet on his head.

"Well, best of luck, Spider. I hope you make it through all right."

"Yes, and you Jack."

A training school instructor's voice called out. "Squad, Squad, shun."

Jack recognised the voice, he looked to the left to see the drill instructor was SO White, one of the few that survived the shake-up. The ten probationers came to attention and looked across the drill ground at the one hundred foot tall double fronted drill tower on the other side of the drill yard. How many times would they climb it today? The instructor's voice called out once more.

"Squad number."

"One, two, three, four." The chorus rippled down the line of recruits to number ten.

"Squad in crews of four number."

"One, Two." The end two men stood silent.

This was a well-rehearsed piece that would divide any amount of men into groups, this time it was crews of four.

"Squad one, form up at the base of the drill tower, remainder stand at ease."

Wolf, Webb, Edison, and Harvey ran to the base of the tower and stood in a line behind two hook ladders.

Spider turned to Jack and in a hushed voice that came from the side of his mouth muttered.

"Hook ladders. I hate bloody hook ladders!"

"Wolf, Webb. You two men to floor seven of the drill tower and back in unison, Wolf window left, Webb window right, do you understand?"

"Yes, Sir."

"Away you go, lads."

Jack and Spider picked up their light wooden ladders and flicked out the two foot long hardened steel hooks and checked they had locked it into place. The ten sharp teeth and the six-inch bill on the end is all that would stop them from

168

falling the eighty feet to the ground. The principle was simple they would walk up to the building, lift up the ladder until they held it by its base, the top section with the steel hook would then be put through the first floor window the hardened teeth would bite into the window sill and the fireman would climb the hooked on ladder. When they reached the window opening they would put one leg through, leaving one leg outside running down the face of the wall, sitting on the sill they would lean outward, unhook the ladder and pass it hand over hand raising it up to the next window above, putting the hook though a widow once more, they would swing free from their perch, for the process to start again. This was scary enough to do alone but to do it in unison usually took practice, one man should take charge and count off their moves ensuring they stayed together in time, they were both right handed so each would face the same way. Jack would see Spider, Spider would only see his ladder and fresh air, logically Jack would be best placed to time the moves, the sub-officer had not given any instruction on who should lead, he wanted to see what the recruits did on their own initiative.

This was a test of nerves, leadership and team. Who would take charge of the climb? Who would trust whom? They had to 'Walk the wall', no safety lines, no net, just the light flimsy wooden ladder. Spider looked hopefully at Jack. Jack knew he was the obvious one to lead, he could watch Spider and adjust the timing to suit Spider's pace.

"Don't worry, I've got this Spider, follow me, I'll call the moves. And lean back, arms out straight the further you're out, the safer you are. Happy?"

"No, I feel sick and shaky, but let's do it."

Once more, they checked their ladder hooks had clicked and locked into place, Jack looked across at Spider, he did seem rather pale but hook ladders did that to some people. Jack started in a clear controlled voice.

"Into window one. Hook on, by the left step one, two, three, four…"

Jack counted the climb out, he was almost singing the steps like a metronome, the rhythm was flawless, even if you didn't know what was coming next, by the rhythm you knew when it was coming.

"Nine, ten, eleven, and stop, grasp ladders horns, lean back, left leg in, sit on sill, turn to the right, raise ladder and one and two and three and four and turn hook in, pull down, weight on, and swing out, by the left climb, one, two, three, four…" The rhythm went on, the same at each floor, they were 'walking the wall'.

The drill instructor below walked backwards across the yard, he had not taken his eyes off the two men climbing the face of the building, one false move and he would shout the word 'STILL'. This was the command on the drill ground which meant imminent danger of serious injury or death, everyone within earshot would freeze instantly, they would stop whatever they were doing until the danger had been pointed out to the individuals at risk.

The drill instructor had walked back almost to the squad line where eight faces were raised up watching the two men scaling the tower in perfect harmony. It was pretty to watch, they could not hear the metronome calling the moves, they just watched as two men seemed to climb the tower without effort.

When Spider and Jack got to the seventh floor, both men climbed to the head of their ladders and stepped in through the windows. The drill instructor turned to the squad line.

"There you go men, it's that easy, you will all do it in turn."

The instructor walked forward having given the two at floor seven a moment to catch their breath. Looking up, he bellowed.

"Aloft there, two ladder men dismount."

On the seventh floor, things were not going well. Jack looked across at Spider who was standing in the corner of the small brick room avoiding Jack's gaze.

"Spider, are you all right? You don't look good…Spider."

Spider turned to face the wall. As he did, he held his hand up to Jack in a move that said, 'Give me a moment'.

"Aloft there, Dismount." The Drill instructor was repeating his order.

"Spider we have to go, you can do this."

Spider held his hand up once more towards Jack, but still had his back to him. Then, as Jack watched, Spider threw-up emptying the contents of his stomach over his highly polished fire boots. The pitter-patter of a regurgitated full English breakfast and the stench of fresh vomit, made Jack's stomach turn.

"Aloft there, is there a problem?"

Jack patted Spider on the back turned and lent out of the window.

"No problem, Sub-O, Firemen Webb is just adjusting his fire kit."

"Very well, down you come lads."

"Spider, do you want to walk down the internal staircase? I'll walk with you, we can do this another time."

"No, no, I must do it, Bianchi said no second chance, he's watching me; fail this exam and I'm out."

Jack looked at Spider, what he just said didn't make sense. Only minutes ago Spider had told Jack that Bianchi was in prison, how could he be watching him? Jack frowned as he looked at the pale Spider.

"Bianchi's not here, he's not in charge anymore, he's gone, you can have another go later. I'll do it with you, there's no problem if you're ill."

"I ain't ill Jack, I'm shit scared. Can't you see me shaking? Them ladders are gonna kill me."

"They won't kill you, ladders don't kill people, even the fall won't kill you, it's hitting the ground after you've fallen that kills people."

Spider spat an uncontrolled laugh. Then strangely he said. "Why? Who did?"

"Spider focus, focus, do you trust me? I know you can do this, I watched you all the way up here, you're good, you never missed a beat, you never slipped, you never put a foot wrong, I believe you can do this, you aren't afraid of heights or ladders you're afraid of failing this exam and I'm not going to let that happen. We came up here together and we are going down together on the outside or the inside, but together. Look at me spider, trust me, together Spider, we will do this together. RIGHT."

"Jack? Jack!"

Jack watched Spider as he made a grab for the internal staircase handrail, as he took hold, his legs buckled, he briefly waivered then sank. He dropped to the floor like a sack of potatoes. He lay at Jack's feet in a cold faint, Jack looked down on him in disbelief then turned and lent out of the window once more.

"Below there, Sub-O."

"What is it, Wolf?"

"We're coming down the internal staircase, Sir. Fireman Webb is not well."

"Very good, get yourselves down here."

Jack knelt by the side of Spider Webb, he held his chin and called his name but there was no sign of consciousness. Jack slapped his face, he'd seen it done in the movies, it seemed a reasonable thing to do so. When the light slap had no effect, a few harder slaps followed, unfortunately they had no effect either. Jack stood up and looked down upon the unconscious Webb. He decided to have a conversation with somebody who was out cold.

"Well mate, it looks like I'm going to have to carry you down the stairs, are you sure you won't wake up? No, Oh thanks, I need the exercise, having just climbed up the outside of the tower I'm really looking forward to carrying you all the way back down the inside."

Kneeling, Jack took hold of Spider by the right arm and pulled him up to the sitting position, then lifted him, at first onto his knee then in one gut-straining move onto his back. This was his first real fireman's lift of a genuinely unconscious person, it was more difficult than lifts he had practiced in training, but at least Webb was on his back and now he took his first steps down seven floors carrying his man down.

"Aloft there, Fireman Wolf, aloft there."

Jack ignored the call of the drill instructor he was on floor five and running, no time to stop and tell the officer something that would come bloody obvious any minute. Floor four, floor three, floor two, Spider's head was close to Jack's face, he was still unconscious and dribbling down the shoulder of Jack's tunic. Jack slowed to take a look at him, it was then he smelt a weird smell coming from Spider, not the smell of vomit but the sweet smell of pear drops or was it cellulose thinners? He knew what it was. Floor one and then the ground floor.

Jack made his way out of the wide drill tower door and walked around to the front of the tower with Spider still on his back, he laid him on the wet granite cobbles where they had started. He heard the sub-officer ordering the squad, "Stand fast," before he walked over to the base of the tower to look down on them.

"What's happened, Wolf?"

"Fireman Webb, Sir, he's collapsed, I think he's in a diabetic coma, can we get him some help."

"What are you talking about Wolf; he's fainted, did it last time according to his records. That's why he's here; he'll come to in time."

Spider murmured and moved a little but was not coming around.

"I don't think so Sir, we need an ambulance."

"What? For this fainting prat."

Spider stirred once more.

"May I get someone to look at him? I think I've seen something similar before, my auntie is diabetic."

"You're who? What the hell have your relatives got to do with this? Wolf, what are you talking about?"

"Sub-Officer, I don't think this is a faint. I think he's diabetic, he was pale, shaking, he was confused, he threw-up, then he passed out. That's not a faint Sub-O."

"Oh, very well." The drill instructor turned to the squad line.

"You two men give Wolf a hand and take Webb to the mess-room, get him some sweet tea that'll sort him out. Double away lads."

Spider was scooped up by the three men then they ran, carrying him unceremoniously across the drill ground to Centrals' mess-room.

Spider was laid on the floor of the mess room, he was pale and cold, the two men with Jack tried their hardest to bring him around, talking to him and sitting him up against a chair did nothing. Jack drew back and looked at the scene, then turned and walked to the wall mounted phone and dialled zero the fire stations emergency number that went straight through to fire control. A woman's' voice answered.

"Fire control."

"Hello control, I request an emergency ambulance to station 1 Central's mess room. We have a fireman who's collapsed and in a diabetic coma, he has been unconscious for approximately five minutes, and shows no sign of recovery. This is not a drill."

There was a short pause.

"Okay Central, Red ambulance is en-route, who is requesting this attendance?"

"Fireman Wolf. 1834."

"Very well, Fireman Wolf, stay with the casualty, ambulance is seconds away."

There was a click in the earpiece and she was gone. The other two firemen were kneeling either side of Spider. They looked quizzically at Jack. Jack realised one of them was Spider's crewmate from Kings Norton. Eddy spoke as Jack looked at him.

"Should you have done that? Shouldn't we get an officer to look at him first? Shouldn't you get permission? The sub-officer said sweet tea would fix him."

"I think he needs insulin not sweet tea, he's ill, he needs medical attention now, we don't have time to discuss it."

The two recruits looked at each other, they were not convinced.

Within minutes, two ambulance men came through the mess room door pulling a gurney.

The first ambulance man through the door went straight to the side of Spider and lay him down without saying a word, the two recruits pulled back letting the second medic in, at last he spoke.

"How long has he been like this?" he asked.

Jack answered. "Ten minutes, no more."

The first medic turned to his colleague.

"DKA. Let's get him across the road to the general hospital, he needs a shot of insulin at least, maybe some potassium."

No sooner had they come through the door than they were making their way back out with Fireman Webb strapped to the gurney. The three recruits with very serious faces followed them out through the door, the ambulance crew pushed Spider's gurney into the back of the ambulance. The driver quickly jumped in the cab and started the engine leaving the attendant to secure the gurney, once again Jack found himself at the back of an ambulance watching a fellow fireman being prepped for transport to hospital.

The drill sub-officer was all of a sudden beside them.

What's going on here? Who requested the ambulance?

Jack went to speak, but the ambulance man spoke first.

"Hello Sub-O, your man here is not well, DKA, he needs attention quickly, good call."

"What's a DKA for god's sake?"

"Diabetic Ketoacidosis, your man here is diabetic, got to go." He pulled the rear doors shut and the ambulance drove out of the yard a little too fast for the Sub-O's liking.

The three recruits looked at each other and smiled a satisfying smile but said nothing. The sub-officer watched the ambulance as it drove out of the station yard he then turned his attention to the three men who all looked a little self-satisfied.

"What are you three grinning at? You look like Cheshire cats, get back in the squad line…No wait, Wolf and Pearson you two, can you see the tower?"

"Yes, Sub-O," came the harmonic answer.

"Can you see what's wrong with it?"

"No, Sub-O."

"Nor me, Sub-O."

"Can you see two hook ladders hanging from the seventh floor windows doing sweet FA?"

"Yes, Sub-O," came the harmonic answer once more.

"Well, don't just stand here grinning like school girls, get up there and bring them down, and I mean climb down, down the outside using the ladders, lets finish the drill. Move."

Once more Jack was climbing the tower.

All day, the drills kept coming, hose running, ladder running, pumping from hydrants, pumping from fire wells, it just went on and on. Jack reckoned he must have run the fifty-foot escape, seven or eight times, once carrying Eddy Pearson. He had lost count of how much hose he had run out, drained and re-coiled, foam branches, basement branches every ladder of every size he had climbed more than once, all on a bowl of breakfast cereal.

Lunch was just as light, soup and a brown bread roll that was a little on the stale side. After lunch they went off station to the Birmingham and Fazeley canal where they constructed a temporary bridge out of ladders, made temporary dams out of ladders and even a temporary crane out of ladders. Why? Jack was not sure but the drill sub-officer seemed to be enjoying himself dreaming up different scenarios.

He now had two assistants, two leading firemen were helping and it seemed their role was to dream up even more and more weird problems for the recruits to solve. Late in the afternoon, they were formed up in a squad-line on the canal towpath having just re-stowed all the equipment, the last and final task of the day being a temporary shelter for chemical de-contamination, which to Jack looked very much like half a dozen salvage sheets tied together between two fire engines, but the sub-officer seemed happy with the result.

"Squad, squad, shun." The nine recruits came smartly to attention, however fatigue was beginning to show.

"Leading Fireman Hoskins will walk down the line and ask you all an operational question, you will give your answer and I will mark you on the answer you give, do you understand?"

"Yes, Sir," was the not too enthusiastic reply. "Very well, Hoskins, carry on."

Hoskins approached the first man. Jack was fourth in-line he had time to determine the theme and toughness of the questions.

"Fireman Brown: What is the theoretical height of lift for fresh water?"

"Thirty two feet, Sir."

"Correct Brown, well done."

"Fireman Edison. What is the practical height of lift for fresh water?"

"Approximately twenty five feet Sir, depending on the efficiency of the pump."

"I'll accept twenty five feet, close enough Edison."

Jack, by this time, had worked out that they were all going to be hydraulic questions that any good pump operator should know he was running through in his mind what hydraulics questions could be coming, probably something to do with pumping at distance and friction loss. Hence the next question caught him completely off guard.

"Fireman Pearson, an operational question for you, picture this; you are riding on the back of a pump just four crew and you turn-out to a house fire, the pump escape is on the other side of the station ground at a road traffic accident, your back up trucks are five to ten minutes away, your truck is the first to arrive on scene. Do you understand so far?"

"Yes, LF."

"When you arrive, you see smoke issuing from the upstairs windows and roof of the house, as you run toward the house you are greeted by the homeowner who tells you his two young children are trapped upstairs in their bedrooms and he cannot get to them because of the thick smoke. He also informs you that he is a keeper of exotic animals and roaming free in the house is a full grown male Bengal Tiger...Do you understand, Pearson?"

"Err, yes, I think so, LF."

"Very well, detail your actions from the point of being told of the Tiger by the homeowner. Go."

Jack's head swung around and looked first upon an incredulous Eddy Pearson then to a just as incredulous Drill Sub-O, then lastly to a smug nodding Leading fireman that had just gone completely off message. The whole squad-line, the sub-officer and a nonplussed second LF starred at Eddy. Hoskins meanwhile grinned like an idiot and looked even smugger, if that was possible. Jack could not take his eyes off of Eddy who seemed deep in thought and weighing his options.

"Well, Pearson! We haven't got all day these children are about to burn to death in their bedrooms you need to do something. Come on man, what are you going to do?"

"Hmm, a Bengal Tiger you say LF?"

"Yes, come on man, make a decision."

"Full grown, male Bengal Tiger LF?"

"Yes, a male bloody Bengal Tiger, get on with it man."

"Well...I think I would go back to the truck, get a stun gun out of the rear offside locker, load-up, then fire a stun grenade through the ground floor window, maybe two, just to make sure I'd subdued the ferocious animal, you understand. Then, when the animal was suitably stunned I would carry out the recues as normal…Wait, I may also kick the Tiger in the balls for good measure as I went past it."

Jack looked in amazement at Eddy; nobody said a word, everyone to a man watched LF Hoskins for a reaction, time seemed to be in suspension, nothing moved, not a breath of wind, not a ripple of water on the canal. Silence, just silence. Then.

"Stun gun! Stun gun! What bloody stun gun? When did we start carrying bloody stun guns and grenades on fire engines?"

"Oh, that one's easy LF. It was just after idiots like you started saying we had Bengal tigers in house fires."

The squad line erupted into fits of laughter, the sub-officer turned away hiding his grinning face, he made a short walk along the canal tow path, then when he had managed to compose himself he turned back to the squad.

"Okay, that's enough, that's enough for today, mount up men, let's get back to the station."

Friday Night Is Factory Night

After two days at fire training school, Jack was happy to be back on station for the two night shifts, Saturday and Sunday. According to the off going watch, all had been quiet on Friday night which was unusual as Friday night was 'factory night' as the small factories, of which there were thousands across the city, shut down for the weekend. A piece of equipment somewhere in the city would not be turned off or shut down properly. It would overheat un-noticed by anyone and late in the night it would start a fire. That had been the way of things for a hundred years or more and things were showing no signs of changing. Then there was always the businesses that are doing badly and the owners think that having a fire and claiming on the insurance would be a good way to solve their problems. They also had the habit of choosing a Friday night for some unknown reason, perhaps that was a natural end to the week and in their minds their business, either way the reality was much the same for the city firemen 'Friday night was factory night'.

By midnight, the ten firemen of Blue Watch were fast asleep in the dormitory on the top floor at Aston. Sid was also fast asleep but in the station office where he had a put-u-up bed that hinged down from the wall. A couple of small rubbish fires and a road traffic accident had been all that had broken the evening's routine of cleaning and maintaining the fire engines and equipment. Horace's supper of boiled fish, boiled potatoes peas and bread sauce once more had not gone down well with Jack but the sweet golden syrup sponge pudding had more than made up for the unappetising main course.

Jack was awoken by movement in the dormitory, the door to the dormitory toilet creaked as it was opened casting a beam of bright light across the room and over Jack's bed, a shadowy figure made his way through the doorway. In the few seconds of light before the door closed, Jack had time to look at his wristwatch. Two forty five.

A few minutes later, the figure reappeared, this time the pinprick of a bright red-orange glow was leading the shadowy figure across the room. It was Conker, he returned to his bed and sat upright, puffing slowly on his capstan full strength. Jack watched the glow light up Conker's face each time he took a pull on the cigarette, the tap on the little aluminium ash tray that sat on his bedside chair Jack had heard many times in the middle of the night. Jack rolled over in an attempt to get back to sleep. Just as sleep was coming to him the whole fire station lit up, every light in the station came on automatically after dark, when the fire bell burst into life on full alarm.

Everyone jumped from their beds pulled on their trousers then made their way to the pole drop with a little less enthusiasm than was to be seen during the day. Each man slid down the pole in turn, as they came through the ceiling opening they looked across to the little coloured lights above the engines, all three were lit, everybody goes.

As Jack climbed into the pump the up and over doors were making their familiar clatter as they made their way across the ceiling, as he sat down he glanced across at Conker who was pulling on his bright yellow over trousers still with the cigarette in his mouth.

"Smoke issuing, factory, Lichfield Road, Junction Lovers walk, buckle up boys, and get your BA on."

Sub-Officer Dwyer was wide-awake and surely could not have been asleep, he looked to a half-asleep Jack at any rate, like he had just come off parade. His long sleeved shirt, buttoned at the cuff looked as if it had just been pressed and his jet-black hair was combed with a perfect centre parting not a single strand of hair out of place. Jack watched him put his fire tunic on even the tunic seemed freshly laundered if not new, the two chrome bars of his rank's markings seemed to shine extra bright in the dim light of the crews cab. Jack wondered how he could look so smart in the middle of the night. Jack, for his part, felt awful and still half-asleep. He looked out of the side window as the pump pulled out of the engine house following the pump escape off towards the Lichfield Road the turntable ladder would as ever bring up the rear.

The ride to the Lichfield Road was totally uneventful; the streets of Aston were deserted, nothing moved, there was no need for the two-tones, even the three sets of blue lights passing through the narrow streets and reflecting off of the shop windows along the Lichfield Road seemed weary and lacking urgency. The purr of the Rolls Royce engine pushing the truck along with ease seemed to increase the feeling of this just being a run out to a false alarm. No one spoke, each man sat dressed and ready in his seat being gently moved by the swaying ride of the fire engine, each had hold of something fixed, a door handle, a seat back anything that could steady them on the short routine ride.

Off the Lichfield Road, Lovers walk ran along the side of the railway line that cut its way through the heart of Aston. Many years ago, it may have been the place for a stroll down a picturesque country lane for a young courting couple but, with the coming of the industrial revolution and the railway it had turned into a dingy, dilapidated, slum area where hundred-year-old and many probably older terraced houses had been turned into illegal sweatshops, nothing was legal in these all too familiar places not even the workers, they would scatter at the first sign of anyone with a uniform or any authority from the city council, they would make just about anything; clothing was a favourite.

The pump escape passed the building, stopping just under the railway bridge that crossed the Lichfield Road leaving the frontage free, the pump Jack and Conker were riding, pulled up short, en-route everyone to a man thought this would be a false alarm but as they looked at the old terrace of houses they knew it was cooking inside. Six, maybe eight, houses of the old terrace had heavy smoke pushing out from the eaves, the first floor sash windows of each house had been boarded over with flimsy, now peeling plywood, years ago. The pressure created by the fire found even the smallest of gaps and pumped the black-brown smoke through any opening it could find to the outside. All the windows at ground level had closely spaced steel bars covering them, each bar cemented fast into the brickwork. The house at the centre had the same thick black-brown smoke coming from the ground floor windows, one each side of the only working front door, even that had been covered with a sheet of galvanised steel with two steel bars and heavy duty shrouded padlocks to add to the security, all the other front doors had been bricked up with no attempt to match the bricks or the bond. Sid walked the frontage weighing up his options. The pump escape's crew were running a hydrant supply into their truck as Jack, Conker and 600 did the same to theirs.

"No problem with water here Jack, the water main here's a monster, one of the main feeds into the city."

Sid had made his mind up, he pointed to a bricked-up doorway to the left of the steel covered door.

"Sledge hammers and large axes, we go in through here. T.L. crew knock out all the top floor windows, I don't care how you do it."

Everyone went about their allotted work without question. Jack got to the side locker that contained the breaking in tools, 600 was already there he had hold of the large axe Jack grabbed the sledgehammer.

"Why are we busting through brickwork when we have a doorway in front of us, 600?"

"That's because whoever did the security, wasn't thinking straight, that door has probably got another piece of steel on the inside, the two pieces together making it a steel sandwich. With all those locks and bars, it would take us ten, maybe fifteen minutes to get through, but this crap bricklaying is going to crumble as soon as we attack it, it's not even keyed in, they didn't think anyone would go through a wall to get into the building. It's often easier to go through a wall than a security door."

Jack swung the sledge hammer at the brickwork of the door way, it may be crap brickwork and not look good but it was not crumbling as soon as they attacked it, that was for sure. After half a dozen blows, Jack had made a small hole in the centre which smoke pushed out of instantly and under some pressure, another ten blows made a hole the size of a dinner plate, Conker was now at Jack's side also holding a sledge hammer.

"Take a rest Jack let me have a go." A breathless Jack stepped back and let Conker in.

Conker was like a man possessed he swung the heavy hammer without rest the hole in the centre of the brickwork quickly grew larger, then a crash of masonry as the top section fell as one, thick smoke poured out of the building. Conker then concentrated on the lower brickwork knocking it free brick by brick.

"Okay. Conker let me back in, you have a rest."

"Hang on Jack."

Conker was looking through the opening into the building his head disappeared into the smoke plume, 600 was shovelling bricks away from the soon to be re-born entrance to the building, then Conker drew back.

"I'll get the rest of the bricks out Jack, there's shelving or racking on the inside with stock loaded onto it, I'll get the last of the bricks out then you can move that shelving and stuff to get us a way in."

Conker swung again at the few remaining courses of brickwork. He was now working constantly in the thick brown smoke that poured from the doorway. Jack saw Sid coming towards them he had two men in breathing apparatus and an entry control man with him he talked to the BA men but broadcasting so all could hear.

"Right men when these guys have made an entry point for you, I want you two inside with a main jet okay?"

"Yes, Sir."

"Entry Control. You set up here to the right of the doorway. You three when you're done get around the back and help the sub-officer make another entry point there okay? Yes, Sir."

Sid turned and walked away into the smoke cloud, as he disappeared shrouded by the rolling smoke a loud crash of breaking glass made everyone look along the face of the building the turntable ladder crew had decided to smash the windows with the head of the ladder rather than with a man at the head breaking the windows with an axe. Neither the rotten plywood nor the Victorian sash windows showed any resistance, even more smoke belched out from the newly made openings. The breaking out of the first floor windows did have one noticeable effect on the doorway Conker was working on, smoke no longer came out from the doorway, fresh air was now being drawn in, which made the work outside easier but all six men knew they were feeding the fire with a good supply of fresh air, plus a new exhaust point four houses down and counting as the T.L. crew made their way along the buildings face smashing more windows. This was a dangerous strategy, if they didn't get water onto the seat of this fire soon it could flash-over. Jack was grabbing and pulling out armfuls of brightly coloured anoraks packed five to each clear plastic bag, the footpath and roadway was quickly becoming covered in anoraks of all colours and sizes. Jack stepped inside the building and kicked at the steel shelving which was slotted together rather than being bolted it quickly fell apart when he switched to hitting it with the large fire axe, the entry point was free, the BA men had already started up their sets and were handing in their identity tallies to entry control as Jack stepped back out into the fresh air. The last man going in through the doorway patted Jack on the shoulder as he passed him by, it was only then that Jack realised it was Harry in BA hauling the charged line of hose into the building. Jack hit Harry on the top of his helmet with his axe handle.

Outside Jack looked at 600 and Conker each of them was sweating and breathing heavily.

"Right then, around the back and find the Sub-O."

182

Axes and sledgehammers over their shoulders, they headed off to the back of the building. Conker led, followed by Jack, 600 was last in line, they fell into step as 600's strong Welsh-tenor voice came stealing through the smoke.

"Heigh-ho, Heigh-ho, it's off to work we go, we smash smash with a sledge and an axe Heigh-ho, Heigh-ho." The refrain carried them to the back of the terrace.

The back of the building was in almost complete darkness the three men hadn't realised but the orange glow of the sodium vapour streetlights had lit the front of the building so they had not needed floodlights at the back. The scene was completely different, one lone floodlight lit the entire rear of eight houses that was now a factory, the small rear yards had been levelled, their wash houses were gone, concrete and tarmac now covered the small area with just a couple of wooden sheds looking very sorry for themselves containing who knows what. 600 had stopped singing which was good as Jack thought he had carried on the joke a little too long. The three men looked around but could see nobody in the darkness and swirling smoke.

"Up here, lads."

The three men looked ahead and up through the smoke they could just make out a wooden staircase with a line of charged hose leading up it, perhaps it was a fire escape that led down from the first floor, at the top the sub-officer was with Will and Johnny Johnson. When they climbed halfway up the staircase they could see the three men were trying to get through another bricked up doorway this one was not giving way as quickly as the one at the front, it appeared to be a double course of bricks that had been tied in but at least they had made a small hole at the top that they were making larger. The same black brown smoke pumped out angrily. Conker got the Sub-O's attention.

"Can we help, Sub-O?"

"Not really, lads. Not much room up here on the landing for three let alone six, we thought this would be an easy way in but it's a bastard, it's putting up a fight. Conker, just at the foot of the stairs there, can you see a steel covered doorway?"

"Yes, right here at the bottom of the stairs, I see it."

"Well you boys have a go at that, see if you have more luck than us." As he spoke, the smoke coming from the little opening they had made changed to flame, then almost instantly back to smoke again.

"Watch that, sub-officer, it's rolling above you."

"Yes, thanks Conker, I saw it."

The three looked long and hard at their next doorway, Jack spoke up. "I'll go first."

The sledgehammer had little effect on the door. Jack could see a hasp and staple with a good quality padlock closed onto it and a Yale lock but there was surely more holding this door fast.

"Hold there a minute, Jack, don't hit the locks, hit the other side, there maybe half a dozen locks of different shapes and sizes on the inside of this door but what everybody forgets is there are only two hinges, smash them away and we are in, probably only a few screws holding the other side."

Jack changed his stance it would be easier if he had been left handed but he could get a good swing and land a fair blow although it felt awkward. To Jack's amazement, the first two high blows had moved the door inward, another two low down did much the same, he put all his effort into the following blows and there was no doubt the door was moving.

600 spoke up, "We're gonna need a jet, I'll run a hose line from the front for us." As he spoke, he turned and was gone. Conker tapped Jack on the shoulder.

"My turn, Jack." The sledgehammer weighed twenty pounds and swinging it especially above shoulder height quickly sapped the energy of the user, short bursts of powerful blows were far better than slogging away when tired only landing light blows that achieved little. Conker was back swinging with all his might; the hinges were giving way when an out of breath 600 dropped an uncharged hose and branch at their feet.

"I'll go back and get water; I see you boys are nearly through."

Jack looked up the staircase to the sub-officer and his crew as 600 went once more to the pump escape to get water on. They were still working on their wall the smoke was pushing out above them with even more force.

As Conker gave the door another mighty blow, the door hinges gave way completely.

Conker threw the sledgehammer behind him and linked arms with Jack, like dancers from the London Palladium or the Moulin Rouge, they stepped back together then moved forward and as one, raised their legs to waist height and kicked the door inward. As they did, as if it was planned, the empty hose line came to life filling with water, it became as hard as rock. Jack picked it up from the ground and made his way toward the door, he felt Conker pick the hose up from the opposite side behind him, he slapped Jack on his right shoulder, he was ready. His hand stayed on Jack's back, pushing him slightly forward, ready to take the jet reaction when the hose line was opened up. There was a pulse of heat from the doorway, the smoke was changing to flame, this was not a flashover but the fire was now free, it was taking charge, it was venting and growing, time to hit it hard and knock it down.

Jack went forward through the doorway and into the heavy smoke and opened up the branch; the rope, like one-inch jet of water arched into the heart of the fire. Jack dropped to his knees to get out of the thick brown smoke layer, Conker followed. Below three feet from the floor, the air was pretty clear and fresh but Jack could see no flames, then there was a tremendous crash and a rush of air passed them and out through the doorway.

"What the hell was that?" Jack called back to Conker.

"I reckon a section of roof has caved in, but it's someway off, we're okay here."

Jack shuffled forward on his knees and kept working the jet to and fro, he could feel Conker pulling the hose in for him and taking the weight of the jet reaction; then they moved forward again.

At the front of the building, 600 lay motionless amongst a pile of bricks and roof slates, he had been on his way back to join Conker and Jack when the roof of the centre terraced house collapsed inward. As it did, it pushed a section of the brick corbeled eaves some twenty feet long down onto the street, just as 600 was about to run through the arched entryway.

Toot, Nobby and George saw it happen and were where 600 lay before the dust had settled. They picked him up and carried him away from the front of the building in case more masonry should fall. They lay the unconscious, brick dust covered 600 on the wet roadway behind the pump which was screaming at full revs pumping water, Nobby kneeling at his side took off 600's helmet, Toot had taken off his tunic and was rolling it into a ball to put under 600's head, as he did, 600's eyes opened, he was totally lost. He said nothing but his eyes were wide and questioning where in the world he was. Toot spoke first.

"You okay, mate?"

"I think so, my arm and shoulders, they bloody hurt."

"I'm not surprised, you've just been pummelled by half a ton of bricks."

Sid, who was at entry point one had heard that someone had been hit by falling masonry and was now with the four men.

"How are you, Jones? You look like you've been in the wars."

600 was now wide-awake and his broad Welsh accent was more evident than ever.

"I'm well, as you can see, SO. I'll just get some air back in my lungs and I'll be back in the fight. You can't keep a man from the valleys down with a few bricks."

"Well, I think I'll have you checked over first, an ambulance is on its way, Taylor you stay with him and make sure he gets checked over. Clarke, Harrison, you two get around the back and give them a hand around there. I've made it five so we should have company soon. The circus is on its way."

Jack was working the jet hard, again he went forward on his knees, the smoke was particularly acrid, this was not wood smoke it was plastic smoke, horrible stuff, the stinging eyes and ever-present running nose, Jack was used to, but this shitty plastic smoke was horrid and hurt his chest. He moved forward once more, they were twenty feet or so into the building now and they still hadn't seen any real flames, just the shitty acrid smoke that showed no sign of easing.

All of a sudden, Jack felt the weight of the jet reaction come to him, it was trying to push him backwards. Conker had been taking this weight as Jack directed the jet, now it was hard to hold let alone move around. Then he felt the weight of Conker on his back, it was pulling him over to the left, controlling the jet was becoming harder than ever. Conker must have become distracted, what was he doing? What had he seen that would stop him working?

Conker's body weight was pushing Jack to the left but Jack could see nothing of interest that way, no fire, no nothing. Then Conker slumped forward over the hose, forcing Jack to point the hose almost vertically, the jet of water hitting the ceiling above them deluging the pair of kneeling firemen. Jack struggled to control the jet, he jabbed his hand forward to the control lever and shut the jet of water off, the closing down of the jet shot him forward as the counter balance weight became unequal. Jack dropped the line of hose and turned to look at Conker, as he did, he was horrified by what he saw. Conker was motionless face down in the steaming black run off water, his helmeted head jammed against a metal shelving rack.

Jack grabbed hold of his friend by the shoulders and pulled him into the sitting position. Conker was unconscious. Jack called to him and shook him but, nothing. Jack knew he had to get him out, for the second time in a week, he would have to carry an unconscious firemen on his back, this time he didn't feel the weight, this time there was no onto the knee first, this time he grabbed his

186

friend's arm and tucking his head under Conker's armpit in one smooth move, he brought Conker across his back, without hesitation. He made his way out following the hose.

He saw the entrance door complete with padlock lying in inches of black water, indicating that he was by the doorway. Jack's head was forced down by Conker's body across his shoulders, he was still following the hose line out of the building he was not looking where he was going, through the doorway and onto the yard and fresh air. Jack briefly raised his head to look for assistance. There was nobody to be seen, the length of hose still stretched up the fire escape and into the building but the crew must all be inside.

Jack made his mind up, he would carry Conker to the front of the building without stopping. As he walked forward, there was a crash of falling brickwork in front of him, another piece of corbeled eaves had given way, climbing over rubble, carrying an unconscious person, Jack found it difficult and his ankles more than once complained of the angles and weight they were being asked to bear. As he entered the entryway through the houses, still head down, Jack heard Nobby's voice.

"What the hell."

Jack looked up to see the two men. As he did, Nobby took Conker's arm and he eased the weight from Jack's shoulders.

"What's happened, Jack?"

"I don't know, he just collapsed in the building, he won't come around."

"Let's get him to the front."

The three men carried Conker, Nobby and Jack had an arm each, George had his legs, it wasn't textbook but it was effective. As they emerged from the entry onto the footpath, they saw the cream coloured city ambulance, with its back doors open wide, parked in the middle of the road, they headed towards it. In the back sat 600 with an oxygen mask strapped to his face, when they got to the open doors the two ambulance men and 600 turned to them in surprise.

"What now lads?" one ambulance man asked.

"Overcome by smoke?" the second ambulance man followed his colleagues' lead.

"I don't think so, he's a smoke eater," Jack replied.

"Bring him in; let's have a look at him."

600 stood, complete with oxygen mask to make room for his unconscious friend. The three men laid Conker on the gurney then stepped back to give the

ambulance men room to work, the three decided it would be better to stand outside the rear doors, as a standing patient a lying patient and two ambulance men was easily enough in the back.

The three firemen watched intently as the guys worked on Conker, his fire tunic and shirt were quickly removed, he lay unconscious and bare from the waist up as one ambulance man listened to his chest, the other took his blood pressure. They both looked concerned for their patient, they had a short whispered conversation with each other. The three watching firemen strained to hear but surrounded by the racing fire pumps engines they heard not a word.

"What's going on men?" Sid joined them at the ambulance doors. Nobby replied.

"Conkers collapsed, overcome we think, SO."

The ambulance man with the stethoscope looked up.

"Have you got a police car here?"

"Yes, there are three, they've closed the road off for us," Sid replied.

"Good, get one to give us an escort into town. Your man's not well he's had a cardiac arrest." Everyone scattered quicker than any rehearsed drill, the ambulance doors were slammed closed and within minutes two police cars were escorting an ambulance with blues and twos through the early morning city streets. As they disappeared down the Lichfield Road heading towards town Sid, Nobby, George, and Jack watched in silence.

To Jack, the rest of the firefighting at the anorak factory on the Lichfield Road seemed unreal. He watched BA crews from Central and Handsworth go into the building repeatedly, he helped run in a supply to the turntable ladder so they could pump tons of water into the fire's black heart where the roof had collapsed, but he had no interest in the fire's death throws.

The whole bloody place could burn to the ground for all he cared; he wanted to know how Conker was doing. As he passed his fellow firemen from Aston, they acknowledged each other with despondent frowns. The fire seemed to drag on even as dawn broke and daylight made its way onto the fire ground; the mood didn't change.

At 0800 hours, Sid called the Aston crews together, they gathered by the side of the turntable ladder.

"Well, men, I'm sure you have been thinking of Conker and 600 after they were taken to hospital. As you know, I would get nothing over the brigade radio, however, I did manage to find a phone box down the road and I have contacted fire control. The hospital wouldn't tell me of Conker's condition, I did try them first, unfortunately all control could get was that Conker is stable. 600 was found to have a broken left forearm.

"I'm sorry, I have nothing more for you, so that's it for now. We have done our bit boys, relief crews are on their way, gather up what you can of our gear and stow it away, make ready for going back to station. Jack went about his work thinking of what Sid had said. Jack thought it was interesting that the station officer had been using the men's nicknames."

Back at the station, just before 0900 hours, Jack knocked on the office door. The high-pitched voice bade him, "Come in. Yes, Jack?"

"SO, I will be going to the Conker's house, then the hospital when I leave here and I wondered…I wondered, will Mrs Fowles have been told of her husband's condition?"

"Why are you going to the house Jack? This is by no means the best time to go visiting."

"I have been seeing Fireman Fowles daughter for some few months now, SO and consider myself a friend of the family. It would be wrong of me not to go with Conker being ill and all."

"I see Jack. Well in that case I will tell you what is happening. An officer from headquarters and an officer from 'A' division HQ have been to Conker's house and told Mrs Fowles what happened at the fire. They have taken Mrs Fowles to the general hospital so she can be at the bedside of her husband. I believe the eldest daughter is at home looking after the younger children."

"The twins, Sir."

"Yes, I believe so, the twins indeed, if you are to be of use to the family it may be better helping to look after the children than getting in the way at the hospital."

"Yes, thank you, SO."

Without saying more, Jack turned and walked out of the office just as the fire bell announced the end of Blue Watch's night shift. It was 0900 hours, Sunday morning.

Jack closed the green metal door of his locker and turned the flimsy key in the lock, his wet fire-kit was in the basement drying room and his smoke stained but washed clean fire helmet sat on the top of his locker like all the other lockers of Blue Watch. He made his way through the engine house where the three machines stood resting but re-fuelled and clean. Waiting for their next shout out

189

through the wicket door of the backwash bay and onto the drill yard, the bright sun made his tired, sore eyes hurt. He squinted and dropped his head for shade. As he walked toward the back gates, the station officer drove out of the car park and drew alongside him.

"How are you getting home, Jack?"

"I'm on the bus, SO."

"Then how will you get to Conker's house?"

"Hopefully I can borrow my mother's car."

"Jump in Jack, I'll take you home."

The station officer drove out of the station yard and made his way into town, the two men sat in silence for the first few minutes of the journey. The roads and buildings they passed that Jack had had no knowledge of a few months ago, now seemed like old friends. Down Aston High Street, Jack watched the Bartons Arms slip by, it seemed like a lifetime ago that Sid had bought him a pint for his birthday. Sid seemed to sense Jack's mood, he watched Jack looking out the window at the pub deep in thought.

"We've had a busy old time of it lately, Jack, don't you think? What with Fatal and 600 getting injured, now it looks like Conker's had a heart attack; we are getting a bit thin on the ground."

"Yes, SO," came Jack's monotone reply.

"I hear you had some excitement at training school on Thursday, too."

"Yes, SO."

Sid looked across at Jack, he looked drained and tired. Should he keep chatting and try to bring Jack out of his malaise? Or should he leave him be and let the young man sort himself out? Sid decided to leave him be, the rest of the journey was made in silence. After just twenty-five minutes, Sid pulled up outside Jack's parents' house. It had not occurred to Jack that Sid had not asked him his address or for directions; as the car pulled to a halt Jack pulled the door handle and half opened the car door.

"Thanks SO, it was very kind of you to give me a lift home."

"Not at all Jack, you're welcome, if you see Conker later, please give him my best wishes and those of the lads too. Tell him we will all visit him as soon as we are allowed to and could you tell Mrs Fowles, I'll be in touch."

"Certainly SO, and thanks again for the lift."

"Okay Jack, see you later at the fire station."

As Jack closed the car door he realised he had to be back on duty at the station at six o'clock, they all had one more night shift of the tour to go.

As Jack approached the front door of Conker's house, the door opened, a red-eyed Sophia held her arms out open wide beckoning Jack to embrace her. Jack walked into her open arms and they held each other tightly without a word being spoken. Sophia could smell the smoke of the fire in Jack's hair; to her it was a cruel reminder of what the fire had done to her father.

"How is he? Have you heard from your mother?"

"One call about six o'clock, Mamma says he's fine sitting up in bed and talking, they are monitoring him or something."

"Aunt Isabella is on her way, she should be here in quarter of an hour to watch the twins then I can go to the hospital and sit with Mamma."

The twins had come to the front door to see Jack and were now standing in the hallway listening to the conversation.

"Can we go with you and see Papa."

"No, not yet girls, they won't allow it."

"Why won't they allow it?"

"In the heart ward, where Papa is, it's a maximum of two visitors per patient, no children are allowed. We can all go when he's moved to a general ward."

The twins dropped their heads dejected and walked back into the kitchen without further discussion.

Jack was still in the doorway with his back to the street when Sophia, looking over his shoulder called out, "Aunt Isabella."

Jack turned to see a handsome middle-aged woman walking towards him; his instant reaction was that she looked remarkably like an actress, a film star he knew, whose name totally escaped him.

"Isabella, thank you so much for coming over."

"Nonsense, my darling girl, how's your father?"

"He is well auntie; he's sitting up and talking, that's all we know. Auntie, this is John we all call him Jack, my boyfriend I told you all about him a while ago."

"*Si si, ciao,* John." She held her face forward and waited for a kiss.

Jack obliged and kissed her once on each cheek.

"John, you smell of smoke." Isabella didn't mince her words.

"I'm so sorry, Isabella, I came straight here from the station. I haven't had time to shower."

"I tell you what Jack, you go upstairs and have a shower while auntie and I have a coffee, I'll find a fresh shirt and trousers for you. Would you like a coffee when you've had your shower?"

"Oh yes, please, a good strong coffee would wake me up I'm sure."

Jack and Sophia climbed the wide stone stairs to the first floor of the general hospital. The plastic sign on the wall directed them left to the cardiac ward, as they made their way along the old gloss painted corridor. They looked into each room they passed, at the next room they met a smiling young nurse on her way out with a large grey papier-mâché bottle in hand.

"Hi, can I help you?"

"Hello, yes could you direct us to the room of Mr Fowles."

"Are you related to Mr Fowles?"

"Yes, I am his daughter and this is my husband, his son in law."

Jack looked at Sophia, trying not to look amazed by the speed of her lying response. The young nurse was no fool, she looked Sophia up and down and then in the eye.

"Are you? Are you indeed?" she paused.

"Go right to the end of the corridor, there is a sunroom there, he is there with his wife. You have five minutes, that's all."

"Thank you, you are very kind." Sophia was being as polite as possible, knowing she had just lied to the nurse and was now felling guilty.

Jack led the way. As Sophia passed the nurse, the nurse tapped Sophia's arm and whispered.

"You both forgot to wear your wedding rings in your hurry to get here."

"Thank you, I'm so sorry." Sophia sounded contrite. The nurse smiled once more and was off on her way to the sluice room.

Conker sat in a large metal framed chair which looked most uncomfortable, behind the chair in a bracket was a small black cylinder of oxygen from which led a thin clear plastic tube that ran to the mask that covered Conker's nose and mouth. Beside him, in a smaller but equally uncomfortable looking chair sat a worried looking Giulia who got to her feet as they walked in, the two women said nothing but hugged each other in a long embrace. Conker watched them and then turned his gaze to Jack.

"How you doing, Joe?" Jack thought there was time to use, 'sir' there were times for swearing and there were times for using nicknames, this was not one of them.

Joe removed the facemask. "Felt better, Jack, but they say it was a mild heart attack, not the big one. I'll be fine if I take it easy. They say no more fighting fires though and no more cigarettes. The cigarettes I can do without but, no more fires? I can't do that, perhaps I can have a word with the chief, there must be something an old firedog can do in the brigade, don't you think?"

Giulia broke free of holding onto Sophia and turned to scold her husband.

"Joseph, Joseph, you must listen to the doctors, it's all over for you, no more the fireman. You can do this no more, this job it's a no-good for you, the coughing, the burns, and your friends with the broken bones, enough already. This-is-a-God, this-is-a-God, he is telling you this Joseph, he is saying enough, stop this or I will take your life back to me. No more, please, no more, *e la fine*, it's finished."

She slumped down into her small bedside chair, clutching a clean white but tear-dampened handkerchief. Jack had never seen her emotional, her Italian background had surfaced. It made her pleading all the more passionate and all the more poignant.

Joe, looked at his wife and daughter, he put his hand lightly on his wife's thigh next to him and patted it.

"You are always the sensible one, Giulia, you and the children are the world to me and once again you are right, I know it really. I will retire and we shall live a quiet life in the country surrounded by many grandchildren."

Sophia blushed and looked at Jack. Jack knew it was time to stay silent, he reached out and held Sophia's hand and gave Joe a knowing smile; Conker, his mate, smiled back. The young nurse entered the room the group shuffled their positions, somehow that cleared the tension in the air.

"Okay people, that's enough excitement for now, everybody out, just one visitor at a time tomorrow, then after that we may let two of you in. Say your goodbyes."

"Mamma we will leave you and Papa together to say goodbye. Jack and I will wait at the stairs. Goodbye, Papa." Sophia lent down and kissed her father on the cheek. Jack held out his hand to Joseph who grasped it and held on.

"Did you get me out, Jack?"

Jack hesitated. "Yes, Joe, yes, I did."

"Thank you, Jack, thank you. You're a good man, Jack."

Jack dipped his head in an almost unperceivable nod to his friend, Conker nodded back. Once more they were talking without words.

Jack and Sophia left the sunroom with Joseph and Giulia holding hands, though Giulia's eyes were hot and wet but she was happy, she still had her husband.

Jack drove them back across town in his mother's green Ford Escort, Giulia was in the back seat, Sophia was at Jack's side in the front. The ride back to the house was made pretty much in silence. Giulia didn't seem to want to talk, Sophia tried once or twice to get her mother chatting but all the replies were in monosyllables, she was really saying 'give me a little space'. When they got to the house the two women walked up to the front door Jack stopped short as the front door was opened by a woman that looked very like Sophia Loren, Isabella held her arms out to her sister. Jack turned to his Sophia.

"I have to get my mother's car back to her and I have to go on duty tonight so I better get going."

Giulia, hearing what Jack had said turned to him and lightly grasped each side of his head. She warmly kissed him on each cheek. "*Nostro figlio, nostro eroe.*"

Jack kissed Sophia goodbye, turned and left the three women at the doorstep.

It seemed to Jack, in no time at all, he was on parade in the backwash at Aston. He and Sid had managed to have a few words before the start of the shift and Jack had brought the station officer up to speed with the events of the day. Jack looked down the paraded line of Blue Watch to see a strange face at the end it; it was one of the crew from Handsworth. Blue Watch Aston were indeed getting a bit thin on the ground due to injuries so a 'standby' fireman had been sent to make up the numbers. Tumble detailed the runners and riders and as usual Jack was riding on the back of the pump. Tumble finished by detailing the routines for the evening then handed the parade to Sid.

"Evening men, firstly welcome to Firemen Williams from Handsworth and a thank you Williams for volunteering to stand-by tonight to end this tour."

Williams smiled and waved his hand down the line.

"Division is hoping to sort a more permanent transfer out to help us, as we are now three short. I'll let you know more about that when I know. You will be pleased to hear I'm sure, that Joe is fine, he has had what was described to me as a 'mild' heart attack if there is such a thing, he is sitting up out of bed and chatting with his family. So he's on the mend. If you want to visit him please go through 'A' division HQ as his wife has enough to deal with without dozens of firemen ringing her at all hours of the day and night, okay?"

"I have also been to see firemen Jones. He is home, nursing a broken arm and some good bruising over his back and shoulder. Jones is happy to receive visitors and he wants the plaster cast signed by all so he can keep tally of his visitors. Well, that's it men, let's have a quiet night. Sub-officer, dismiss the men."

"Parade shun, fall in for work routines at 1830 hours, working rig. Parade, dismiss."

Jack looked across the bench seat of the pump at the stand-by from Handsworth, and held out his hand. "Hi, Jack Wolf."

"Hi, Bungy. Bungy Williams." The two men shook hands. "How long have you been in Bungy?"

"Just coming up to four years, and you?"

"Just nine months on station."

"I remember you now. You were at that job in Aston Lane with the stiff, and all that Bianchi business, you were with Conker inside. I was one of the BA men you kept soaking with your jet. We were seriously considering turning our jet on you two when the end wall started to come in on us. Good working job that was. Who would have guessed the Bianchi brothers were up to all that mischief, eh?"

"Yes, who indeed."

Sunday night passed by quietly and uneventful, Monday morning's soggy toast and coffee in the mess room was as quiet as the night. At 0900 hours Blue Watch and Bungy were saying their good-byes and making their different ways homeward.

By ten o'clock, Jack was back at his parent's house, he telephoned Giulia at home to check on Conker, on hearing he was well and recovering, he asked if he could do anything to help the family but Giulia was stoic as ever, she told Jack to look after Sophia, that's all she wanted.

He called Sophia at work, something that was frowned upon by the Birmingham Post but this was an exception, surely they would understand. He promised Sophia he would be in town when she finished work so they could make the short walk to see her father in hospital.

His phone calls finished, Jack sat in his parent's kitchen at home and played with the spoon in his coffee, his mind wandered. The floating man. The footless man, now Conker. Shit.

His mother was at the sink, she turned. "Are you all right John?"

"Yes, fine mom, just thinking about my car, that's all, maybe I'll go and have a look at it."

He got up and went outside to the garage, standing with the cup of coffee in his hand looking at his roadster, he started talking to himself.

"Time I got you on the road. I do need my own transport."

"You do need a car, Jack."

"Hey, that's good. I need a car-jack."

"Let's buy a hood, I'm broke. I can't be broke, Jack I've got some cheques left."

Jack went back in the house, thumbing through the yellow pages, he found the number for Fletchers Autos, on Lawley Street, he rang the number.

"You have? Great, how much? Twenty six fifty, wow, that's not cheap, is it? Any discount for fire brigade personnel? Okay, twenty-five quid, do you take cheques? Great, put it to one side for me, I'm on my way."

Within the hour, Jack was back unloading a large brown cardboard box from his mother's Escort, carrying the awkward sized box past his mother in the kitchen, he threw the escorts keys on the kitchen table which promptly skated at speed over the Formica top falling off the edge and landing in the dog's basket.

"Thanks, mom."

"Is that car of yours ever going to be finished?"

"Soon, Mom, soon." Jack was trying to navigate the large box through the back door.

"Well if you didn't come home off nights and go to bed all the time you might get it finished sooner. You're wasting your life away sleeping in the day. Or you're at that station, earning hardly anything. You could be on good money by now if you had stuck to being an electrician. You should listen to your father, young man, giving up your trade to just be a fireman. What do you do there anyway? Do they let you go to fires yet? John I really don't understand you."

"No, Mom, you're right, Mom. I'm in the garage, love you, Mom."

"Oh, John you are hopeless."

Jack was not really in the mood for another lecture from his mother about how his life should work out. His mother was so kind but she had no idea of what firemen did or for that matter, life in the outside world. Dad had protected her from life, he had kept her from the rough edges of the wider world and sometimes it showed, but hey, both his mother and father were good to him. They let him get away with far too much and they had paid for his new black leather car seats, they looked fab sitting in the car. The MGB would be on the road in under an hour.

Jack paced up and down Printing House Street outside the Post and Mail building, the office tower stretching high above him. It wasn't long until Sophia came walking towards him beaming a wide smile. Jack was just about to tell Sophia of his short uninsured test-drive in the MGB with its new hood but thought again, perhaps that would be crass with Conker being ill in hospital. He asked her how her day had been instead, by the sound of things that had not gone that well either.

It was a short walk down Steelhouse Lane and they were there at the entrance to the general hospital, up the stairs to the first floor where they were greeted by the same young nurse as yesterday.

"Hello, you two, back to see Dad?"

"Yes, if we may, is he okay?"

"He's fine; your mother's with him, so only one of you in the ward for ten minutes, please."

"You go, Sophia, give him my regards, tell him I'll see him on our next visit. I'll wait for you in the cafeteria."

Fifteen minutes later, the three sat in the café sipping powdered coffee that had been spooned from a large metal tin, then drowned in boiling water from an ancient dull chrome gas urn, the addition of cold sterilised milk was the final insult. Giulia was not impressed with the muddy drink, but in herself she looked much better than yesterday.

"What will we do, Jack? How will we manage on a pension? The officer from headquarters said he would get Joseph's pension worked out for us but, it wouldn't be a full pension because he hasn't done his thirty years."

"It will be fine, Giulia, things will work out, he would have retired soon anyway, things are just happening a little quicker than he thought. Knowing Joseph, I'm sure he has a plan already. When he has recovered, I bet he will want to do a little light work in an office or something similar so, with a pension and a light part-time job the money coming in may be much the same as it is now."

"Giulia it could be the best time for you, you can both slow down, perhaps a short holiday a convalescence perhaps you could visit Venice at last. There will be no more working night shifts, no more weekends. He will be home every Christmas, in fact this coming Christmas we are scheduled to work Christmas Day and Boxing Day, he's out of that. The whole family will be sitting around the table eating turkey with all the trimmings and sipping Vin Brule. How fab will that be, and luckily for him, unlike the rest of us at the station, he won't have to suffer the culinary delights of Horace, the boil-everything cook."

Jack was trying in his own clumsy way to lighten the conversation.

"Yes, you are right, Jack, I'm sure he could find a little job, but I'm not going to think of Christmas. That's so far off, like Venice. I just want him well and back home now, so I can look after him."

"We all do, Mamma."

Harry walked across the car park at Aston Station. Having just parked his car he was, for some unknown reason, in full undress uniform complete with cap and carrying his fire-kit. It was half past eight in the morning and Jack had arrived only seconds before him. Jack, for the first time, was driving his MGB, it was polished to a super high gloss, the tyres had been blackened with shoe polish and the re-chromed wheels sparkled in the morning sunshine.

Jack climbed out of the driver's seat which he had been sitting in perhaps a little too long but he was savouring the moment, as he closed the car door he grinned the broadest of grins, then he turned to the approaching Harry.

"What do you think?"

"Well, well, well, this is it then. This is the car you've been boring us all with for the past, I don't know how long. This is the one you bought in bits off some bloke down the Bristol Road?"

"Yep, this is the one. It's the car's first proper run out, finished, taxed and insured it yesterday. So, what do you think?"

They started walking together across the car park, towards the backwash of the engine house.

"I have to hand it to you, Jack, it's a beauty. I never thought you would do it. Has Sophia seen it yet?"

"No, it's a surprise, after the shift today I'm off home to get changed then I'm picking her up, taking her for a drive and dinner at the Dirty Duck in Stratford-upon-Avon. It's all booked and paid for, even the bubbly and a bouquet of flowers at the table, Sophia deserves a little spoiling, she's had a rough time of things lately, with Conker and all."

What Jack had not told Harry was how he had paid for it all. Harry, for his part, had not joined the dots up and questioned the arrival of Jack's newfound wealth, so the conversation carried on unhindered by any probing questions.

Jack had spent an hour sat at his parent's kitchen table trying to convince them to release his grandfather's inheritance early to him. They had power of attorney over the five thousand pounds that was to be held for him until reaching the age of twenty-five. He tried everything he could think of to bolster his very thin argument. The need to get his transport from two wheels to four wheels purely on safety reasons, but they had already contributed to that, his impending betrothal to a girl they had never seen let alone met.

That one didn't go down too well either, he probably should not have included Sophia as a reason. But the wish to get a flat or house of his own did seem to strike a chord.

They discussed his brother and sister, their respective universities and the associated costs, Jack was turning them, they were now sympathising with him. They were definitely melting they were coming around to his way of thinking. His father looking at his mother, nodded acceptance; after what seemed an eternity of deliberation, his father spoke.

"Very well, Jack, we will release the money to you, do with it what you will, but when it's gone, its gone. Do not come to us for money or loans, this is it. I will transfer two thousand to your account today the rest in a month."

Jack was about to ask why he was splitting the transfers but thought again, perhaps best not to rock the boat, if this is what his father wanted this is how it would be. Jack and Harry were now at the backwash wicket door; Jack opened it for Harry to step through.

"How is Conker?" Harry asked.

"He's good. Three days in the cardiac ward hooked up to machines, then yesterday they moved him to a general ward, they won't let him out yet for some reason though. They want to keep an eye on him for another twenty-four hours, just to make sure but hey, you know Conker, he's champing at the bit to get home, hopefully if everything is okay he should be out lunchtime tomorrow."

"That's good news. I didn't think it would be easy to keep that old firedog down. I'll have to go and see him when he gets home."

"That would be good, I think he is looking forward to seeing all the boys, he's definitely looking forward to a pint with them."

"A pint, what a good idea, a pint, a run out in the country with your new motor, top down maybe? That sounds like fun, what about I see if my mom is free and we could make up a foursome for dinner?"

"Err, no. Not a good idea, Harry, it is going to be a little special, in fact extra special, so just Sophia and me, if you follow my drift."

"You mean a ring, a ring thing. You're a ring bearer, you're a Hobbit, Jack you are a fast worker it's only been six months, if that."

"Harry, I'm saying no more, if you even mention this in the station, I'll be feeding you your Cahoonas."

"You can't threaten me, mate I've been threatened by the Bianchi's nothing scares me now. But don't worry about me Jack, I'll keep Schtum, your secret's safe with me."

They walked together through the backwash towards the locker room. As they did, someone shouted from the deck of the turntable ladder, mocking their arrival.

"Okay men, stand easy, Birmingham is safe, the posers of Blue Watch have arrived to save the city or maybe the world, Oh, they're so brave and so handsome and they drive sports cars. Oh, where would we be without them?"

Harry gave a two-fingered salute, but couldn't resist a reply.

"How's the night shift been, men? Have you White Watch boys let any buildings burn down in the night? Made any nice flat ash covered car parks for the council? It is your specialty, after all. I know how you boys struggle at getting things right. Like counting past ten without taking your shoes and socks off and doing joined up writing. It must be really hard on the White Watch."

"Bollocks, Wilson," another voice from somewhere unseen in the engine house replied.

Laughter rattled around the engine house as the two watches prepared for the change of shift. Harry had already forgotten what he was told by the ring bearer.

At 0900 hours, the parade was brought to attention and the White Watch were dismissed. As they left, passing behind Sid and Tumble, but in front of the parading Blue Watch, a few gave a silent two-fingered salute. Blue Watch smiled back in frustration at not being able to respond. The Blue Watch parade was taken as usual by Tumble with Sid looking on; Bungy from Handsworth was with them again. He had volunteered to stand-by for the tour. The runners and riders were detailed and there was no surprise when the riders of the pump were called off, Jack took it in his stride, back of the pump.

"Parade, parade shun."

Just as Tumble said the words, the fire bell gave out its short ring, a fire call was coming through.

"Stand fast men," Tumble called.

The watch room attendant called to them from the watch room doorway.

"Pump only, stand-by duties, A1 Central."

"Okay pump crew, mount up."

Central had something going on and fire control had decided that it was best to bring a pump into the heart of the city for cover. It would be a normal drive into town, no blue lights no two-tone warning horns. As they rounded Lancaster Circus in front of Central Station, Jack looked up at the clock tower, twenty past nine. Hmm, not a bad run in, he then looked across the traffic island to the general hospital where Conker sat impatiently, waiting for the doctor's signature that would discharge him.

Through the wrought iron gates and onto the drill yard, Toot swung the pump around the yard in an arc to line up with their allotted bay. As he did, Jack noticed a group of raw recruits standing to attention under the gaze of a drill instructor, they were all watching the fire Engine passing close to them, Jack looked down from the crew cab upon the innocent faces who looked up in wonder at the 'Real' firemen. Did they really have any idea what they were letting themselves in for? The recruits watched the pump roll through the backwash and out of sight into the engine house, the high brown engine house doors closed behind it.

Central's turntable ladder crew were in the engine house and greeted their friends from Aston.

"What they got boys?" Tumble was the one to ask the question that the Aston lads were all wondering, having heard nothing on the main scheme radio about Central's job while on the run into town.

"Somebody trapped in machinery in Duddeston, going to be there a while by the sound of it."

"We might as well enjoy our time here at the 'Big house' then, can your mess stretch to tea for the five of us?"

The seven men walked through the engine house chatting as only old friends can on their way to the first floor mess room. Four teas and one coffee were carried from the kitchen on an old aluminium tea tray. Just as the tray was placed on the mess table, the fire bell sounded full alarm, the seven men made their way to the pole drop, the pole drop door was opened by one of Central's fireman, he turned to Jack just before he made the jump to the pole.

"Don't forget to look up before you mount the pole, don't forget there's another floor above us where others can get on." As he said the word, 'on' he shot out of sight through the floor. In the engine house, one of Central's men was holding a piece of message paper in the air waiting for Aston's officer to take it from him. As Tumble approached he offered him the message.

"Sods law, Tumble, it's a house fire, persons reported, back on your own ground."

The crew climbed on board their Pump as the doors were opened for them, it was a long run to Birchfield from Central, but Toot had a fast stretch of road on his route out of town where he could let the Rolls Royce engine have full throttle, they were on the Birchfield Road and the speedo was just nudging sixty miles an hour when the main scheme radio came to life it was Sid's voice, he had arrived at the address but it was the next sentence that slowed Aston's pump.

"No sign of fire at Birchfield Road, please verify the call."

That's all it took. Tumble looked across the cab at Toot and made a cutting gesture across his throat with his right hand, the experience of both told them it was a false alarm. Toot lifted his foot off the gas and let the speed fall away. He left the blue lights on but was now only traveling just above the speed limit. Cars they had passed only seconds before were now passing them, their occupants looking at the fire engine as if the driver had gone mad and was just playing with the traffic.

The radio came back to life calling Sid's fire Engine, Sid, by the speed he answered, was obviously sitting in the cab waiting for control to call back with verification.

"Go ahead, control."

"Call was made by a youth in a phone box situated on the Soho Road, Handsworth at the junction with Nineveh Road."

Sid now knew this was definitely a bogey and not a mistake in the address, as the supposed incident and the kiosk were miles apart the kiosk was just down the road from Handsworth Station, someone who didn't know the fire station's ground probably made the call expecting to see the engines from Handsworth turn-out, they would be disappointed when the station remained quiet.

Sid immediately replied and booked the call as a false alarm. That stood down all responding fire engines and ambulances.

Tumble, for his part, was straight on the radio calling the control room, as Aston's pump was back on their own ground but had been standing-by at Central, were they to go home to Aston or to resume the stand-by duties at Central? A

202

few seconds passed the control room was obviously working out cover moves. The order came. 'Return to home station'.

That's pretty much how the crews day played out, runs out on the station ground but nothing of interest. At lunchtime Jack was surprised by being given a baked potato for lunch by Horace. As he was last to get to the kitchen it was waiting for him on the small kitchen prep table, just one white dinner plate with a large slightly overcooked baked potato on it.

"Is that it, Horace?"

"Nope, there's a bowl of grated cheddar cheese on the table in the mess room, help yourself."

Jack sat at the mess table looking at the potato he had just cut in half; he picked up the saltcellar in front of him and sprinkled a little salt over the opened spud. He thought of the potato man that once stood at the top of Stephenson Street in town with his coal fired oven on a handcart he would be there come rain or shine, in the winter he also sold roasted chestnuts. His mother would buy him a baked potato with a little salt on their weekly shopping trips in town. For him, that was a treat, the highlight of his week when he was ten years old, but now it was the epitome of Horace's cooking skills.

Looking down the table he saw the cheese bowl in front of the newspaper reading Harry who had a huge pile of grated cheese in a mound on his plate totally burying his potato.

"Slide the cheese down, Harry."

Harry looked up from the newspaper and without moving the bowl along the table, he tipped it up slightly showing Jack the lack of contents.

"It's all gone mate, you should have got here sooner."

He let the bowl go, turned a page of his newspaper and carried on reading. Jack let out a small sigh then dug his fork into the white flesh of the potato.

The afternoon passed as uneventfully as the morning; the off-going parade was also a quiet affair not even the slightest of banter between Blue and White watch. Within five minutes of the end of shift, Jack was in his MGB and on his way home to get changed for the big night out. A quick bath, change of clothes and he was back on the road in less than thirty minutes, much to his mother's dismay.

"John, you treat this place like a hotel, now you have money in your pocket you're never here, where are you going now?"

"Just out for dinner in Stratford, don't wait up I may be late home tonight."

"John, you're wasting your life away, you need to grow up young man, take some responsibility for once in your life. John, John,, are you listening to me?"

"Yes, Mom, you're right. Soon I will, I promise, love you Mom, bye."

He was dressed once more in his one and only mud brown suit, bright yellow floral shirt with matching tie and his favourite boots, the only difference this time being what he was carrying. He had a little plain white envelope and a small red leather covered box, the box had a gold inlaid inscription that read, 'love is a fire' the envelope and the box sat in his right hand coat pocket. He tapped the pocket once, checking they were in place, things were going well, he would propose to Sophia tonight, and when Conker came home from hospital tomorrow, lunchtime, they would announce the news and show them the ring.

That would, by his reckoning, make Conker and Giulia happy and a great start to the new phase of their retired life together, hopefully a quiet retirement.

There would be one last surprise, the little white envelope with two 'flexible' air tickets to Venice. That would be his engagement gift to the two of them. Sophia knew nothing of his organising any of this. It was perfect, it was to be a surprise for them all.

He drove into the small *cul-de-sac* pulling-up outside the Fowles' house. Stepping from the car, he straightened his suit and tapped the pocket once again for good measure. As he approached the front door, it was opened by a tearful, distraught Isabella.

"Jack, Jack, they are at the hospital, the hospital called you must go there. It's Joseph, he has had another heart attack, he is not good. Go, go, you must go. Sophia, she is there with Giulia, go."

"Isabella. What has happened? What did they say?"

"The telephone, the hospital, they rang, they just say come now, he is not well. I know no more."

Jack parked the car outside the hospital. It could have been on a yellow line but he was not really taking much notice of parking restrictions. He ran to the main entrance and once more, he climbed the wide stone steps to the first floor but this time, to a large adjacent general ward. The entrance to the ward was as before deserted, no nurses, no visitors, nobody to be seen anywhere. He started to walk forward into the ward; as he did a voice from behind him called.

"Can I help you?"

Jack turned and saw an older nurse emerging from a side room he had just passed. She still had her hand on the door handle she had not quite closed the door shut.

"I'm with the Fowles family. I've come to visit Joseph Fowles."

"And you are?"

Jack knew the relatives only routine and the maximum two at the bedside rule, there was nothing for it, he would lie to get to see Conker and the family. His borrowed white lie would make him feel better.

"Son-in-law, I'm his son-in-law."

"Have you been made aware of the situation?"

"Yes, indeed, I received a phone call." Lying to the nurse was easier the second time.

She hesitated, then beckoned him forward to her. She whispered, "Be strong for them." As she did, she opened the door, he stepped inside and his world fell apart.

Giulia was knelling at the bedside praying. Sophia was at the foot of the bed, her face buried in a handkerchief, she was sobbing uncontrollably. Joseph lay dead on the bed. No tubes, no machines, no bleeping monitors. Just a thin white sheet covering all but his face. As Sophia turned to Jack, she dropped her hands to steady herself, holding onto the metal bed frame still with the handkerchief in hand. Through the tears she just managed to get the words from her lips.

"He's gone Jack, he's gone."

Jack couldn't believe what he was seeing or hearing, he walked slowly up to the bedside. He reached out and put the palm of his hand on Joseph's forehead. It wasn't cold but it wasn't the right temperature either. His face had shrunk, it was cadaverous, this was not what his friend should look like. He kept his hand on Joseph's forehead, he could hear his voice. "Morning, 'Conkers' the name, pray tell, who may you be, my good fellow?" It echoed in the room bouncing from the walls.

Jack realised he couldn't control his breathing, he gulped at mouthfuls of nothing, the air caught in his throat it would not go down into his lungs, a devil unseen had stabbed him in the heart and was twisting the blade.

A feeling of melancholy, of hopelessness, welled up inside him, surely this hurt he felt would soon show. His eyes reddened with the pressure that was building inside them, they were about to burst, his hand shook on Joseph's forehead as a tremor took his body. As he drew his hand away, a single tear rolled down his face.

He couldn't take much more death and destruction. Giulia had fallen silent, she had finished her first prayers, now Sophia was kneeling with her mother, both in silence. Jack knew he could not fail them, they needed him now. He brought himself back from the edge.

"Giulia, there are things that must be done. Would you allow me to tell the family of your loss and help take care of the initial formalities, so you can stay here with Joseph for a while?"

He felt like a coward leaving them with Joseph. Was he running away or was he doing the right thing? Joseph was dead, they needed someone to help them through this. He wanted to do it for them and for Joseph, he was being practical. He was not running, but it felt like running.

Giulia nodded. Sophia rose to her feet and walking around the bed, she kissed his cheek.

"Do what you can, Jack. I shall stay here with Mamma for as long as we are allowed."

"If you need anything, ring home. I will see to it that either Isabella or myself is there."

Jack got into his car outside the general hospital, he sat for a moment looking through the windscreen of his car into nowhere. He could not see the traffic or the pedestrians, he heard nothing, he just sat.

A few moments, yet a short lifetime slipped by in his memory, emptiness filled his very being, what now? He slipped his hand into his right jacket pocket and pulled out the small box and envelope, he looked at them and gently stroked the two as if they needed comfort.

He was still looking at them when a sharp metallic rap came on the windscreen breaking the trance he was in. A man dressed in a blue/black uniform with a yellow band around the cap bent down and peered through the side window, Jack's blank face turned to face him.

"Move along, son, you can't park here outside the hospital you're on double yellows."

Jack acknowledged the man's instructions with a confirming nod. He held the little box and envelope a little longer then he lent across the inside of the car and opened the small metal lid of the glovebox. He laid them inside and gently patted them, slowly he pushed the lid shut, the catch caught with a light snap.

His hand automatically found the ignition key, he turned the starter, once more he nodded an acknowledgement to the traffic warden who was waiting for him to move on.

He drove off towards the house where he would break the news to Isabella and the twins.